Praise for Doc Macomber

"Insanely entertaining!"
– Editor, *The Skin Game*

"Doc understands the seamier side of life.
His characters are complex, loaded with contradictions and
wholly believable."
– Dan Schilling, Former Special Ops Commander, Co-author,
The Battle of Mogadishu

"As addictive and satisfying as my first tattoo ... *Wolf's Remedy*
left me craving more."
– Lyle Tuttle, Tattoo Legend and Historian

"Hard men, Wild women, and even a Love-sick
Alligator ... it's a killer!"
– Retired Marine Capt. W.A. Montgomery

"It's always enjoyable spending time with Jack Vu."
– Bill Johnson, Teacher, Screenwriter, Author,
A Story is a Promise

"An intriguing read that will hold your attention as investigators
come up against dead ends and lies...where people aren't always
what they seem. A fun read and
something different by a talented author."
– Murder and Mayhem

"Adventure abounds in Costa Rica ... In his latest Jack Vu
mystery, best laid plans for a quiet vacation get shattered when the
drug trade becomes a genuine threat to the peace and tranquility of
this otherwise idyllic country. Jack and Betty soon find themselves
back on duty... Once again, Mr. Macomber has scored a winner!"
– Harley L. Sachs, Author of the Mystery Club series.

FLOATING WORD PRESS

River City

Also by DOC MACOMBER

The Killer Coin
Wolf's Remedy
Snip
Riff Raff

River City

(A Jason Colefield Mystery)

Doc Macomber

Floating Word Press, LLC
Portland, Oregon

Floating Word Press, LLC

1017 SW Morrison Street, Suite 215

Portland, Oregon 97205

Floating Word Press logo is a registered trademark. For information about special discounts for bulk purchases, please contact Floating Word Press, LLC, Special Sales at 1-877-356-9673 or fwp@ floatingwordpress.com.

COVER DESIGNED BY DIVERSITY DESIGN STUDIOS

Editor: Martha Cowen

Author photograph Copyright © 2014 by Ty Hitzemann Cover photographs Copyright © 2014 by Doc Haake Productions

Manufactured in the United States of America

Printing Number

9 8 7 6 5 4 3 2 1

First Edition

Library of Congress Control Number: 2014935687

Soft Cover: ISBN –13: 978-1-941297-00-1

For my good buddy, Jimmy.
I miss you man...

1

The line that divides is often invisible. An unseen separation. An imaginary barrier. That was the case in the waters surrounding Sauvie Island the morning the body was discovered.

Sentinel seagulls cawed in protest and fled their roosts as the motor sputtered and the hull scraped aground. Deputy Jason Colefield scrambled out of the River Patrol boat ahead of his younger partner and sloshed ashore, bowline in hand. The latest storm system had lifted, leaving behind a muddy beach strewn with piles of decaying vegetation and bird guano. After kneeling down to tie off the boat around the exposed roots of an undermined cottonwood, he stood and surveyed the scene.

The last time he'd been on the island it was sunny and forty degrees warmer, and all he'd been packing was a cooler of cold beer and a fishing rod.

Even then, it had been an uncomfortable return.

As the fog lifted, he could see willow trees lining the narrow channel, which provided fair wind coverage for the duck hunter blinds. Since waterfowl season was in full swing, he was relieved to see no shotgun barrels.

"Bart!" he yelled to his partner. "Grab our orange vests."

Colefield paused to get his bearings. Inland, pastoral farmland stretched for miles crowned by old Victorian homes, red barns and picket fences. A paved road dead-ended at the northwest tip. From there one could either turn around and head across the island toward Collin's Beach, the nude beach, or south toward more expensive real estate perched atop the banks of the Columbia River, affording spectacular views on clear mornings of four snowcapped peaks – Rainier, Hood, Adams and St. Helens.

An old fisherman once told him that Sauvie was the largest island in North America, bigger even than the isle of Manhattan. That may be true, but the two couldn't be more different. Sauvie boasted bucolic fertile environs, not concrete and skyscrapers.

Colefield studied the steep riverbank and swift current. He wondered if a body could even wash ashore here. Yet nothing was impossible. The job had taught him that. Bodies often appeared in odd places. They might sink at first, bump along over the rocks or get snagged on reeds for several weeks before enough bloating occurred for them to resurface, sometimes miles from the point of entry. Then it was just a matter of time before the River Patrol received a call.

This morning both rivers, the Willamette and Columbia, were running high from recent rains. Because of the swollen waters, the deputies had made two sweeps of the area, maneuvering around tank-sized flotsam, before coming ashore. If the body was supposed to be here, they hadn't spotted it.

But tides rise and fall. Shorelines morph and disappear.

He radioed dispatch and asked them to patch him through to the 911 caller who had agreed to stay at the scene. Turned out the body wasn't in the water after all, but land bound. He was in for a hike.

Behind him, his young partner slogged ashore, wearing two orange vests and juggling a heavy forensic kit. Sweating, he heaved the evidence locker to the ground and shed the extra clothing, tossing it to his partner.

"Do we have any heavy rope in there?" Colefield asked as he slung the vest over his jacket.

Bart grunted and started rummaging through his gear. "This should do the trick." He handed a thick coil of knotted rope to the deputy.

"Wait here until I figure out where we're supposed to be."

"Works for me." Bart flopped down on the box, whipped out his phone and began texting.

Colefield turned back to the task at hand. He knew from experience that once he reached the top of the rise, he would be at the county line. Dispatch was waiting for his determination of whether the body was located in Columbia or Multnomah County. Truth was neither jurisdiction wanted the case. Even interviewing witnesses was problematic when neighbors resided in different counties. At this point the only thing clear was that the body was in a field and not in the water.

The muddy embankment didn't look that difficult to climb but the rain had made the ground slimier than an oyster shooter. Colefield tied the rope around his waist and struggled up the steep bank, his boots nearly sucked off his feet, his gloves and knees soon covered in slick goo. As he crested the ridge, the mud gave way to grass and brush. Standing 100 yards away, he spotted a man with two large dogs, waving in his direction.

In his hunting jacket and baggy jeans the guy looked harmless enough until he spied the shotgun resting on his shoulder. Colefield wiped his gloves on the grass, secured the rope to a willow, and then tossed the line back over the embankment to his partner.

"You missed me, asshole!" Bart laughed.

"Keep your vest on. There're hunters up here."

"Roger that."

As he approached the hunter, Colefield's irises widened in recognition of his childhood nemesis. He'd been carrying a shotgun then too. Colefield flinched and involuntarily ducked as the memory seared through him. Hammered off his Hodaka Super Rat as he spun donuts in a fallow field, he'd hit the earth hard, the smell of seared flesh filling the air. It felt like a baseball bat had slammed into his head and chest as his riderless motorbike gained traction on his sprawled legs before careening into the dirt, its throttle stuck open. He'd tried to run, but his legs hadn't responded to his emergency signals, and so he had cowered in the dirt not sure what had just happened. When he'd heard the voice and saw the shotgun he was convinced he was going to die. Truth be told the shooting did signal the death of his innocence.

Everything happens for a reason. His mother's words echoed.

His stride became more assured as he mentally prepared to revisit his childhood boogeyman as an adult. Colefield glanced down, grateful the orange vest covered his give-away name tag. At 6 feet he bore no resemblance to the gap-toothed child that had flown across his land. He had braced for this often imagined confrontation, but the old hunter didn't seem to remember him. The man shifted his shotgun to his opposite shoulder and extended his hand. Removing his gloves Colefield reciprocated.

"Under better circumstances, I'd say nice meeting you." The hunter's grip was still firm. "I'm Hank Scarbough."

"I'm Deputy Coleman." He surprised himself at the ease with which the spontaneous lie rolled off his lips. "What's the shotgun for?"

"My dogs and I were hunting this morning."

"That how you found the body?"

"I wouldn't have spotted it in the tall grass otherwise."

As he glanced across the field the Lab on the right zeroed in on his bum knee while the black Lab with the greying muzzle enthusiastically nosed his crotch. He was more worried about his knee than his balls. But soon enough both dogs were intently sniffing the smeared goose shit on his legs – frosting on the cake for a bird dog.

"Were you the one who said the body washed ashore?"

"I told them it was along the east side of the channel. Apparently, someone got their wires crossed."

"Evidently. Why don't you take point, Mr. Scarbough? When we get close, keep your dogs back. We'll need to tape off the area."

The hunter stared back toward the river. "Is someone else coming?"

Colefield glanced over his shoulder. Bart was straining to pull the evidence locker up the bank.

"My partner will catch up. Lead the way."

While Scarbough set the pace, Colefield studied the fresh tracks in the tall grass. They could have been made by the hunter and his dogs or another person leaving the scene via the river. He'd check the bank for evidence later.

"You live nearby?" Colefield already knew the answer, but wanted to get a feel for the man after all these years.

"Toward the Point," the old man motioned to a big red barn and some wooden outbuildings off in the distance. Over the years the trees had enveloped the property, but it was mostly how Colefield remembered it.

"It's been in my family for generations. Back when the island was owned by the French."

"You still have family on the island?" Colefield's face twitched as he realized he'd tipped his hand.

Scarbough stopped and looked directly at him but Colefield doubted he'd recognize him as the redheaded kid who'd raced his dirt bike across his fields. He tugged his cap down tight over his close cropped hair. The moment passed.

Scarbough's expression turned inward. "My wife passed winter before last. Kids are all grown. I live alone now." He paused. "You from these parts Deputy?"

Now was not the time to reintroduce himself.

"I grew up in Portland. After high school I joined the Navy to see the world. After my discharge, I'd seen enough and couldn't wait to get back home."

"Some of the finest land this country has to offer," Scarbough agreed.

Colefield couldn't argue that. "How many residents currently live on the island?"

Scarbough thought for a moment. "Two thousand give or take. A fair number are retired. Pumpkins, corn, onions and herbs are still the staples for the south side. But things have changed over the years. Now there's a group of young people carving out a life for themselves growing organic vegetables, raising chickens, and catering to city folks from Portland who want to experience "country life" firsthand. They've built quite a following."

Colefield pulled out his notebook. "Any recent hunting

accidents?"

"A few months back at Bedford's farm, a guy shot himself in the foot. Nothing serious. Blew off a toe. Outside of that, let me think. Oh, there was a little mishap in the number eight blind last week. Two hunters knocked over their camp stove and burned it to the ground. That was a real disappointment. It was a dandy spot to bag Canadian geese."

As they resumed their hike, the older dog kept sniffing at Colefield's ankle. He couldn't seem to shake him. And then when he wasn't looking, the dog nipped at him. Colefield flinched. The hunter pulled back hard on the dog's collar.

"Sorry about that. She meant no harm. When Sadie was a puppy, my wife taught her to grab shoelaces and untie people's shoes. I've never been able to break her of the habit." Scarbough stroked the dogs as he continued. "My wife spent endless hours with them when they were pups. Named them after her grandmothers, Sarah and Sadie. But she never was very keen on the girls once they were grown."

While they waited for Bart to catch up, Colefield bent down to check his ankle and retie his boot.

It didn't appear as though there had been a lot of activity in the area. Dense blackberry briars and tall grass competed for space with reeds and marsh.

"While you were hunting this morning, did you see anyone else?"

"No. But from that blind there to as far as you can see the land is mine."

"You allow other hunters on your land?"

"Rarely."

"Anyone lately?"

The man thought it over. "Couple last week, couple this week."

"Do you post no trespassing signs?"

Scarbough shrugged. "Who pays attention to signs?"

Colefield considered the question based on his own history with the man as Bart struggled over, lugging the evidence locker with him.

"Mr. Scarbough, this is Deputy Bart Ryan."

Winded, Bart nodded to the hunter and knelt down to pat the Labs before looking back at Colefield who was staring toward the shore.

"Did you see that fresh trail a few hundred yards back?" Colefield asked Bart.

The deputy nodded.

Then as if on command, the dogs began pulling on their leashes, tails wagging.

"They've caught the scent. Shouldn't be much further, Deputies."

The hunter was right. About thirty yards into some tall reeds they came upon a trampled down area. Colefield asked everyone to stay back. Just ahead, he found what they were looking for. He paused, listening.

"You hear something Bart?"

"No."

"I don't hear it now." Colefield took another step forward. An iridescent bird shot out of the brush, soaring skyward like a clay target sprung from its trap. The dogs went crazy – barking and straining against their leashes. The pheasant's lamenting cry through the gray sky left Colefield unnerved. He had instinctively reached for his sidearm. He wasn't the only one the bird spooked.

"Holy shit!" Bart yelled as he uncoiled from the crouched position his body had assumed.

"You two would make fine bird dogs!" Scarbough chuckled.

Ignoring the sarcasm, Colefield told his partner to get him some gloves from the forensic kit. Still rattled, Bart opened the lid and fished around inside.

As Colefield approached the body and the scene came into full view he removed his cell phone and began snapping photographs. Engrossed, he didn't notice the deputy as he walked up from behind.

Bart waited gloves in hand. Finally, Colefield turned toward him, exposing the body to the young deputy.

"Christ! It's a kid?" Bart uttered. His partner stood frozen, eyes locked on the bloody tableau.

Colefield nodded. From what he could see, the victim appeared to be a fair skinned Caucasian boy with sandy hair and a thin build. Twelve or thirteen at most. Facedown, his back showed a dozen entrance wounds just below the shoulder blades, most likely from a shotgun blast. It was hard to tell if this center of mass shot was the fatal one because the victim also had massive head trauma. Powder burns on the clothing and blood splattering on the ground suggested the boy had been shot at close range. Colefield reflected on his encounter moments earlier with the pheasant. *Instinct takes over. This could be a hunting accident.*

He pulled the gloves from Bart's clenched hand. "Looks like the Multnomah County Sheriff's Office 'tags and bags' this one. Get them out here."

Colefield pulled on the gloves. "Then start taping off the perimeter. And keep your eye peeled for any spent shotgun shells."

Bart nodded; appearing relieved to have a job that kept him occupied and away from the blood soaked body. Though he was well-trained and had handled many drownings, this was his first shooting.

"Should I start a Sign-In Roster?"

His training was kicking in.

"Roger that. But mark off the area first."

The boy probably had been dead a day or more. They'd had a cold snap. Nighttime temperatures had been in the low thirties, barely climbing above that during the day, which would explain why the body wasn't covered with insects and flies. A warm day and the remains would have appeared otherwise.

Colefield took in what the kid was wearing – worn leather boots, denim jeans, a red flannel shirt, and a camouflage hunting vest too large for his small frame. The collar of a thermal undershirt showed at the neckline. An orange hunter's cap lay on the ground beside the body. Given the cold winter weather, the boy had on appropriate hunting attire.

If his take on the entry wounds was accurate, the hunter could have been about twenty feet behind the boy when the trigger was pulled. He surveyed the surrounding area. The placement of the hands and the angle of the feet suggested the boy crawled along the ground either before or after he'd been shot, making him invisible in the tall brush.

He knelt down and examined what was left of the face. Next he studied the boy's hands. The kid was a nail biter. Colefield curled his own hands into fists, an involuntary reflex he'd developed over the years to hide the same condition. If the hunter had moved the body, he couldn't see traces of it in the grass.

Without disturbing the evidence he took a closer look at the body shot. The back of the vest displayed a symbol of some kind. Colefield's childhood vest had borne the image of a motorcycle. Leaning down to examine the design more closely, his stomach clenched. Unless he was wrong, the boy's symbol looked like it had been applied after the shooting. Colefield jotted notes and photographed everything.

Homicide would process the scene, but he wanted a record in case someone down the line got sloppy. Bart had finished cordoning off the area around the body with police tape. As he marched back over to his evidence kit to stow his gear he glanced over at his partner.

"Will our office assist on this?"

Colefield stopped writing. "What?"

"You're going to a lot of trouble for nothing. Isn't this Homicide's case?"

Colefield didn't respond. His attention was focused on the boy's untied shoelaces.

He stopped writing. Behind him Scarbough paced.

"Did you disturb the body in any way, Mr. Scarbough?"

"I checked for a pulse."

He signaled Bart to join him with the old man. On a hunch, Colefield squatted down and looked the Labs over. Sure enough, there was blood on Sadie's muzzle and feet.

"Sadie went for the boy's shoes before I could stop her," Scarbough admitted.

"I need to see your shotgun, Mr. Scarbough." Colefield's tone hardened.

Since Bart was closer, he retrieved the gun. The hunter surrendered it willingly. Bart held it out to Colefield.

"Just see if it's been fired."

Bart checked the chamber, cleared one round, and then sniffed the barrel. He nodded to his partner.

"Could you empty your pockets for me, Mr. Scarbough?" Colefield studied the hunter.

Without objecting, Scarbough turned his pockets inside out. Both were empty.

"Your hunch is I shot the boy, Deputy?"

"Did you?"

Scarbough clenched his jaw.

Colefield stooped and picked up the ejected shotgun shell. He pulled out an evidence bag, dropped the shell inside and slipped it into his pocket. He had an idea about the shell that he wanted to check out personally.

"When was the last time you fired your shotgun?" Colefield asked.

"Right before I called 911. The dogs flushed a pair of grouse. I thought I winged one. Dogs went in. But the bird flew off. That's when I found the body."

Colefield glanced down at the man's tan boots and seemed to be making a visual comparison to the impressions in the grass by the body when a bloodstain on the right toe caught his eye. Colefield pointed at the bloody smear.

Scarbough glanced at his feet. "That could have come from most anywhere. These are my hunting boots."

"It looks fresh," Colefield said.

The man stooped down to see for himself. Bart put his hand on the Scarbough's shoulder. "Not so quick sir." Scarbough shrugged him off and stood. He stared at the older deputy.

"We're gonna need your boots too," Colefield said.

Scarbough scowled, but remained silent.

Colefield glanced back at the body for a moment. "Did you hear any shots yesterday from your farm house?"

"It's hunting season. What do you think?"

"Have you ever seen the boy before?"

Scarbough shook his head and sighed.

Colefield thought it over hard for a few moments and then told Bart to turn the gun over to the lab techs when they arrived. He was unsure how to process the dogs.

"You're making a mistake, Deputies."

"Just following protocol," Colefield explained. "If you're cleared, you'll get your gun back."

"Don't you mean when I'm cleared?"

"I said it right the first time."

2

The dogs were the first to hear the noisy approach from the opposite end of the field.

"Here comes the Cavalry!" Bart shouted, returning his cell phone to his jacket pocket. Three four-wheeled quads bounced over the rough terrain. Each had a rifle attached to the front and equipment attached to the rear rack.

Colefield thought he recognized a familiar face among the helmeted riders. Bart fumbled around with his clipboard and seemed nervous about what to do next. Colefield quickly assigned him a task.

"Stand guard," Colefield said. "Ensure no one goes in or out of the scene without signing your log sheet."

Scarbough, who earlier had been told he couldn't leave with his dogs until a detective spoke with him, found a stump where he could sit down, hold the dogs at bay and wait. Rattled by all the police activity, the barking Labs fought their leashes. Scarbough on the other hand, silently sat.

Colefield strolled over to greet his old pal, Detective Harvey Feinstein. The stocky detective climbed off the first quad and began removing his gloves and helmet.

"Damn, Jason, could you have picked a more remote location?" The detective dislodged a hunk of mud from the corner of his eye before peeling off his riding jacket. "I hear River Patrol has been working a lot of overtime lately."

"You could say that," Colefield smiled. It was well known that Portland's bridges provided more than an expansive view to those despondent enough to end their own lives.

"Five jumpers just last week? Gotta be a record."

"It's the holidays," Colefield said. "Happens every year. We'll see another surge end of January when the credit card bills come due."

Harvey wagged his head. "Every month when my credit card statements arrive I know I want to jump off a bridge."

Colefield smiled, remembering Harvey bemoaning what it cost to clothe a teenage girl these days.

"Hey, which reminds me, my daughter wants to go on a ride-along. Think you can arrange it?"

"I'll set it up ... after things slow down a little."

"Great. So what kind of mess we talkin' about here?"

Colefield pointed toward the taped off area. "A boy's been shot twice with what looks like a 12-gauge. I haven't rolled the body. He's on his stomach just like we found him. The cheek that hasn't been blown off still has some baby fat on it. I'd put his age around twelve or thirteen. We'll compare notes later."

"Find any spent shells?"

"Not yet."

"Is it still hunting season?"

"Until the end of the month."

"Who's the grumpy guy with the dogs?"

"He called it in. Name's Hank Scarbough. He lives on the island."

"His story check out?"

"It's a stretch. But 60/40 says he's not telling us everything."

"He recognize the kid?"

"Says no, but with the boy's face all shot up, he might be telling the truth."

Harvey looked back over at the hunter about the time Scarbough lit a cigar.

"Well, don't let him wander off. I'll want a word with him later."

"His dogs were with him when he found the victim and might have compromised the scene."

"OK. I'll make a note not to look for a killer with paw prints.

Anything else?"

"I bagged grumpy's boots. I think there's a recent blood stain that might be of interest, and figured you'd want to make a size comparison with the imprints around the body."

"OK." Harvey switched gears. "So it sounded like Dispatch said the body was near the riverbank. So why are we in the middle of a friggin' field?"

"Dispatcher error."

"How fresh we talking?"

"One day – two tops."

As the two approached the body, Harvey's assistants hefted their cases down off the racks and got to work. After the techs finished their preliminary examination, Feinstein waived Colefield over.

"Could be an accidental shooting. Yet boys will be boys. They like to hunt and kill things at this age. Interesting time for a kid. He's old enough to have a Youth Permit, but I didn't find one in his pockets. Found a few coins and some chewing gum. No wallet. He's probably too young to have an interest in carrying one yet. Kid could have been taking a shortcut to the river and some hunter shot him by mistake. 'Course the grass isn't over four feet tall. A hunter would have seen the back of his head especially since he was wearing an orange cap. Unless, the hunter was extremely short. Any midgets on this island?"

Colefield couldn't tell if he was joking or was actually pondering the possibility.

"What's your take on this?" Harvey asked him.

"If the boy was hunting, where's his shotgun?"

"How about the marks in the dirt?" Harvey continued.

"It looks like he was crawling."

Harvey pointed to the drawing on the kids vest. "What do you make of this?"

"Looks like an infinity symbol."

"Thanks, sport, but I wasn't being literal. The bigger picture…"

"I think it was made after the kid was shot," Colefield squatted down by the body. "See how the paint penetrates the gunshot wounds?"

Harvey joined Colefield for a closer look. "So we concur this could be a possible homicide?"

"Looks that way to me."

"Help me roll him over." Harvey slid his hands under the legs. Colefield took the spine and head. "On three, ready? One, two, three..."

Trapped air released from the body as they eased it onto its back. Both of them stared at the bloody hole where his cheek should have been. Colefield stepped back. He'd seen enough. The frail boy with long eyelashes closed over a ravaged face struck a familiar chord. Colefield rubbed the scars on his own cheek. *Another inch and that could have been me.*

Harvey poked around the sinus cavities and then completed his examination of the body.

"It is odd – that symbol." Colefield pondered. "I think it means 'without end'."

"Death is a pretty final end." Harvey didn't look up from the body. "My guess? The symbol is part of a bigger picture. We got a memo last week asking to report any deaths involving letters, numbers or symbols to the FBI."

Harvey studied the boy's neck and hands. "Rigor mortis has set in. He's been dead at least twenty-four hours." He took a closer look. "It doesn't appear that he fought with his killer."

"No. It just looks like he was trying to get away."

Bart, who was standing off to the side listening, turned to the technician, "You think you can get a brand of spray paint off the vest?"

Colefield looked over at Harvey. He was shaking his head like it was the dumbest thing he'd ever heard.

The technician strode over. "Maybe. I'd like to try."

"What were the symbols found at the other murder scenes?" Colefield asked.

"Don't remember the specifics." Harvey stepped aside to allow the techs to move the body. "Body looks like it has been out here overnight. Kind of rules out your suspect unless he came back today to throw us off the scent."

"He could have painted the symbol so it wouldn't look like a hunting accident," Colefield mused.

"His shotgun been fired recently?" Harvey asked.

"Yeah… What do you want to do with it?"

"Deputy Ryan said he was shooting grouse?"

Colefield nodded.

"I think we've got probable cause to hold it." Harvey turned toward the hunter. "If he puts up a stink and lawyers up, we'll have to return it unless there's other evidence linking him to the scene. We'll check him for paint residue. Anything else I should know about your 60/40 suspect before I have a word with him and his two dogs?"

Colefield spied Harvey's neatly tied shoelaces and smiled. "Nope."

3

It was another hour before Detective Feinstein had finished questioning Scarbough and cleared the Medical Examiner to transfer the body to the morgue. The best way to do that was by air transport. A helicopter was dispatched. Within minutes, it had circled overhead and landed. Colefield studied the ground beneath the body. It revealed nothing new.

He turned back toward the chopper in time to see Bart and a rookie paramedic struggling with the litter, trying to lift it through the chopper's small door. Colefield hustled over to give them a hand.

Together they slid the stretcher inside without incident.

"Thanks for the assist. I tweaked my back yesterday." The paramedic winced as he pulled himself up inside the chopper, waved goodbye and closed the door. The deputies stepped back as the whirling blades picked up speed and the helicopter lifted off.

Scarbough, shoeless and exhausted, left the area propped up on the back of a quad, his Labs leading the way home.

Colefield told Bart to wait by the tree while he went over to talk with Harvey one last time.

When he returned, Bart was leaning against the trunk relieving himself.

Colefield spied the spent cigar butt. "Hey, don't piss on that." He pointed to the inch-long stogie. "Bag it and let's go."

Bart finished, put on gloves and scooped up the evidence. Colefield was already on the move. Bart picked up the forensic case and hustled after him. "Learn anything new from Feinstein?"

"We compared notes. We're going to take a different path back to the boat. Follow me."

"Shouldn't we see if any of the neighbors heard or saw something?"

"Harvey's handling that. We're gonna have a look down by the riverbank. We have jurisdiction there."

Colefield cut through the brush in a zone all his own. His mind took in the sound of the geese flying overhead. The way the grass and twigs scraped his pant legs. The sound his boots made as they sank into the mud. He spotted a number of broken twigs and down by his feet the grass had been flattened. In some areas it was springing up again, toward the rays of sunlight filtering in through the dense brush and cottonwoods. It was clear to him that someone had recently made this path.

When Colefield reached the river, they came out at a lower section of the island. Still plenty of room for a boat to pull ashore and with fewer embankments to climb. Bart stopped and set the case down. He stood back while Colefield searched down to the waterline.

Bart shouted. "Should I wait here?"

"Yeah. Take a breather. I think we can slip around this ledge and get back to the boat without backtracking. There's something I need to look for."

Bart squatted down on his heels and watched the deputy search the riverbank for God knows what.

At one point Colefield knelt down and studied something resting atop a stump. He pulled out a Ziploc bag and placed what looked like a cigar butt inside. He studied and photographed hull markings along the bank and footprints left in the deep muck. Markings that, because of the rising and lowering tides, had already lost much of their original shape.

"You want to grab some food on the way back?" Bart shouted and then mumbled something about being able to devour an entire cow. They had gone hours without eating, but the job wasn't always conducive to a timely appetite.

Colefield continued to focus on the riverbank. Awhile later, he hiked back up the ridge.

"What'd you say about food?" Colefield asked and handed Bart the evidence bag with the cigar butt inside. Bart opened the lid on the forensic case and stuffed it inside an empty compartment, pulled out a log sheet, made an entry and closed the case.

"You up for some chow?"

Colefield glanced at his wristwatch. "Lieutenant is expecting us back at the office. We can follow the ridge from up here. You're still good playing pack mule?"

Bart nodded.

Colefield led the way again and after a few strides along the ridge, his partner asked, "What were you looking for down there?"

"To see if any boats have come ashore recently. Hull marks mostly. And footprints."

"I don't suppose the cigar butts are for your homeless pals down on Burnside?"

"Bart, you might want to start paying more attention to your surroundings."

The exhausted deputy stumbled over a rock. "Guess you're right."

"Didn't you notice that Scarbough was smoking a cigar?"

"Yeah – so … not a crime to smoke yet, is it?"

"And no harm in collecting butts either. It could be nothing but what are the odds that we'd find a cigar butt along the riverbank, especially with the fluctuating tides?"

Bart thought a moment. "I don't know. Probably about as good as me finding my future wife in a titty bar."

4

The River Patrol building sat at the edge of the Columbia River. Windows faced the water, framing a view of Mt. St. Helens. From inside the deputies could see the public boat ramp and several enclosed floating garages that housed patrol boats and a boat for the fire department. In the summer the scenery markedly improved. The nearby beach filled with sunbathers. Nothing took a lawman's mind off a dull day better than watching bikini clad women lolling about in the sun.

As the deputies pulled the boat up to the dock, loud cursing spewed from inside one of the boat houses. The men headed toward the commotion. Colefield pulled open the battered door and peered inside.

One of their boats was taking on water. A lot of water. Deputy Larry Weaver was down on all fours near the stern. The portable bilge pump they had dropped inside the hull had stopped working and he was frantically twisting wrenches to revive it. Tony Parker, the other deputy, was inside the cabin, cussing up a storm.

"Weaver! What's the matter?"

"That you, Colefield? Go get your wet suit."

That was about the last thing he wanted to hear. "Thru-hull fitting?"

"Yep. Busted off at the base. Tony's jamming a rag in the hole but it's not working. I thought if I could get the water pumped out, we could seal it up with Instant Seal. But nothing seems to be working right today. Think you can go down and hammer a plug in from the bottom? The fitting's too damaged from our end."

The boat had always been a problem. They desperately needed

a new one, but budget constraints necessitated that this one still float as a backup.

"There's another pump in the other boat house."

"Not anymore," Weaver said, standing up and mopping his sweaty face. "I trashed it last week on that schooner taking on water. Remember?"

"Shit. That's right. Didn't Becker fix it?"

"He had to order parts. It'll be another week before it is back in commission."

"Get the hand pump from our boat," Colefield said to Bart.

"I'll be right back," Colefield told Weaver.

Tony popped his head up. "It's a two-inch fitting."

Colefield left the garage and headed up to the main office and his storage locker.

Lieutenant Daniel Briggs, was built like a fireplug, and only wore button-down shirts for meetings with the Chief. He stood jiggling some wires on the back of the two-way radio. When that didn't work, he slapped the front of it with the palm of his hand.

"Doesn't anything work around here anymore?" Colefield asked as he opened the front door.

"Have Bart take a look at this will you?" Briggs put his fingers inside his collar and stretched his neck out.

"Who you calling?"

"You! We need a diver."

"So I heard."

"I'd let that piece of shit sink if it was my own boat, but for now we need to keep the damn thing above water."

"Where's Becker?"

"Responding to a service call."

"We have any of those two-inch fittings lying round?"

"Check his storage locker."

The Lieutenant's phone rang. He dropped the microphone, headed toward his office, slamming the door closed behind him, a habit to which the deputies had grown accustomed.

As Colefield pushed through the door to the locker room, a

pain shot through his back. Every day his aches and pains seemed to increase. Still at this point it was nothing a good masseuse couldn't fix.

He headed to the garage where each deputy had a locker for equipment storage. Colefield had the luxury of two because he was the only certified diver on the team and needed the extra space.

He changed out of his tactical gear and into his wet suit, grabbed fins, a mask, and a five-minute air bottle. He collected some basic hand tools and a fitting from Becker's area. He then headed back down the ramp to the boat house.

Bart was back, knee deep in water inside the boat, working the handheld bilge pump like his life depended on it. Water flowed in spurts out the nozzle and back into the river.

"Hurry it up!" Tony shouted.

Colefield sat on the wooden floor and pulled the fins on his feet. He had the hammer and a tapered wooden plug stowed inside a water-proof pouch hooked on his dive belt along with a flashlight.

"You owe me a beer for this," he said to Weaver and then stuck the regulator in his mouth and dropped down into the frigid water.

The world went murky and dark. But he was experienced. He'd logged at least a hundred dives over the years, and taken all the specialized courses the Navy had offered, providing lifesaving knowledge time and again.

There was a strong current underneath the boat. The garage had been built on floats and there was no protruding water-block on the structure. The river ran under it like it would out in the middle of the Columbia. Because of this Colefield had to hang onto the hull as best he could and patted his way over to where he suspected the thru-hole fitting was located, kicking his feet to tread just below the surface.

The job took less than five minutes. He jammed the tapered wooden plug into the hole and hammered it until it met resistance. He gave it another hard blow and assumed now the rest of the damaged fitting could be removed from inside the hull. He resurfaced and told the guys they could ease up on the pumping.

The plug was secure.

Tony suggested they replace the old fitting on land. Once the water was pumped out of the hull, they could run the engine, motor around to the boat ramp and pull the boat out with the trailer. No big deal.

An hour later after he had showered and changed into street clothes, Colefield looked out the window as Bart trudged up the ramp, hauling fifty feet of water hose and the old portable bilge pump. From inside the warm office Colefield heard the garage door open and then close. A few minutes later, the sloshing sounds of wet boots filled the air as Bart appeared.

He was soaked from the waist down, his shirt muddy and his hands covered in grease.

Instead of cleaning up, Bart collapsed into his chair. "I'm more tired than after a day of chores on my folk's dairy farm." He looked down at his belly and sucked it in and out a few times. "I think I lost some weight today."

"Your chores aren't done yet." Colefield pointed to the squawk box, which was flickering between static and frequency. "Lieutenant wants you to take a look at the radio."

"Now?"

Lieutenant Briggs' door opened. "I'll need your reports on the Island case by end of day."

Colefield glanced at his watch. "End of day is in five minutes."

"Not for you two. The Chief's chomping at the bit on this one."

"I was thinking I could write my report tomorrow," Bart said.

"I need them both done today."

Colefield slid back from his desk. "What's your definition of done?"

The Lieutenant frowned.

"Look, Bart and I were talking earlier. I think our office should take the lead on this case. It'll improve morale. And be good PR. It's technically an island, which involves plenty of water. We could make it fly."

"Not a chance. It's Homicide's, especially since the FBI is now involved," the Lieutenant said. "If Homicide needs an assist, they'll call."

"So in the meantime, we spend our time checking expired tags while some child killer is at large?" Bart was full of righteous indignation.

The Lieutenant rubbed his eyes. "With my luck we'll end up with the case anyway."

Colefield sat up. "Why's that?"

"Detective Feinstein called a few minutes ago. He said you know the agent the FBI has assigned to the case. An Agent Costa?"

Colefield's face tightened. "What'd Harvey tell you?"

"Just get me your reports." The Lieutenant's telephone rang again. He stomped back to his office, the door banging shut behind him.

Colefield sat forward and planted his feet squarely on the chipped linoleum. He felt light headed. He hadn't eaten all day. Breathing the rank air from the portable tank and seeing the boy's destroyed face had left him queasy. He leaned back in his chair and closed his eyes, taking a few deep breaths. It wasn't really about the murder or the day. It was the unexpected mention of FBI Agent Tamara Costa. That painful relationship bubbled its way back into his thoughts. Colefield wondered what planetary shift was occurring in his life. First Scarbough's unwelcome return and now Tam...

Wet boots and faulty wiring were a bad mix but Bart began fiddling around with the loose connection on the marine radio.

Anything to avoid writing a report, Colefield mused.

The radio blasted nail-biting static until Bart twisted the squelch knob and the soothing sound of barge traffic filtered in on Channel 12.

Colefield faced his computer and began typing. His fingers pounded the keyboard so hard the tips went numb. Eventually, the report was done and he sat back and read it. Halfway through he got an idea and began searching online. Next he downloaded his notes and crime scene photos. He printed out the results and along with his report, slid the documents under the Lieutenant's door before heading toward the locker room to get his jacket.

Meanwhile Bart stared forlornly at a blank computer screen. He laid his hands over the keyboard as if willing the powers above to help him start typing.

When Colefield returned from the locker room, he told Bart if he finished before midnight to join him for a beer. He pulled back the sleeve of his peacoat, a holdover from his Navy days, and glanced at his watch. He'd have to hustle if he wanted to catch the end of Happy Hour.

The night air swiped at him as he stepped outside, but the sky was clear. Weather guys called it wrong again.

Colefield zipped his jacket. Traffic was heavy on both sides of Marine Drive. An endless stream of blinding headlights made the short route to Sextant's Tavern dangerous if you weren't paying attention.

He hugged the shoulder listening to the gravel crunch underfoot and thought about the kid. According to his pal at Homicide they had begun inquires but were coming up empty determining the boy's identity. What with their caseload, and the face mincemeat, no surprise there.

Still nobody had filed a missing person's report, which seemed odd for a child his age. The Medical Examiner had determined the body had been dead for more than 24 hours. You'd think someone would have noticed a child missing for that long.

The press had gone ahead with the story on the five o'clock news, but as far as he knew, no one had come forward with information for the police.

Colefield cut across the grass, skirting the busy parking lot, under the green neon glow of the tavern's sign. As he hopped up the front step, the door swung open and a group of half-sloshed regulars poured out and patted him on the back. Apparently the River Patrol was mentioned on the news broadcast. He ducked inside before any of them could ask about the case.

Case? What case? The Lieutenant had put the kibosh on that.

The bar was jammed and the crowd seemed rowdier than usual. Every table had stacks of empties. He looked for a seat at the bar. No luck there. The butts were wedged together so tightly it would have taken plastic explosive to clear a space.

He smiled at his girlfriend Jill behind the bar, twirling bottles with the dexterity of a gunslinger. He loved the curve of her neck and the muscles flexing down her toned arms. She wore a racy black top, one of his favorites. He'd given it to her on her 35th birthday. It showed off just enough skin to keep the men amused and the women jealous.

She turned her blonde head and big green eyes in his direction and winked. It gave him an enviable jolt. Then her slender arm shot out like a sideline pass to reach for a bottle. Without a word she returned to the hectic pace of serving the crowd before the end of Happy Hour.

Colefield managed to snag the sleeve of a harried waitress whisking by and asked if she could deliver a couple beers to him.

He found a vacant table in back by a window. Five minutes passed, then ten. The longer he sat, the more prone he was to dredge up old shit. Today had torn the scabs off several painful memories.

He stood up to better survey the crowd. Jill was making the final round with the patrons at the bar.

So where the hell was that waitress with his beers?

Before he could find out, two deputies from the River Patrol arrived. Colefield waved them over. They were no fools though. They headed straight toward the bar to place their order before taking a seat at his table.

Across the room he ferretted out the waitress in question bursting from the kitchen while juggling a tray of food and frothy beers. She spotted him and fought her way toward the table.

"Three beers, right?"

"Two."

"You ordered three."

No point in arguing. Someone would drink the extra.

"Sure."

"Sorry it took so long," she removed the pint glasses and dropped them in front of him on the table so hard that liquid sloshed over the tops.

Colefield picked up one of the beers. "First Friday night Happy Hour?"

"First night in Hell, you mean."

The waitress balanced her tray on his table and half-heartedly sopped up the beer with a bar towel pulled from her hip pocket. "I'll be back in a minute to collect. I need to deliver this hamburger before it's ice cold."

His co-workers cruised over with their drinks and flopped down.

Colefield noticed Weaver had been looking frumpier than usual. Being married with three kids could explain it. He also had the world's hairiest body. And his attempts at trimming all that fur produced a scraggly molt guise. Weaver claimed that after sixteen years of police work, things happened to the body that he would never have imagined. Tony constantly gave him shit about his unkempt appearance, nicknaming him "Hobo".

Tony was the office gadfly, always singling out the new waitresses even though he was in a committed relationship. Tony's pants were pressed and sharply creased, and his dark hair was always styled and trimmed. He never wore a hat even when it rained.

Tony took a sip of his draft and looked around at the crowd. "Who's the new waitress?"

"Don't ask. I don't think she'll be here after her shift ends."

"You received a call after you left," Weaver said.

"Who?"

"Some chick. An Agent Costa from the FBI."

Colefield's chest fluttered. "What did she want?"

"To talk to you. Has something to do with the shooting out on the island. She wants to set up a meet tomorrow back at the crime scene."

Weaver unfolded a crumpled piece of paper he removed from his jacket pocket and dropped it on the table in a puddle of beer.

You would have thought the paper contained the winning Powerball numbers Colefield moved so quickly to pick it up.

"The Lieutenant brief you guys on the case?"

Tony answered. "Yeah. A child shotgun vic. Possible murder."

"Did you tell the FBI agent that the case had been turned over to Homicide?"

"Yep," Weaver said. "That didn't seem to matter to her. Said it was important you contact her personally. Said to call her tomorrow, first thing."

"You mention that tomorrow is Saturday and I'm going skiing with Jill?"

"Hey, asshole, I'm not your personal secretary."

Colefield pulled out his cell phone went outside and placed a call to the telephone number that the beer had made nearly impossible to read. He wondered how she figured into the island shooting. Was this part of a bigger picture? Part of him hoped she just wanted to see him again. Who doesn't have an unrequited love in their past? When he returned to the table and sat back down, he appeared to be mulling something over in his head.

"You get ahold of her?" Weaver asked.

"No."

"I told you she said to call her in the morning."

Tony stared him in the eye. "So you canceling the big ski trip with Jill now?"

Tony liked to stir up trouble.

Disrupting their conversation, a women's voice shouted above the roaring crowd. And for a moment, the room fell silent, everyone's attention focused on Jill castigating a rowdy customer.

"She look like someone you'd screw with?" Colefield paused. "If I need to I can take care of business in the morning and we can be on the slopes by mid-afternoon."

"Sure, you could if you were running the show," Tony said.

"You better call it off before you blow your good thing with her." Weaver scratched his scruffy chin. "I need another beer. Anyone want another round?"

Weaver looked at the pair of untouched beers in front of Colefield, then at Tony.

"Sure, take em." Colefield slid the beers across the table. As the men tipped them back, Jill looked over and waved.

"She makes this place, doesn't she?" Tony said, grinning.

Colefield flashed him the evil eye.

Truth was everyone knew she was the main attraction at the bar. But she had confided to Colefield on several occasions that the job was burning her out. She was considering a change. Colefield didn't know if he would be included in the reordering of her life.

"Well this might be your chance," Weaver broke the silence at the table. "Jill looks like she's got a few minutes so you can go deliver the bad news."

"Great."

The loud cadence of Happy Hour was petering out. The waitress wandered over to the men's table and held her hand out toward Colefield.

"Time to pay up." She tapped her toe.

Colefield looked from Weaver to Tony for their donations. They smiled back in response as he reached for his wallet, pulled out a ten and a five and handed them to her. Her look said it all. He fished out a couple more dollars. Disgusted, she snorted and stormed off.

"She's kinda cute." Tony checked her out across the room. "And she's taken a real shine to you."

Colefield finished his beer and stood up.

5

There were no witnesses in the kitchen when Colefield delivered the news. He'd figured he could always hide behind some pots and pans or make a dash for the walk-in cooler and wait it out until she calmed down.

Jill's full lips pinched into a tight frown as she shot him a vile glare. Fortunately, they were at opposite ends of a butcher block when she grabbed the knife.

"Jill?"

"I can't decide. Cut up these limes, or cut off your dick?"

"I'd like to offer a suggestion…"

"I'm all ears."

"We can be out of town by noon at the latest. We'll still have the room booked at the lodge. We'll go night skiing. Have champagne afterward. How's that sound?"

Jill hesitated, thinking it over. Then she glanced down at a lime on the cutting board and jammed the pointed blade through the center of it. Juice squirted everywhere including his right eye.

He squinted but kept talking. "Night skiing. Romantic. Not as crowded. Warm and snuggly afterward."

"This about the kid on the five o'clock news?"

Colefield held up three fingers. "Scout's honor."

"And it's important you do this tomorrow morning?"

He searched the counter for a towel as his eye teared. "It is."

Jill finished dicing the lime into little wedges and then set the knife down on the counter. She pulled down a plastic container from an overhead shelf and scooped the chunks into it with her palm.

"Scouts always keep their word," she warned.

* * *

When he got back to the office everyone was gone. He sat at his desk and searched all the missing persons reports filed over the last twenty-four hours. Nothing.

Why did he always feel like one big letdown to Jill? Or was this just some blowback from the return of Tamara Costa?

He found his work jacket, removed the shotgun shell from his pocket and transferred it to his windbreaker before shutting off the lights and heading out the door.

Colefield's old Ford F-100 pickup was the only vehicle in the parking lot. He climbed behind the wheel and stuck a bent key into the ignition.

He took the long way home, staring at a sliver of silver surrounded by a few glittering stars. He wondered if the stars would look larger up on the slopes?

By the time he arrived at the Portland Rowing Club the moon had disappeared behind a bank of clouds. Earlier the weather guys had called it wrong. Were they correct now? He hoped not. Rain would wipe out any remaining evidence. He climbed out of his truck and hiked down the gangplank to the small houseboat he rented from a crotchety old pirate named Montgomery.

The tender sat still in the water, deck lights off.

His landlord lived in the front houseboat, ten times the size of his. Montgomery did things in style. Owning the largest houseboat at the marina was just one needle in a haystack of excesses the old man claimed.

Colefield wasn't ready to turn in just yet. If Montgomery was still awake, he had some business to discuss.

Down by Montgomery's door he heard the familiar sound of a faucet running. He peered down to the end of the walkway. His landlord was up to his old tricks. The eighty-five year old was swaying back and forth on tiptoes with nothing on but a bathrobe held open while he peed into the river.

Colefield caught him off guard. "You could get arrested for that!"

Startled, Montgomery looked up and grinned. His frizzled snow white hair and full beard glowed in the dim light. "I'm going to rust this rail in two before I die if it kills me!"

Even with marginal lighting from the entryway, Colefield could see where the paint on the metal handrail had flaked off and freckly pitting marred the surface. Years of pissing had paid off.

"It looks like you've nearly succeeded. What will you piss on next?"

"I'm sure I'll find a worthy cause..."

Montgomery finished his business and retied his bathrobe. He smiled over at Colefield and picked something from his front tooth.

"For a few weeks, it'll be no tinkling in the river for me or you."

"What are you talking about, Bill?"

Montgomery steadied himself on the handrail. "The dreaded dredging starts next week. Electricity and plumbing kaput! You're going to have to vacate the premises for a spell. A friend of mine might have a place in the Pearl District for you to drop your duffle during the move out. Interested? Or are you going to shack up with that bartender floozy?"

Colefield had totally forgotten that the month-long dredging project was happening so soon. It had been in the back of his mind but he thought it was at least a couple of weeks off. He never understood why there wasn't an easier method to remove built up sand from the river without disrupting entire communities from their homes for weeks at a time. Some type of vacuum system a diver could use underneath the houseboats instead of scooping it up one bucket at a time from below the water's surface. He was going to research that when he first heard about the coming dredge but had spaced on it.

"Hell of a time to dredge," Colefield mumbled. "Dead of winter..."

"Deadly wiener?"

"I said – dead of winter."

The ex-marine, if there was such a thing, crinkled his forehead, smiling. He had not heard him, of course. Served as a lieutenant in the Korean War or was it WWII? Years of firing every imaginable firearm known to mankind not to mention a small armory of explosives upstairs where he toiled away late into the night working on God knows what gun or device, had left him with about twenty-percent of his hearing. Yet he refused to wear hearing aids for "personal reasons", claiming it came in handy on dates.

"Can't hear you, but I'm all for you," was Bill's answer to most questions.

"Goodnight Bill. We'll talk in the morning. And get me the number of your friend."

Montgomery raised his right arm. "*Ora pro nobis...*"

Colefield fingered the shotgun shell absently as he headed home, thinking his Latin was about as rusty as the pissed-on railing. He managed to recall the well-worn phrase as he neared his door. "Pray for us."

Inside, Colefield flipped on an overhead florescent, opened the refrigerator and removed the last bottle of ale from the bottom shelf. He twisted off the cap, tossed it across the room and nailed the sink for a three-pointer. The ale was not nearly as tasty as the draft at Jill's. Next he rummaged for some beef jerky. Armed with dinner, he moved to the living room.

The hardwood floor squeaked a familiar hello as he flipped on a lamp. Tonight the room seemed smaller than normal, and colder. He noted his shallow breathing. Agitated and restless he flipped on the TV. Nothing interested him. He moved to the window and turned on the XM radio. It was tuned to a mellow station.

His grandfather once told him that in order to protect his emotions and hide any inner weakness; he needed to develop a strong physical persona. He took the advice to heart, first as a college quarterback, and later in the military and as a patrolman, where the ability to be viewed with respect and fear trumped parleying with an opponent any time.

He picked up his 50 lb. dumbbells and began working out to the music. A Leonard Cohen song was playing. *"We find ourselves on different sides of a line that nobody drew. Though it all may be one in the higher eye, down here where we live it is two."*

Colefield paused.

The words struck a familiar chord. Family, work, lovers … he had always struggled with relationships. Then the tempo changed. *"Mack the Knife"* came on.

His face twisted up into a crooked smile. *A knife, really Jill?* She was feistier than the Lab that had nipped at his leg. He loved that about her.

Warm thoughts flooded through him, a momentary distraction which quickly faded, leaving a deadly hollow in its wake.

6

"Meet me at 0900 at the country store on Sauvie Island. We'll have coffee and then drive out to the crime scene," Agent Tamara Costa said on the telephone the following morning.

"What evidence do you think we missed?"

"Things always look different in the morning," she replied.

"It'll be good to see you, Tam." Instead of a response, dead air.

Not exactly the way he had envisioned them chatting after so many years. No, Colefield – better to let sleeping dogs lie. Rekindle that teenage bonfire and someone gets burned. He had tried before. Once during leave. Another after his discharge. With his career starting off and training to attend, a permanent arrangement never materialized. Then she met someone else.

He put his cell phone down on the kitchen counter, refilled his coffee cup and opened the refrigerator to look for the carton of half-and-half. Stirring in the cream his mind began to wander.

Her reappearing out of the blue unsettled him and though Harvey had said it was fate that she had been called in on the case, he wasn't sold on that notion. Still the line between his past and present seemed to dissolve the more he worked this case. Facing Scarbough after all these years, why had he hidden his identity? Was a terrified boy still buried inside him? If that was true, he'd have to jettison that weakness and fear to solve the boy's murder.

As he opened the door to fetch the newspaper, the breeze off the river had a bone chilling bite. A northwesterly was pushing a bank of threatening clouds inland. It looked like rain, maybe even snow on the valley floor by Sunday. Whatever surprise the low pressure system building off the coast had in store, there was a sure chance of snow in the mountains and fresh powder on the slopes.

The pass through the Cascades would probably require chains, but conditions would be ideal for skiing. He remembered the last time he and Tam had gone skiing. Back when it didn't cost a week's salary for a lift ticket. Those were the days. The slopes weren't crowded. Even underage they toted little flasks of whiskey to sneak a drink up on the mountain. Everything was about the adventure … and that it had been.

He and Jill had never been skiing together. This was to be their first trip. How would it measure up?

He picked up the newspaper and closed the door. Sitting at the kitchen counter, he opened it and looked to see if *The Oregonian* had a story about the boy. He found a small article inside in the Metro Section which added no new information. He tossed the paper aside. Where had he laid his jacket and sidearm the night before?

He found both by the bookcase, put them on, and headed out.

To his surprise, his landlord was hobbling toward the parking lot. Montgomery wore baggy jeans and his favorite filthy blue sweatshirt, with USMC lettering on the front. The right pocket of his nylon jacket sagged – a Smith and Wesson – Colefield figured.

He had stopped to catch his breath and was leaning against the ramp railing with a cane in his hand, when Colefield caught up to him.

Montgomery raised the cane, pointing upriver. "Look!"

A flat barge hauling an enormous dredge that looked like some eerie carnival ride crawled toward them. This protruding metal apparition, rusted and menacing, had a large conveyor and oversized steel buckets for teeth. The industrial device belonged in a sci-fi film, not at their moorage.

"We're about to be invaded," Montgomery said.

"About that friend of yours … the one with the loft in the Pearl … tell her I'll take it!"

"Chicken shit! This could be the perfect time to move in with your bartender. Make an honest woman of her."

"Funny. You have her telephone number on you?"

Montgomery hobbled onward leaving Colefield behind, wondering if he'd heard him or not. He followed him the rest of the way up the ramp and into the parking lot before he brought the subject up again.

"Hey, if you want me out, I'll need your friend's number."

"Well, my friend Sally will take care of you."

They stopped beside Montgomery's old beat-to-shit blue sedan with the sprung trunk lid, the hinges bent from the last incident. The lid bounced up and down as he drove down the street like a big metal clamshell snapping open and closed. Montgomery had tried to secure it with a frayed rope, but that failed to hold it in place. Besides the trunk issue, the driver side front fender and door were caved in. The entire car was sprinkled in dents like it'd been hit with shrapnel. The passenger side had a long yellow crease that ran from the front fender all the way back to the rear quarter panel, courtesy of the Portland Street Car Montgomery had collided with on his way to the Multnomah Athletic Club.

It was pointless but he put his hand on the trunk and attempted to force it closed. No luck.

"You want me to get a bungee out of my truck?"

Montgomery rubbed the stubble on his chin. "Fuck it … I'm just going to the liquor store. Let it flop around. By the way, your name's in the paper. You're giving us hunters a bad rap."

"I don't believe it was a hunter who shot him."

"Who then?"

"Good question."

Colefield had nearly forgotten what was in his pocket. He reached in and pulled out the evidence bag with the shotgun shell and dropped it into Montgomery's hand.

"Christmas has come and gone my boy…"

"I'll need the pellet size and count. From the lines on the casing I'm pretty certain it's a home load. If you can determine the type of reloader used – all the better. Make a note of anything out of the ordinary."

"Do I sense underbelly tactics, here?"

"The lab would take weeks to get results. It won't be admissible as evidence but it will give me leverage, should I need it."

"Well, old boy, I can't seem to locate my good cheaters. My BB count may be off a wee bit."

"Buy a new pair. I'll reimburse you."

Colefield leaned on a post and waited. Watching Montgomery maneuver his gimp leg into the front seat was painful. Grimacing at the effort, he extracted a crumpled scrap of paper from his back pocket.

"No hanky-panky with her," he pointed his finger at him, frowning. "She's mine…"

Colefield took the old sales slip, turned it over and looked at the scribble on the back. He assumed it was Sally's contact information.

"Where are you moving?" Colefield folded the paper and tucked it inside his pocket.

"I can't hear you, but I'm all for you."

Colefield raised his voice. "When do I have to be out?"

"You want to make out?"

"Forget it – I'll call Sally today."

"Whatever flips your wick!"

Colefield only made it half a car length when the all-too-familiar sound of click, click, click, came from under the hood of Montgomery's pockmarked heap.

He reluctantly walked back over to the driver's side door. Montgomery shoved it open so they could talk.

"Pop the latch," Colefield said. "I'll go get my jumper cables."

"I owe you one, old boy…"

Colefield returned with his truck and pulled in beside Montgomery's car. Leaving the engine running, he climbed out, opened the hood of both vehicles, and stretched jumper cables across battery terminals.

He stepped out from under the hood and shouted, "Give it a try!"

The engine groaned but didn't start.

"Let it charge for a minute."

"You're going to charge me?"

"The battery." Colefield pointed to the engine compartment. "Let it charge! I'm going to climb inside my truck and rev the engine so the alternator can do its thing..."

Montgomery didn't seem to get any of what he had said, but he was willing to wait until further notice from the rank and file.

After five minutes of idling, he figured there was enough juice in the battery now to turn over.

"Try it again!"

This time the engine sputtered to life and the old pirate hollered, "Thar she blows!"

The engine ran rough. "Keep it running," Colefield shouted over the chugging.

While he disconnected the cables and stepped back, Montgomery kept pumping the accelerator. Each time he'd gun the pedal, the fan belt fired a shrill screech in protest.

Colefield closed the hood on both vehicles, stashed the cables behind the seat of his pickup truck, and walked back over to Montgomery's driver side door. "Drive around the block a few times before you turn off the engine. Better yet, leave it running at the liquor store. It needs time to charge."

"God and country thank you!"

As he pulled out of the parking lot, Colefield checked his watch. He was late. If it hadn't been for Montgomery he would have been on time. He could use that as his defense if need be. After all this time, he didn't want to resume things on the wrong foot with Tam.

The drive to Sauvie Island took about a half-hour. Although traffic had been light along the way he seemed to hit every red light. He picked up his phone and dialed her number but got her recording.

The steel bridge crossing the Multnomah Channel to the island had recently been remodeled. Extra lanes were added, making an ideal speed trap. A patrol car sitting alongside the shoulder of the ramp, window down, aimed a radar gun at oncoming bridge traffic. Colefield let up on the accelerator.

At least he thought he had. It's tricky to drive 25 mph with a lead foot. Yet, for both Tam's and Jill's sakes, he'd tried to keep within the posted speed. A citation would mean precious minutes cut from his time on the slopes. A chatty patrolman that sucked up time or a citation that sucked up a pay check. Neither was acceptable.

He drove by the patrol car and kept his fingers crossed. Glancing in his rearview, he didn't see any flashing lights. He checked again after the bridge. Just to be certain. Coast looked clear.

Traveling on the island offered options to a visitor. One road veered to the left and headed south out toward the famous Pumpkin Patch, unending farmland and cornfields. The other road continued north, straight down the bridge ramp, past the country store to the left and followed the channel. According to his watch, he should have arrived at the very spot where he was to meet Tam twenty minutes ago.

He pulled into the crowded parking lot and killed the motor. There were hordes of bicyclists and sleek racing bikes of all kinds stashed here and there. The spritely riders were standing around or sitting on wooden picnic benches alongside the building, sipping water, talking, and devouring nutritional snacks. All wore skin tight garments he wouldn't be caught dead in. Racing shorts, cleated bicycle shoes, jerseys, all sorts of pointy helmets. The expensive bicycles were made by foreign manufacturers whose names he could barely pronounce.

Unfortunately, none of the automobiles looked like anything a federal agent would drive – the lot was filled with Volvos, Mercedes, and Priuses. He got out of his pickup and entered the store.

It was different than he remembered as a boy. Cyclists of all ages and ethnicities were milling about a beverage counter and snack area. None of the faces resembled that of an FBI agent. Nor did he see anyone resembling her by the magazine section, or in back by the beverage cooler. The cooler clicked on and let out a loud hum just as he passed. He stopped at the bait freezer. A stout deliveryman wandered through a back door carrying frozen packages of bait and headed toward him. Colefield glanced down inside the big compartment at frozen herring and several different cures of salmon eggs. He stepped aside so the man could get by and returned up front, thinking he might have missed her in the crowd. Two shapely women in black bicycle shorts filled Styrofoam coffee cups at the beverage counter. He moved in behind them and waited his turn to fill two cups, one black and one loaded with cream and sugar. He couldn't remember how Tam took hers.

Colefield sipped the bitter coffee and lined up at the counter where an Asian woman rang up his purchase.

"I'm looking for someone. Has a woman been in asking questions?"

"Many woman, yes…"

"This one might have flashed a badge."

"She leave."

"How much for the coffee?"

"Two dolla."

Colefield paid with cash. Afterward he handed her his business card. "If she comes back, give her this. OK?"

The Asian nodded twice. "Yes, yes, OK."

The woman set the card on the register where she could easily see it. Colefield went back outside and struck up a casual conversation with a middle-aged guy in spandex, standing next to a seven-thousand dollar bicycle. Turned out the man was part of a local riding club that met at the store twice a month to tour the island. Today was an official race that was about to get underway.

The guy didn't stop there. Colefield was going to mention he had once lived on the island but the bicyclist wanted to tell him all about the island's wildlife before he got the chance.

"I've seen everything from bald eagles to black-tail deer. One time I almost ran over a raccoon or a possum, I couldn't tell for certain. It was near dusk. That same day a peregrine swooped down and snatched a mouse from the Pumpkin Patch."

"That so?"

"You ever been on the island before?"

"Not in a while."

"Well, this is why I moved here from California."

After the man left, Colefield pulled out his cell phone and dialed Tam's number again. He figured on driving to where the road ended to see whether or not she had gone ahead without him. Still no answer. He dropped his phone back into his pocket.

Before he had driven a quarter mile past the fork which veered to the other side of the island, flashing lights lit up his rearview mirror. His first thought was another speed trap he'd somehow missed. But it turned out to be an unmarked gray sedan, its flashing blue and red lights tucked secretively behind the grille.

He pulled over to the shoulder and stopped. The sedan pulled up behind him and a plain clothed policeman got out and headed his direction. The tall broad shouldered black man wore a standard two-tone gray suit with a detective's shield displayed on his left pocket. Out of habit Detective Daryl Redden unbuttoned his jacket as he approached. A wind gust snapped the jacket open, exposing a concealed weapon in a shoulder holster.

"Hey, Red!" The detective stuck out his hand. "I thought that was your old rust bucket."

"What are you doing on the island?" Colefield asked.

"You heard about the shooting here, right?"

"Sure. I was the first on scene."

"Hell – that's right. Harvey mentioned it in his brief."

"Where is Harv?"

"Harvey had a death in the family – an uncle, I think. He took a red-eye flight at midnight last night to New York to make funeral arrangements. I'm pulling some overtime. We got a possible hit on the kid's identity. I'm heading there now to see if it's legit. Reportedly, his mother lives on the island."

He wondered how they nailed the kid's ID.

"Who came forward?" Colefield asked.

"No one. ME found a hunting license tucked down inside the kid's sock. We tracked down the address on the card to the kid's grandparents. According to a neighbor they're in Reno. But they told us the mother lives on the island too and they left the kid with her on Wednesday. He fits the description. Want to break the news with me?"

Colefield looked at his watch. "Have you spoken with FBI Agent Costa this morning?"

"Sassy?"

Colefield hadn't heard that name in years. "Yeah. You know her?"

"Sure. We went to the Academy together."

"I was supposed to meet her about a half-hour ago. We were going to go back out to the crime scene."

"Well, I'd appreciate the backup on this. Hell, Sassy can come along too. Call her and tell her we are making the notification."

Colefield thought it over. "Why the hell not..."

"Appreciate it! This is the part of the job that never gets any easier. You never know how the family is going to react. It's back the other direction on Reeder Road, near the trailer park. You can park your truck or follow me, your choice."

"I'll follow you. I gotta split by noon."

Colefield had forgotten how picturesque the eastern side of the island was. The miles of open fields, the well cared-for farmhouses, the rural road winding its way through dogwoods and oaks all brought back pleasant memories. He'd spent plenty of time riding his dirt bike around these parts. It had been a great place to spend his youth. He regretted that he had caused his family to leave.

He eased off the accelerator as the unmarked sedan turned onto a dirt road flanked by tall trees and leading to a rundown farmhouse. He turned in and followed the sedan to the road's end and parked.

The residence had seen better days. It sat on the bank of the Columbia River. Nestled down in a grove of trees and well back from the main road, it had a creepy, almost haunted quality. The neighboring properties were a good distance away.

Siding was falling off. The roof sagged under a heavy moss canopy. The yard was overgrown. A patio swing on the front porch sat still. Rusted bicycles lay in the yard. No automobiles sat in the drive. The place looked abandoned.

The detective climbed out and Colefield met up with him as they approached the entry and rapped on a torn screen door. After no response, they tried knocking harder. Still nothing.

"Let's check around back," the detective said.

The back of the house had several fruit trees not yet in bloom scattered among an old swing set and broken appliances. A tilting outbuilding had probably held a well or septic pump in its day. By contrast, the house had a well maintained private slip. A fiberglass boat with an outboard sloshed back and forth in the current, clanging against the dock.

"Nice view," the detective said, looking at the river. "Wonder who owns the boat?"

"Doesn't seem to belong to this place, does it?" Colefield agreed.

Obviously, children once lived here. The swing set indicated that. The men headed toward the back door when, to their surprise, it creaked open.

A scrawny woman of indeterminate age wearing torn jeans and a tattered flannel shirt stepped out from the shadows and flipped a cigarette butt into the yard.

It was as if the men were invisible to her. In a stupor, she looked right through them, staring off at the muddy river. Her eyes were lifeless orbs. Her limp hair was thin as fishing line. On her cheek a fresh bruise bloomed. How the woman hadn't known they were on her property was beyond him. They had knocked loud enough to alarm the neighbors a quarter-mile away.

"Ma'am!" the detective shouted. "Would you be Anita?"

The woman, vague and rummy, eventually focused on them. "Get lost!"

"Ma'am we're with the police department. I'm Detective

Redden. This is Deputy Colefield. May we come in for a moment?"

"If you're lookin' for my no good son-of-a-bitch husband, I don't know where he ran off to. Bert's Tavern probably..."

The men approached the door. "Ma'am?" Colefield got a closer look at her face. He also noted bruising on her wrists. "Who assaulted you?"

The woman ignored the question, turned around and went back inside, leaving the door wide open. The officers looked at each other and followed.

The house was a dark cavern. Blinds were tightly drawn and the place reeked. It took Colefield a moment to realize they were standing in the kitchen.

A double sink held dirty dishes piled high on one side and blood encrusted carcasses of what looked like partially plucked ducks on the other. Red ants swarmed the walls and counters. He batted a few flies away. Feathers were strewn about the counter and floor.

The woman picked up a pack of cigarettes off the table, pulled a lighter from her shirt pocket, and lit one. The trail of smoke did nothing to kill her rank body odor and putrid breath.

Her hand trembled as she raised the cigarette to her lips. Colefield guessed she had been drinking for days.

"My know-it-all step-son call you?" The detective glanced at Colefield while she fumbled with the refrigerator door, and pulled out a beer, flinching as she pressed it against her swollen cheek.

"No one called us, Ma'am."

The woman sagged against the wall. "The bastard..."

"Do you want us to contact someone for you?" Colefield asked. "Social services? Or the paramedics?"

The woman wagged her head. She guzzled her beer and followed that with two deep drags from her cigarette. "Always ... always ... always after he comes back from the farm," she muttered. "The bastard..."

Colefield and the detective shared a perplexed look.

"You mentioned a step-son, Ma'am. Is he here?"

Colefield caught sight of a cereal box on the counter, an open jar of peanut butter, a half-eaten loaf of white bread. He reconsidered what was lying in the sink, smelling up the place.

"Ma'am, does your husband keep any guns in the house?"

"They're his fuckin' mess. I told him I'm done cookin' his stupid birds."

"Is that what the fight was about?"

"The bastard has our bedroom smelling like a gun shop."

"He keeps his guns in your bedroom?" the detective asked.

"Inside a locked cabinet. I should know. I tried to shoot him once. It was my dumb ass luck it was locked."

"Who else is in the house?"

"His brat daughter is probably somewhere painting her fuckin' toenails. I don't know where the hell his son is."

"What are their names?"

"Penny and Jeb."

"Do you have a son named Timmy, Ma'am?"

Her lips quivered. "I did."

"You did what?"

A dark cloud floated over her expression. "Had a son named Timmy, but he's gone now."

Detective Redden rubbed his chin, thinking. "So you know what happened to him?"

"It wasn't my idea…" she said.

Detective Redden reached for his weapon and signaled for Colefield to check out the rest of the house while he stayed with the woman.

Colefield entered a room off the kitchen – sort of a dining room slash living room. And like the kitchen, it hadn't been cleaned in months. There were moth eaten taxidermied trophies on the wall. Mismatched furniture and rotten food littered the landscape. The recliner was torn up. A filthy throw rug lay rumpled by the front door. Rat turds were everywhere.

Watching where he put his feet Colefield moved down the hall, poking his head into a bathroom, which was worse than any skid row toilet he'd experienced. A boy's bedroom came next. Blankets folded, bed made, clothes put away, and like the boat docked outside, in distinct contrast to the rest of the house. The bedroom at the end was probably the master. The door was ajar. A gun safe sat in the corner. He picked his way passed the stripped bed with the stained mattress, avoiding the filthy clothing and beer cans strewn about the floor.

He tried the handle. Locked.

The last bedroom to check was opposite the master. He listened at the closed door and then put his hand on his gun.

He nosed the barrel through the door crack and eased it open.

7

Seeing movement, the girl shoved the naked boy off her and screamed. The boy tumbled off the waterbed to the floor. He scurried toward a pile of clothing in the middle of the room, found a pair of dirty jeans and got all twisted around trying to pull them on.

Jeb? Colefield wondered.

No. This was obviously a girl's bedroom. Pink walls decorated with Hollywood posters and stuffed animals. She looked to be about fourteen, the boy, her age or older. She bolted upright, pulling a dirty sheet up over her bare breasts. She looked nothing like her stepmother in the other room. She had dark skin. Maybe traces of Aleutian or Indian bloodlines.

The thin sheeting couldn't hide the fact that she was skinny for a kid her age. Her lips looked deformed and swollen, but some of that was probably just smeared plum colored lipstick. The boy had hickies on his neck and purplish lipstick on his chest and stomach. A piercing festered in the corner of her mouth.

"You Penny?"

"Yeah. Get the fuck out!"

The deputy conjured one of those looks suggesting the strange factor had just doubled-down. He turned his attention to Redden who had showed up at the door to see what the commotion was all about. The boyfriend, still trying to jerk his jeans up, looked scared shitless. The detective holstered his gun.

"I'll go ask the stepmom if she wants us to detain the boy."

Colefield looked at the girl. "Put some clothes on. We're police officers. We have a few questions to ask you."

The girl threw back the covers and marched naked right in

48

front of him. That's when Colefield got a whiff of something sweet smelling like coconut. On the floor by the bed was a tube of sex lube. This wasn't her first time.

The boy, his pants hanging low on his ass gangster style, grabbed his shoes and T-shirt and attempted to slip by Colefield who was having none of it and blocked the exit.

The kid tried a fake right. He easily reached out and grabbed the boy's arm, spun him round and flattened him against the wall. "Easy does it tough guy. You heard the detective. We need to check with the mother."

The girl flung a pillow across the room at the deputy. "Let him go, asshole!"

"C'mon, man," the boy pleaded. "You're hurting me."

Colefield flipped the kid back around.

"Chill, dude! We were just screwin'…"

The boyfriend puffed out his chest. Suddenly, he was no longer intimidated by the deputy. Before he could do anything about the attitude adjustment, Detective Redden reappeared. "He can go. Tell the girl to meet us in the kitchen." Colefield looked back at the boy. "I see lube, but no condom."

"I pulled out."

"You did this time, dumb ass." Colefield cuffed the kid up the back of the head. Nothing like the sight of a gun aimed in your direction to ruin a perfectly good hard on.

The boyfriend sprinted barefoot down the hall and out the front door

At that age, Colefield thought he might have made out with a girl. *But sex?*

He checked the girl's window for a possible escape route before leaving the room and closing the door.

"Get dressed!"

A large heavy object thudded back.

Eventually, the door opened and the teenager wandered out. She looked different clothed. She had on a pair of torn jeans, an oversized sweatshirt with "Harvard" pasted across the front, and a pair of flip-flops. On her head sat a knit skull cap like those worn by rap stars, thugs and NFL players. She reminded Colefield of one of those kids on a reality TV show. A shiny tongue piercing bobbed about as she spoke.

She flipped Colefield the bird. "Where's Bobby?"

"He hit the road."

"Where's my alcoholic stepmom?"

He pointed toward the kitchen.

Detective Redden stood by the wall keeping an eye on the stepmother sprawled across the table when they entered the kitchen. The teen refused to sit down in the empty chair beside her, slouching against the wall.

"Where's your brother Jeb?" Redden asked.

"You're the cops, you tell me."

"Cut the crap." Colefield warned. "We need to find him."

"Whatever, dude," Penny feigned boredom. "He's probably with Timmy."

"I don't think so." Detective Redden roused the slumping drunk.

"Anita, did you shoot Timmy?"

The woman's eyes widened. "What are you talking about? I didn't shoot anyone."

"Your son, Timmy. You said it wasn't your idea? Who pulled the trigger?"

The teen reacted to the news. "Timmy's been shot?"

"You'll have your turn in a minute," Detective Redden said to her. "Anita – consider what you say carefully. What do you know about your son's death?"

"He's dead?"

"Yes ma'am," Colefield said. The men looked at each other. It was clear that they had misconstrued her earlier statements.

"So you're saying you didn't know about your son's death?"

"No! How could I?"

Colefield looked over at the trembling teen. She had sunk to the floor.

Detective Redden told them the basic details, leaving out the most disturbing aspects that could wait until later.

"Can we call someone for you?" Colefield asked.

"Who? My worthless husband?"

"Another relative, perhaps?"

"That rotten no good two timing prick! He's off with that blonde bimbo again. I know it! And detectives? He's the one you should be harassing! Not me! Go arrest the big hunter!"

The woman swiped at the tears running down her face.

Penny stood up and moved over by the table near her stepmother. "When did it happen?" Her voice barely a whisper.

"When did you last see Timmy?"

The tough streetwise girl had given up. Penny tried to grab Anita's hand for comfort but her stepmother was having none of it. She pushed the teen away and swayed to her feet.

Detective Redden put his hand on the mother's shoulder. "Ma'am, I'd feel more comfortable if you sat back down."

The woman shrugged him loose, picked up the loaf of bread off the counter top and began savagely screaming while shredding it and hurling it in every direction. Only then did she return to her chair, as if some relief had been gained from her outburst. She sagged down, her battered face as white as the bread she'd just attacked.

Detective Redden took the lead.

"Anita, you said Timmy lived with his grandparents. When did they drop him off?"

"How can I know that if I thought he was with them?"

Penny shouted. "You were here when they dropped him off!" The angry teenager was back.

Colefield counted at least a dozen or more beer bottles and cans lying around. No telling how much Anita had consumed over the last couple of days. At least a case, he assumed.

Colefield looked at the girl. "When did the grandparents drop Timmy off?"

"Wednesday — Wednesday night, late."

That seemed to fit what Detective Redden had told him earlier.

"You're positive it's Timmy?" The mother tilted her head, eyes closed.

Detective Redden stepped toward the table. "Well, Ma'am, we'll need you to come down to the morgue to ID the body to be certain. That is, after you've had a chance to sober up." The comment didn't seem to penetrate her pained face.

"It can't be my son."

Colefield looked at the detective. Detective Redden reached into his jacket pocket and removed a Ziploc, then held it out for the woman to examine.

"Do you recognize this?" Detective Redden stared at her. "We believe this is your boy's signature."

Her eyes briefly glanced over the hunting permit and shotgun certification visible through the plastic before looking elsewhere.

"Had your son ever gone hunting on the other side of the island before?" he asked.

Before the woman could answer, the teen interrupted. "Tell them Timmy only went hunting because he hated it here. How else was he supposed to get away from this house?" She began to cry.

Anita shot her a look. "No, you're wrong. Jeb hunts with him and so does your bastard father."

"That's a load of crap!" Penny snapped.

"Who shot the ducks in the sink?" Redden asked calmly.

"I don't want anything to do with him or his stupid birds."

"Did you find a shotgun?" the teen asked next.

The two men looked at each other. Since it was Redden's case, Colefield held his tongue.

Anita reached toward her beer bottle and accidently knocked it over, the foamy river streaming across the table and straight onto Colefield's pants.

Sighing, Redden righted the bottle. "I'm going to look around."

Detective Redden left. While he was away, Colefield studied the girl. She seemed to be caught half-way between wanting to be helpful and wanting to fuck the world.

"I need to lie down." The stepmother's eyes drooped.

Her head wagged from side to side like a bobble head doll. It was all Colefield could do to restrain himself from placing his hands on her head to hold it still. He could hear the homicide detective opening and closing cupboards in the next room, rattling doors. The teen went over to the sink and stared repugnantly at the birds. "These are disgusting!"

Colefield moved next to her. "Who else knew that the grandparents were dropping Timmy off for the weekend?"

"Just Jeb and me."

"You're certain?"

"Look, once upon a time, he lived with that wreck over there. That's when she and dad were first married."

"What happened?"

"They started fighting all the time."

"And?"

"And what?" She glared back. "She and my dad fight constantly, you know. It's her fault dad's a drunk. I blame her for this whole mess. She gave Timmy away."

This must have been the point the woman was trying to make when she said she didn't have a son anymore. That she valued her relationship with her husband more than she did her kid.

"So the grandparents were raising him?"

"I said that."

She glanced back down at the sink. "She doesn't do anything around here but drink."

The teen plucked one of the ducks by the neck and tossed it out the front door into the yard. She did the same with the second bird and then returned to the kitchen, agitated.

She squirted a glob of soap into the sink, constantly biting at her piercing – a nervous tick. When she was done cleaning the sink but not the dishes, she backed herself into the corner digging at her lower lip with a soapy pinky finger, looking distraught.

"What's going to happen now?"

"We'll need your mother – stepmother," he corrected, "to come downtown and identify the body when she sobers up. Are there any pictures of Timmy in the house? "

"I don't think so." She paused. "Wait. I think I've got one on my phone." She reached into her pocket and after a few strokes held up a photo of her and Timmy dressed up like superheroes. "That was taken at Halloween this year."

Colefield stared at Spiderman and Wonder Woman. With his face covered in blue Timmy was still a faceless child. Colefield couldn't stop his mind from substituting his own features for Timmy's. Something about the look in his eyes. Perhaps they shared more than gunshot wounds to the face.

The girl stared at him. "I'll do it."

"The boy's in pretty bad shape."

"What do you mean?"

"He doesn't look the same."

"They shot him in the face?"

Colefield nodded.

"The fuck!"

"When Detective Redden gets back I'll talk to him. See if he thinks it's a good idea for you to go downtown."

She turned and stared toward the living room. "What's he looking for anyway?"

"He's just doing his job."

A few moments later, Detective Redden returned looking disgruntled. Apparently the detective had not found a weapon that would link someone from the house to the boy's murder.

"Ma'am, do you know where your husband keeps the keys to the gun safe?"

The woman didn't open her eyes or look at the detective.

"Answer him!" The teen slapped her stepmother hard across the face.

"You hit just like your bastard father."

8

Gravel crunched in the driveway. The men looked at each other.

"I'll see who it is," Colefield volunteered, unbuckling the strap on his sidearm as he headed to the front door.

Peering out the screen door, Colefield smiled. He'd recognize that determined Italian face anywhere. He stayed put for a moment admiring the view, amused at the pissed-off manner in which she fussed with her dark hair. He was certain she was primping for him. Finally, she exited the car and headed toward the porch. A tailored blue suit highlighted her long legs.

Colefield secured his weapon and opened the door.

"Hello, Jason." Agent Tamara Costa smiled.

She raised her arms as if she expected a hug. Colefield, however, aware of Detective Redden's presence, didn't reciprocate. A hurtful expression flashed across her face but didn't last.

"I'm sorry we missed each other this morning," Colefield began.

But Costa was staring past him at the disheveled house.

"I got your call that Redden had found the mother and needed help identifying the body."

When she finished speaking and looked him in the eye, his knees nearly buckled. She still got to him.

"It's been a long time, Tam."

"Yes it has, Jason."

Colefield stared at her for a moment, allowing his memories to fill the gap.

Finally, he said, "So you work for the Feds? How are those pussies treating you?"

"Like my shit don't stink. How about the river rats down at county?"

"About the same."

Her eyes crinkled as she smiled.

"How's married life these days?" The question came out awkwardly. He wanted to take it back. Costa hesitated, needing a moment to gather a reply.

"Mark and I split the sheets three months ago. He wouldn't leave a job in D. C. when I got transferred to Seattle. So I packed up the cat, wiped a few tears away and left."

"Sorry to hear that."

"So was the cat."

She paused a moment. "We haven't filed divorce papers or anything, but that's coming. I'm just glad we never had kids." She shook it off. "How about you? Did you ever marry?"

The comment took him by surprise. He laughed at the thought.

After seeing Colefield's reaction, it was back to business for Agent Costa.

"Shall we go in?"

Detective Redden brought her up to speed. She wanted to conduct her own interview. In the end, the teenager had gotten her way. Since the stepmother had been in no condition to do it, the girl had volunteered to identify the body at the morgue. It was an iffy call, but Redden wanted a positive ID before they went any further. Costa would handle the females from this point and transport Penny and Anita.

It was decided that Redden and Colefield would check out the tavern in search of Anita's husband, who could also provide an identification. Costa and Redden exchanged cell numbers and Costa said she would follow them. No telling what trouble they might find if the hubby got out of hand. The man was clearly a wife beater. Often these short fused situations blew up at the slightest provocation. They needed to find out if he knew where his step-son Jeb was. There was also the more important question of whether he killed Timmy. At the very least, he was a person of interest.

As Colefield followed the sedan down the winding road the local tavern came into view. A neighborhood joint which once sported a big neon sign, it no longer resembled the place he remembered from his youth. The current sign hung from a rusted frame on the roof. It had more bullet holes than a WWII fighter plane. It had been used for target practice by generations of kids and drunks alike. Admittedly, Colefield had shot a few BB rounds of his own at it.

At one time, the sign read "Bert's Tavern" but now most of the "B" and "Tav" had been shot out and so it read "ert's ern."

Colefield pulled in behind the detective's car and parked. In the space beside his pickup was a muddy 4 x 4.

He climbed out and joined the detective at the sedan's back door. Agent Costa's car pulled alongside. Leaving Penny and her stepmother inside, Costa joined the two men.

"Anita identified that 4 x 4 as belonging to her bastard husband." Costa laughed. "And that kid's a handful. She just told me to fuck myself when she heard me call Child Protective Services about her."

Colefield hadn't considered that Penny might soon be chewed up by the foster care system. In many ways he sympathized with the girl. Living under the roof of abusive parents was tough duty. The path she was on would lead to the same self-destruction as the stepmother's unless she received help soon. He made a mental note to call his friend at CPS to see if he could help smooth that transition and get the teen some counseling. If nothing else, the friend could see about getting her medical attention for the lip piercing, which he was sure was infected. And while they were at it, perhaps some birth control.

"So what's the plan?"

Colefield glanced over his shoulder. The tavern had a front and rear door and sat at the edge of a cornfield. At this time of year, the field was just a flattened mess of rotting husks and tall grass. Good for rodents to hide in, but little else.

"OK," Redden began. "We go inside. We play nice. We ask a

few pertinent questions. We don't like what we hear, we slap cuffs on him. Sound reasonable?"

"You think the wife will agree to press charges?" Costa asked.

"Those are long odds," Colefield said.

"Keep your cool in there. As much as I agree with you about this asshole, we need to do this by the book." Redden checked his weapon.

"I'll provide backup for you two cowboys," Costa said.

"Hold up," Colefield said, getting an idea. "I want to check something first."

Since the windows were down it would be a cinch to search the glove box of the 4 x 4. He reached in through the open window and popped the glove box latch. He fished through the junk papers and hand tools, but didn't spot a weapon. He pulled out the registration, glanced at the name, and looked disturbed.

He rejoined the others at Costa's car.

Motioning for the girl to roll down the window he leaned inside. "Is your last name Scarbough?"

The girl appeared suspicious. "Yeah. Why?"

"Are you related to a Hank Scarbough?"

"Yeah, sure. He's my grandfather."

"The same Scarbough that lives on the island?"

She nodded.

"Did he ever take Timmy hunting?"

"Grandpa would never hurt Timmy." And with that the girl clammed up.

Colefield glanced at Anita passed out and slobbering in the front seat.

"Stay here with your stepmom. We're gonna go get your dad. Then we'll all head downtown together."

So the grandfather knew the victim even if he claimed to not recognize him. His list of suspects continued to expand. Colefield's mind made mental links as they opened the tavern door.

The inside of the bar looked as trashed as the sign. Between bar fights and general neglect, the place had taken its fair share of abuse over the years. Faded posters plastered along the walls hid large holes in the sheetrock. A fixture of fluorescents had burnt out over the bar. Upholstery was torn and tables and chairs were nicked and broken. At the bar men in dirty work clothes nursed their beers, their eyes glued to the big screen TV mounted on the wall. The men didn't seem to notice the three strangers that had just entered their watering hole but several of the women noticed Agent Costa. It was in their DNA to spot potential interlopers. Costa hung back by the front door. The Oregon vs. Oregon State game was on, which explained why everyone was intently watching the TV.

Colefield scanned the crowd while Redden spoke to an employee. The barmaid pointed out their target – a large man sitting at a table in back stacked with empties. His pals, two middle-aged redwoods in greasy overalls, sat hunched over the table alongside the man, throwing back pints as fast as the skinny barmaid could deliver them.

The men headed toward the back while Costa took a central position, but they had waited too long. The man in question had a sixth sense like many criminals do. He jumped up with a full beer, lobbed it at Colefield and bolted out the emergency exit.

His companions rose from the table puffed up like roosters and blocked the door. Hearing the commotion, some men at the bar were jumping to their feet.

Costa didn't hesitate. The situation was escalating by the second. She pulled her gun and displayed her badge. "Everybody calm down. This is police business."

The two hulks moved forward, their intent clear. Colefield knew the look. To them a fight trumped a college game on TV any day. Head down he charged toward the exit door.

His head and shoulder collided with the first man's gut. Something he'd done hundreds of times before with favorable results. But this farmer was a walking, talking Peterbuilt who barely flinched when he slammed against him. The guy's feet certainly didn't buckle like Colefield had anticipated. His big buddy just grinned like Colefield had gone and made a really bad decision.

The man leaned over and wrapped his grizzly bear arms around Colefield's torso, throwing him over a table as easily as tossing a bale of hay into the bed of a pickup truck.

Redden and Costa stepped forward and ended the fun. Redden calmly drew his Glock, pointing it in the big guy's face. Costa swept the crowd by the bar.

The big men froze. "We're just funnin' here."

Redden glanced over at Colefield who was on his feet, brushing a decade's worth of dust off his pant legs.

The men kept their distance. Using his weapon as motivation, Redden waved them clear of the exit. The men sheepishly shuffled aside like chorus girls. As Costa backed out the front door, Redden and Colefield made their exit through the back.

The light outside was blinding. Colefield squinted across the field at miles of open corn stalks. Penny's dad was nowhere to be found out back. They ran toward the parking lot just as Costa screamed: "Stop! Police!"

With gun drawn Costa aimed across the parking lot. The girl's father and the teenager were already in the cab of the 4 X 4. Before shots were fired, the truck sped off, rifling the officers with bits of debris and gravel.

Redden rubbed dirt from his eyes. "What a shit show!" Turning to Costa, he yelled. "Call for backup!"

Costa nodded, holstered her weapon, and pulled out a cell phone.

Colefield and Redden ran for the sedan, pulling to a stop at the flat rear tire. Someone had stuck a knife blade in the sidewall, tearing a gash clean through. They also spotted a fresh cigarette butt smoldering on the ground beside the rear door, traces of purple lipstick on the filter. Colefield stomped the cigarette out with his toe. The men looked at each other. Was she or her dad responsible for this?

"Looks like I got this one!" Colefield scooped up the girl's knit cap lying on the ground where it had fallen off and hustled toward his pickup with Detective Redden a step behind.

"Stay with the mom!" Colefield shouted to Costa as he spun out of the lot.

* * *

On the narrow twisting road up ahead, Colefield spotted the tailgate of the 4 X 4 barreling through the blind turns. The truck was heading to the south side of the island. Colefield ground gears trying to close the gap.

"Damnit! They're losing us! This tub go any faster?" Detective Redden braced his hand against the dash staring out the windshield as pavement whizzed by.

"It's past its prime, but it can still haul ass."

"Prove it."

"Do you think the girl went willingly?" Colefield asked

"Hard to know. Would you choose to go with your drunken dad who may have killed your stepbrother, or prefer to identify his mutilated remains and then go into the foster care system?"

"I should have disabled the car." Colefield wagged his head in disgust.

Colefield struggled to make out the 4 X 4 as it swerved back and forth through a series of tight corners. As the teen's head turned to look out the rear window, the man grabbed a fist-full of her hair and pulled her back around.

A sharp bend in the road appeared, flanked by tall trees. Colefield couldn't see beyond the corner. The speedometer was still climbing when he hit the brakes. A large group of cyclists suddenly appeared around the bend, peddling in the center of his lane. The 4 X 4 had blazed by them, causing several to swerve in all directions. One rider careened into a ditch and crashed head over heels. He cranked the wheel hard veering onto the opposite shoulder to miss the others by mere inches. He kept his focus on the speedometer and pressed the gas pedal to the floor, leaving the screaming cyclists in the dust.

Several turns later they came upon a large open field off to the north with rows of rotten pumpkins as far as you could see. There was a shortcut across the field and in its day, the old pickup would have traversed it without any trouble. So when the 4 X 4 veered off the paved road into the muddy field Colefield followed.

"Hold on!" he shouted as they bounced up and down on the springy seat as the truck swerved off the road in hot pursuit.

The old pickup truck followed the same deep ruts but didn't have enough clearance to avoid the smashed pumpkins. It began sinking into the soft dirt, losing precious time. The tires sank deeper and deeper until the truck's axles packed with mud became anchors. The motor overheated.

He floored it, as the front end plowed the earth and nosedived into a hollow crevice that turned out to be an irrigation ditch covered in flattened corn stalks.

Colefield's chest slammed against the steering wheel so hard that something cracked. Redden banged his shoulder against the door leaving a dent behind. He let out a cry and clutched his shoulder, wincing in pain.

Colefield gasped a few shallow breaths and then shut off the ignition switch. He looked across the cab at the detective.

Redden just shook his head.

Colefield climbed out to survey the damage.

Wheels were buried in mud up to the frame. He limped over to the front of the truck and glanced underneath. The steering mechanism had snapped. A piece of broken tie rod hung down from the undercarriage.

Detective Redden looked ashen as he climbed out and clutched his shoulder. He hobbled over to Colefield and stared off toward the field where the 4 X 4 had rejoined the road and disappeared from sight.

Redden was pushing buttons on his cell phone with his good arm. "We lost them, Costa. They are headed East on Reeder Road."

Colefield was pissed. A hissing sound underneath the hood increased as steam began to roll out and fill the sky. A radiator hose, he figured. He started to pop the hood open and immediately gave up when the pain in his ribs made him involuntarily clutch himself.

"I caved in my ribs and my truck."

"I can beat that," Detective Redden said. "I think my shoulder's broken."

9

The men slogged through the ruined pumpkin patch toward the main road as the sun nudged out from behind the clouds.

The whole area smelled like pumpkin pie.

"You married, Redden?"

"Was? You?"

"No. Kids?"

"Two. Boy and girl. Eight and ten. You?"

"No."

Colefield scraped his heel over the edge of the asphalt while he stared off into the distance. Across the open field barely in view sat a decrepit house. Abandoned and long in need of repair, the once bright azure paint had faded and peeled. Colefield's childhood home hadn't been occupied in years. Built after the Second World War, the wooden structure was a cheaper version of colonials you find back East or even down South. He'd never liked the house. It had been built with second-grade lumber. Always bitter cold in winter, sizzling hot in the summer and connected to too many disturbing memories. Over the years, he had carefully encapsulated his childhood recollections to exclude this house that languished by the road. His mother had loved it, and she never blamed him for causing them to leave.

"What are you looking at?" Detective Redden raised his good arm above his head as a test, and then attempted to do the same with the other. He elevated it slightly before he stopped, grimacing in pain.

"Just getting my bearings," Colefield said. "Hand me your cell a minute. I wanna give Costa some more information."

"While you're at it, tell her to come get us."

Colefield took the cell from Redden and called Costa. When she answered he said: "If the officers can't locate them on Reeder, tell them to search near Cunningham Slough. If it hasn't changed, there's a dirt road. They may try using it. Oh, we're on foot and need a ride." After a long pause he just said "Fine."

He passed the cell back to Redden, shaking his head. "Let's start walking."

"You're shitting me … really?"

"The mother barfed all over the car. A dozen cyclists are getting patched up by the locals from the bar, and everyone has decided to file police reports against us for reckless driving and assault."

The men started walking along the shoulder of the road. Colefield studied the detective holding his body at a funny angle. "How's the shoulder?"

The detective smirked. "Nothing a handful of Vicoden and few cold beers won't cure. What about you, tough guy? How are the ribs?"

"Only hurts when I breathe."

Just then, a John Deere tractor rumbled up from behind. It began to veer clear of the men. Colefield jumped out into the center lane and waved the driver over to the side of the road. The tractor slowed down, stopping along the shoulder, its big diesel engine idling down to a purr.

"We sure could use a lift!"

The farmer studied him for a moment. "Was that your truck back in the pumpkin patch?"

Colefield nodded, looking embarrassed. "We sort of ran aground."

The young man in overalls laughed. "Never heard that one before. Can your friend climb aboard? He looks pretty banged up."

"Hell, he's John Wayne."

But Detective Redden was having a hard time keeping a straight face as Colefield boosted him up onto the hard fender. He slumped down and let out a deep sigh.

Colefield limped around to the opposite side of the tractor and hoisted himself up onto the fender fighting back the sharp pain in his side.

"Where to?"

"Bert's Tavern."

The tractor jostled along and it seemed to take forever to crawl down the rough road. Every little speck of gravel that the big tires rolled over caused him agony.

To get his mind off it, he struck up a conversation with the farmer.

"Sure," the young man was saying, "I heard of Scarbough. Who hasn't? His grandfather was one of the original founders of the island. Came over from Ireland as a poor boy and made millions in the shipyards. Willed it all to the son when he died."

"When was that?"

"I guess Scarbough would have been twenty when the dad died."

"What'd he do with the inheritance?"

"What land he didn't inherit he purchased when prices were still affordable."

"What do you know about his son, Dave?"

"Son's been in and out of jail more times than I can count. I don't know if they still have much to do with each other. His dad tried to disown him a few years back after the son divorced his first wife. I don't think he stuck to his guns because the son remarried a few years later and I heard they had patched things up. I guess Scarbough gets along fine with the new daughter-in-law. He got two grandkids out of the first marriage and I think he'd like to have more. But I'm not sure if it's meant to be. That's about all I know. They live over on the eastside of the island somewhere."

Detective Redden seemed to snap out of his pain and craned his neck around. "What'd he do time for?"

"Assault. Man's got a temper. Add alcohol, you get fireworks."

"We witnessed some of those about an hour ago," Redden said.

"What about the daughter-in-law?" Colefield asked.

"Can't say I know much about her. But people talk."

"What kind of talk?"

"I shouldn't say. My wife told me once, but asked me not to spread it around."

"Spread what around?"

"Rumors mostly."

"This conversation ends with us," Colefield said. "What kind of rumors?"

"Oh, hell – the wife can't have any more kids because she had a miscarriage that went south, if you get my drift."

The man paused and glanced back at them. "So who were you chasing across Fred's Pumpkin Patch?"

"Who said anything about a chase?" Detective Redden blurted out.

"Well, I know Fred – the farmer's field you mowed down – and he don't take too kindly to people tearing up his fields."

Wonder if he shoots at them? Colefield mused.

"Tell him I'll pay for any damage."

"I'll let him know."

Colefield looked at Detective Redden who rolled his eyes. Even with one good arm Redden struggled to hang on. His mind seemed rooted elsewhere.

It was time to change the subject. "So what do the islanders think happened to the little boy found dead out in the field yesterday?"

"It's weird, if you ask me. Hunters are pretty respectful in these parts. The game wardens keep an eye on things. Some of them think it was just a freak accident. Either of you hunters?"

Redden shook his head.

Colefield nodded. "I've spooked a few Ruffed Grouse over the years. You?"

"Grew up hunting. If you've done much of it, you know how easy it is to get turned around. You think somebody is in one spot and then you find out they aren't. My theory, someone shot the kid and didn't even know it. Once they see the news and figure it out – they'll come forward."

Up ahead, the road veered and the tavern came into view. Colefield considered the man's theory as the tractor pulled into the tavern's chaotic parking lot.

"You can let us off here," Colefield told the driver.

"Looks like a few cyclists ran aground today as well." The farmer laughed as he pointed out bent and twisted bicycles perched on bike racks. Costa was handing out her business card to a man covered in road rash.

The men climbed down and shook off the rough ride. The young man smiled and looked at Colefield. "If you need a tow or any repair work I do that on the side. I've got a large shop at the back of my farm. I'd be happy to take a look at your old rig. Otherwise, the town of Renton is about the closest place to find a garage on Saturday. You'd better hurry though cuz it closes at noon."

Noon! Jill! Colefield felt an old familiar detachment grab hold as soon as the thought left his mind. "Thanks," Colefield said. "Yeah, if you've got the time today, I'd appreciate a tow." Colefield reached into his pocket and handed the key to the driver.

The man put the key in his pocket. "Know if you bent an axle?"

"I don't think so. But look it over, will you? Something's busted under there."

"You in a hurry to get it back? Might take me a week or so."

"That's fair enough. Just do whatever it takes."

He figured by the time he had it towed into the city and rounded up parts, he'd be time and money ahead to leave it in the farmer's capable hands. In the meantime, he could borrow Montgomery's old shit box on wheels.

Colefield pulled out his wallet and gave the man one of his business cards with his contact information.

The man glanced at it and let out a chuckle. "River Patrol, eh? Guess you weren't kiddin' when you said you 'ran aground'."

"Let me put your number in my phone." Colefield began

patting his pockets. After a moment his face registered a weary resignation. The damned thing was gone. He was pretty sure it had been lost in the bar encounter. Sighing, he pulled out his notepad.

After the exchange, Colefield, thanked the farmer for the lift and the old tractor drove off as Costa made her way over. Detective Redden had staggered toward the sedan. When they wandered up Redden was glaring down at the flat tire. He braced himself on the trunk as his shoulder spasmed. "Will you give me a hand, Colefield?"

"Sure. In a second. I'll be right back. Somewhere inside that tavern there's a cell phone with my name on it."

"Then I'd better come with you."

"You're not going anywhere." Costa stepped up. "Stay with the Mother of the Year and I'll provide backup for Butterfingers here."

As the two opened the tavern door, the entire bar turned and stared. The bartender was messing with the TV. The picture was flickering on and off. The drunken crowd, which now included pissed off and entitled cyclists, was agitated. Head down, Colefield moved quickly to the back of the bar. At the back table the two rednecks looked pained to see him again. The stack of empties on their table had doubled. Colefield figured that if he did have another go at the men, their reaction time would be slowed by the alcohol. It just might give him an edge. But, as it turned out, the fight in them had played out. And really, he could have no more fought a man than hitchhike to Mars.

Over by the wall Colefield spotted something that resembled a cell phone in the corner. Out of spite he slowed as he passed by the men's table and picked up the pieces. He held onto the broken mess figuring he could always throw it at anyone who got in his face.

At the door Costa asked, "You find it?"

"What's left of it."

They went back outside to the parking lot. Detective Redden seemed impressed by the hunk of crushed plastic that Colefield showed him. His smart phone was no longer smart. Instead, it was a pile of broken parts held together by wire threads made somewhere in China.

"Must be your karma today," Redden said. "Everything you touch is going to shit."

"You want to go back in and roust those two for busting up your phone?" Costa asked.

"I doubt anyone in there would sign on as a witness on my behalf."

"Point taken," Costa said. "I made the call to the Sheriff's Office. Columbia County dispatch sent a deputy out to look for the 4 x 4. Apparently the slough is their jurisdiction. If you want I could drive us back out to the house?"

"Look, someone has to take Redden to get his shoulder looked at. Call dispatch again, see if they've heard anything from the deputy while I change the tire. If they have news, we'll call an ambulance for Redden here, and you and I can head out, collect the girl, and have a nice long chat with the hubby. Oh, shit, wait. Anita still poses a problem. Hell – as much as I hate the idea, we'll let them handle the girl and her father for now. If Anita is still conscious, escort her downtown. Someone's still got to ID the boy."

He turned his attention to the detective. "Give me ten minutes to change the tire and then I'll drive you to the ER."

"You're the boss." Redden was in no condition to argue.

Zip – those were the odds he gave any patrolmen of finding that 4 x 4. There were a million places to hide. The 24,000 acres on the island were sprinkled with lakes and surrounded by water on all sides from which to make an escape. There were also dozens of abandoned houses and outbuildings. The guy was sure to know the cops would come looking.

"Let me have the key to the trunk," Colefield said to Redden, "I'll see if this government piece of shit has a spare."

Not long after, Colefield parked the sedan in the emergency lot of Emanuel Hospital and helped Detective Redden inside. As they stood at the check-in desk, a sharp pain buckled his knees but he didn't whimper. Indeed if his rib was broken there was absolutely nothing that could be done about it. In the old days they used to wrap the ribs with an elastic bandage but that practice had been abandoned after someone sued the hospital over a broken rib puncturing a lung.

The Admitting Nurse jotted down the detective's insurance information and then told the men to have a seat in the waiting room. Someone would be along shortly.

As the men sat down, Detective Redden pulled out his cell phone. "I'd better call the ex, break the news to her that I can't take the kids for the weekend."

"Need some privacy?"

Redden shook his head. "Hell – I've got a message." Redden punched a few buttons and listened to the playback. He hung up and turned toward Colefield. "That was the Sheriff's Department. No surprise, but the house was empty. No sign of the vehicle yet either. They're searching the island, but they figure they're long gone."

"I'd bet my bottom dollar he's still on that island somewhere."

Colefield busied himself while Redden talked with his ex-wife. He checked out some of the other patients waiting to see a doctor. There was an Asian woman clutching her very pregnant belly. She looked both uncomfortable and worried. Fear in her eyes suggested that at any moment the baby would squirt out onto the linoleum. Opposite her sat a homeless guy. Rags for clothing. No shoes or socks, his lobster feet covered with open sores. Near him sat a young mother with a sick toddler with a loud barking cough. Back in the corner sat a retired couple, the husband gasping for breath as if the oxygen bottle at his feet was running on empty. A plastic tube ran from the bottle to a mask strapped to his face. He kept tugging on it.

Detective Redden finished his telephone call and offered his cell phone to Colefield.

"I'm going to step outside."

Colefield stood under an awning to make his call. He checked the time on his wrist watch. It was almost 4 p.m. when he dialed Jill's number. The phone rang and rang and rang and then went to voicemail. Leaving a message seemed like a chicken shit thing to do, but he needed to let her down as soon as possible. He kept it brief and said he'd explain everything that evening at her place.

He returned inside, gave Redden his phone back, and sat down. The detective looked at him.

"You know, Colefield," he said. "This shoulder is going to take me out of action. With Harvey out of the office and now this, I'm going to suggest the case be transferred to you. I read your file. You were a diver and did demolition work during your stint in the Navy. You logged five years on the street before you went to work for the River Patrol. You're a good cop. I'd like you to be lead man. You down with that?"

"If the Lieutenant signs off," Colefield said, "we're good. I may have a very pissed off girlfriend over this but I'll make it up to her somehow."

"Doubtful," Redden moaned.

10

By the time Colefield borrowed Montgomery's car and reached the condominium on Tomahawk Island Drive, daylight was fading. Jill didn't wield a knife when she answered his knock, but her hip blocked the threshold and she refused him entry. Rain poured down, dumping on the front porch and soaking Colefield. She seemed happy about that. A car drove by, the tires sloshing through the standing water on the pavement.

"Can I come in?"

"No."

"Jill, I'm sorry."

"I had my heart set on this trip."

"So did I – I'll make it up to you."

She didn't believe him.

"I knew last night you'd bail on me."

"I tried to call you when it all went to shit…"

"The only call I had today was an hour ago."

"My cell phone got smashed while in pursuit of a suspect." He lamely held up his baggie of parts. "I borrowed a phone at the hospital where I took my injured partner following said pursuit which also destroyed my truck. I borrowed the car I'm driving. It all sounded so crazy I didn't want to leave a long message on the phone. I figured I owed you a full explanation in person."

She wasn't buying it. "They serve beer in hospitals now?"

"No."

"Then why do I smell alcohol?"

True enough, he could smell it too. "A drunken woman spilled a beer on me. Then I was in a barroom brawl that smashed my phone. Could be either or both you smell."

"Got to be in a bar to be in a barroom brawl." She was still having none of it. Her mind was set. He could see it in her mocking expression.

"You promised me this wouldn't happen, Jason. In the short time we've been dating, you've cancelled three dates because you had to work some case or another. I've always tried to give you the benefit of the doubt but this beats all. I rented skis. I arranged to have Julie cover my shifts at the bar. I went out of my way to make this happen. You didn't. I own a business and found time for you but you can never find time for me. It's like there's this invisible line you can't cross whenever you have to choose between me or the job."

"I know it seems that way right now."

"So what do you expect me to do?"

He shrugged. "At least let me reimburse you for the ski rental." As he reached for his wallet she physically recoiled.

"This isn't about money." She studied his wet face. "I took a chance with you, but you just blew your last one."

"Jill…"

Shaking her head with an emphatic "no", she closed the door.

He didn't blame her for being angry and disappointed. Everything she'd said was true. It was tough dating a cop. Crooks and dead bodies get priority seating when you're a cop. He'd change it if he could, but he wasn't the one in charge. Or would he? In a rare moment of self-reflection Colefield had to admit he identified more with the victims of this world than those pulling the strings.

He stood there looking at the brass number plate on her door. The cold rain rolled down the back of his neck. Rain. Not sleet or snow. If things had gone as planned, they would have been feeling the light dusting of soft flakes on their shoulders as they glided up on the chair lift. Hand in hand. Instead that pipedream was replaced with the heartbreaking memory of a child slaughtered, his siblings missing, and a new love lost.

It wouldn't have mattered how long he stood there in the rain,

Jill wasn't letting him in. He knew that about her. She was a pull-the-trigger type. He didn't believe she would give him a chance to make it up to her.

As he stepped away, he remembered the first night they had kissed under her porch light. Not all that long ago. The kiss felt real. He thought he might have found something special in the saloon owner.

On the street in front of her condominium he climbed in behind the wheel of Montgomery's old beater. At least Montgomery had come through....

He tried the ignition. The engine turned over slowly, sputtered but wouldn't fire. He tried it again. Same thing happened. Colefield recalled Redden's earlier comment about karma destroying everything he touched. He said a short prayer and choked it back one more time. The motor sparked to life.

If it was only that easy to jump start a life.

Admittedly, he felt pretty low. The fact of the matter was he about to be homeless because he still hadn't lined up where he was going to stay while the dredging took place at the marina. His phone was destroyed, which was going to cost a week's salary. His girlfriend had dumped him. His pickup truck was sitting in a pumpkin patch with the linkage dangling in the mud. Another expense he hadn't counted on. He had the equivalent of a six-inch thorn in his side every time he breathed.

To top it off, Tam had shown up, churning up all sorts of emotions. He was driving a piece of shit car that didn't have a working defroster, forcing him to drive with the windows down in this hurricane. That part was OK because he stunk to high heaven – a combination of sweat, stale beer and dead ducks. Not to make a big deal about it, but he wouldn't be getting another day off until they had a suspect in custody for the boy's murder. A good cop was counting on him to come through and so was a fourteen year old girl who actually gave a shit about her dead stepbrother. All in all, it had been a pretty rotten day.

And it wasn't over yet.

First things first. Get a working cell phone. Luckily, there was a Verizon Store at Jantzen Beach. Just down the street in a mini-mall.

He parked in the lot in front of the store and went inside carrying his bag of parts. He dumped the contents on the counter in front of a sales clerk. She had a pink ear bud sticking out from under purple hair that she kept poking at as she looked down at the mangled phone.

"Not your day, is it?" she said.

"Anyone ever tell you you're psychic?"

As she leaned forward to have a closer look, she caught a whiff of Colefield and pulled back to allow some fresh air to come between them. "Did you take out insurance on your bag of parts here?"

"I think so. Look my account up on your computer."

"What's your telephone number?"

He said it aloud and she punched it into her keyboard. She let out a little Ughhhhh… "Sorry – looks like it expired last month."

"Is there a grace period?"

"Afraid not."

"No special consideration for police officers?"

"Nope. We offer a ten percent discount to military. You military?"

"Not in quite a while."

"And just so you know, we're out of your model," she sighed. "We're waiting for the new edition to come out which should be any day now. The release date was originally scheduled for last Friday."

"You have a loaner I could use in the meantime?"

"Afraid not."

"Is there another store nearby where I could get one?"

"Let me check for you."

The clerk was all business. She found him a phone across town near the Fred Meyer on Northeast Broadway. She turned and looked at the clock on the wall behind her.

"They close at 6 p.m. on Saturday. If you hurry, you might make it."

"Can you call them – tell them to stay open until I get there?"

"I can call them but I can't guarantee they'll still be open after closing hours."

She punched in numbers. The clerk said they would be happy to stay late, if they only had that particular model in stock. The last one just walked out the door a few minutes earlier. A college student had his telephone stolen. A car break-in...

His next best chance at getting his model of smart phone was in Gresham or Beaverton.

"But—"

"Don't tell me, if the store is open..."

"Would you consider purchasing a different model?"

"No. It took me two months to figure out this one."

"Well, then. I suggest you try our sister stores. Monday would probably be your best bet."

"Great."

He thanked the clerk for nothing and left the store with his measly bag of parts in hand.

Just as he stepped out from under the building's awning, the sky unloaded a frigid mix of snow and rain. The cold front had finally arrived in full regalia. The wind had shifted to the south. Never a good sign in January. Only in the Pacific Northwest could the weather change from warm and sunny to cold and shitty within an hour.

Colefield pulled his coat collar up around his neck and jogged over to Montgomery's car, trying his best to stay dry. The door lock didn't work right so at least he didn't have to mess around looking for a key.

He slid in behind the wheel and wiped his wet face on his sleeve. Locating a pay telephone in the mall was an option but that would require going back outside. The office was only a few miles away. There, he could use the landline and reach the Sheriff's Department to find out if a patrol car had been able to locate the teen or her father yet.

By the time he reached his office, it was dark out. Dime-sized raindrops were falling out of the sky as he swung out of the car and darted toward the door. Bart had apparently come in on a Saturday to get caught up on work because the office was warm and toasty inside. He thought he passed his Nissan heading west on Marine Drive.

After showering and changing out of his trashed uniform, he settled in at his desk to make a few calls, the first being to the Sheriff's Department. Dispatch gave him the number of the deputy who had responded earlier. He eventually reached him on the officer's cell.

"This is Deputy Ross…"

"Ross, this is Deputy Colefield from the River Patrol in Portland. A detective Redden called earlier…"

Ross knew all about it. "Sure. We got nothing yet."

"No teen? No stepfather? No car?"

"No. Nothing."

"Let me give you a number where I'll be for the next few hours. If you hear anything, could you give me a shout?"

"Sure. Fire away."

He gave the deputy his office telephone number and hung up.

He intended to check in with Tam and the body identification, but realized that her number was in his defunct phone.

He dug through his pockets, pulling out Kleenexes, gum and two scraps of paper, each containing a phone number.

He dialed Tam first, leaving the office phone number when she failed to answer.

Next he tried Sally, Montgomery's friend.

A woman answered on the third ring. "Hello."

"Sally?"

"Yes. Who's calling please?"

"Deputy Colefield."

"Who?"

"Jason Colefield. I'm a friend of Bill Montgomery's."

"Yes?"

"Bill indicated that you may have a loft where I could hang my hat while they're dredging over at the marina?"

"Oh, you're his tenant in the tender?"

"Yes, ma'am."

"Bill mentioned you. Any other time it would be fine for you to stay at the loft. However, I've just received a call from my daughter who will be in town with her children. I feel it would be best if she stayed at the loft while she's in Portland visiting."

"How long will she need it?"

"Oh, at least through the end of the month, possibly longer.

"Mr. Colefield if you still need a place come mid-February, you're welcome to call back. I would be happy to discuss it with you then. I'm afraid there's someone at the door. I'll need to hang up now."

Three strikes and you're out. Colefield placed the receiver back in its cradle.

11

The wind rattled the building's windows. Heavy gusts sliced through every crack and crevice in the old structure.

Colefield shut off the computer and rubbed his tired eyes. His stomach growled. He had worked well into the evening looking up old case files and reading the FBI reports that Redden had forwarded to him, detailing the previous accidents which were now being considered as the work of a serial killer. Colefield figured if they could solve Timmy's case, they might solve them all and right now he felt that he was all the kid had. So far he had found nothing that might provide insight into the boy's death or the mysterious family that from time to time had entered the boy's broken life.

The farmer had been correct. The boy's stepdad had a rather extensive record: assault, abuse, drunk and disorderly. The list of incidents was varied and exhaustive. The boy's real father had no record nor did the grandparents. Anita, the boy's mother, had two drunk-drives and hadn't held a job in the last few years. Penny, the fourteen year old, had a number of run-ins with the law for shoplifting. Her older brother Jeb had a clean record. The only thing Colefield could find on him was a brief article in the local newspaper that listed him as the winner of the 2011 Bass Fishing Competition. He would schedule an interview with Jeb as soon as he found the kid. The brothers probably talked. Colefield remembered late night whispered discussions with his own brother when he was Timmy's age.

Even Scarbough Sr. – a respected Scout Master – had a blemish or two. Assaulting a boy about the same age as Timmy and assaulting a woman outside a tavern. Both had taken place a long time ago. In both instances the charges had been dropped.

No need to do any more research on the boy because he remembered every detail of the shooting incident. One doesn't forget being shot.

He had been all of twelve then when Scarbough had fired a load of rock salt at him as he tore across the farmer's fields on his dirt bike. He'd been warned many times before and probably had it coming. But it left facial scars he nicked shaving nearly every day. It had been an extreme measure taken for simple trespassing – the final straw that sent his family packing.

He had never seen Scarbough after that day until yesterday.

As Colefield slid back from his desk, the lights flickered. Went out and came back on. Went out and came back on again. The wind was picking up, howling through the trees. The front door shook against the jam. The noise grew progressively louder by the minute.

Now it was a banging sound. Who was beating on the door at this hour?

Colefield thought about getting his gun, but it was lying out on a fresh towel inside his locker, drying out. Right next to Penny's knit hat which now smelled of gun oil. The Glock had taken a beating in the rain. So he'd wiped it down with a fresh coat of oil. He figured the hat would survive.

He got up from the desk and opened the door. Wind and rain rushed in along with Agent Costa. She was the last person he expected to see. Her long wet hair and dark overcoat glistened under the office lights.

She put her hand up to her face to block the glare. "I got your message and was in the neighborhood so thought I'd drop by."

She immediately took off her wet coat and slung it over the back of a chair, looking around the cramped space. She'd changed clothes and looked out of place in her expensive red dress and high heels. After a moment, she turned and smiled. Her eyes were warm and inviting. Her lips were wet and as tempting as twenty-year-old whiskey swirling in a sparkling glass.

"You look nice." Colefield held open the hinged gate to the small office area.

"I had to change. After my visit to the ME's office I literally smelled like death warmed over."

"Did Anita make the identification?"

"No. She was too wasted. Hank Scarbough ended up making the identification. I called him to come pick up Anita."

"So the guy who said he didn't recognize the dead boy ends up identifying him?"

"Strange, I know, but so far everything about this case is skewed." Costa looked around at the desks stacked practically on top of each other in the cramped space.

"You share this cubicle with how many other deputies?"

"Six."

"You sit on each other's laps?"

"I see you're still kinky."

She ignored the statement. Her restless nature took over and she ambled over and played with the marine radio dials, then squinted through the window at the river. It was too dark to see anything, even if there wasn't a severe storm pounding the hell out of everything. Colefield allowed his eyes to roam over her body.

"I was actually at your crib when you called. Your landlord's an interesting old flirt. He offered me a drink and a personal tour of his hot tub. When I said I didn't have the time, he offered me a rain check."

"I'll bet he did," Colefield said, and then moved in closer, catching a whiff of her perfume. Something behind her eyes seemed untamed and he liked it very much.

"Did you happen to mention you were the daughter of a decorated admiral? That would have really impressed him."

"He didn't need any more encouragement."

She glanced at his computer where he was writing an email to Bart and Weaver relaying when they would be meeting at the office on Sunday.

"If you're wondering why I went to such efforts to find you, I got a call from my boss. You've been assigned to the case."

"I know. I've been reading the files sent over by Homicide. Three teens all died on the same day one year apart, which doesn't fit with Timmy's case. He's out of sync with the others, and his death can't really be mistaken for an accident."

"There are other things that could tie them together."

"You're talking about the symbol on his back?"

"Yes. Look I can bring you up to speed over dinner. You interested?"

"Sure. I haven't eaten all day."

She poked her head inside the Lieutenant's office. "Truthfully, eating alone sucks. It's the one thing that I can't seem to get used to."

Colefield marched over and took her by the arm, pulled her out of the Lieutenant's office and closed the door.

She took no offense and began to read items on the bulletin board. Tamara Costa graduated at the top of her class for a reason.

"So can I trust you to behave for a minute while I go hit the head," he said. "Then I'll change out of this sweatshirt and be ready to go."

"Yeah, sure," she grinned.

He didn't want to admit it to himself, but he was glad she had shown up. Catching the scent of her intoxicating perfume triggered a few great memories – a happier time in his life, even if he hadn't been equipped to appreciate it back then.

As he squeezed by her their shoulders brushed and their eyes met. Looking into her sable eyes was like a big shove back into the past.

On his way to the restroom he started to have doubts about what he was feeling. Was this attraction some deluded fantasy that he was holding onto from a time long gone?

A few minutes later, while he was in the locker room changing out of his shirt, the door opened behind him. Bare-chested, he turned. Costa stared at him from across the room.

"I'll just be a minute," he said.

Her face blushed. "You can't blame me for sneaking a peek. I haven't seen your body in years, even if it is kinda beat up."

He glanced down at his black and blue torso as the overhead lights flickered on and off. Her smile disappeared into darkness.

"Looks like they're setting the mood for us," he said.

When the lights flickered again, it was like one of those strobe dance floors where the person is in one location and then a second later in another. She had moved in beside him, her fingertips grazing his bruised ribs. As the lights flickered off again and didn't return, they slipped into silence.

The building's electricity had gone off.

Colefield went over to the small window and peered out. The streetlights were off. So were the lights in the buildings in the neighborhood. Everything was black. Probably a downed power line or blown transformer somewhere.

"It looks like we're going to have to camp out here for a bit..."

When Colefield turned around Costa pressed him against the wall and planted her lips on his. Lightning unleashed inside him and he lost control. She unzipped his pants and ran her warm hand down inside the front of his jeans. He slid his hand up under her dress to the small of her back and down over her butt, hooked the corner of her panties and slid them down. Then he kissed her hard.

She breathed heavily into his ear. "I so missed this Jason..."

Her breasts pressed against him. He leaned down and kissed her neck, down her chest to her erect nipples. He bit one and then the other. She let out a moan.

He backed her against the locker, slid down his jeans, and then lifted her right leg off the ground and held it there for a moment before she braced her heel on the bench, opening herself up wider for him. The rain thundered against the rooftop and lashed the windows as the storm intensified.

He caught a glimpse of the hunger in her eyes as a passing motorist's headlights spilled into the room.

She released a loud cry and dug her nails deep into his bare back as years of pent up emotion flooded through him. He kissed her softly before they dropped down on the bench sweaty and panting.

The room abruptly burst into glaring light, revealing the reality of what they'd done, and the mystery of their conjoining escaped.

Colefield stood up and fumbled with the buttons of his jeans. Costa ran a hand through her tousled hair and smoothed out the front of her dress. They exchanged awkward smiles.

Colefield could still taste her on his lips. He started to say something when the lights blinked off again.

"I'll get a flashlight," he uttered instead.

He dug around until he found one in his locker and then turned it on. He turned around and shined the light toward where he had left her sitting on the bench. She was no longer there. He pointed the light across the room. The beam caught her shadowy figure slipping into the outer office.

There was a lantern in the storage locker in the hallway. He retrieved it and carried it over to his desk. She was standing by the window, looking out.

"Where's that noise coming from?" Costa asked. The mood was gone.

He listened. She was right. It sounded like the storm had knocked a gutter loose. The metal banging against the siding made a horrible racket.

"I'll go take a look."

"Leave me the lantern, please."

Colefield carried it over and handed it to her. She moved over to his desk and sat down.

"I'll be right back."

Colefield shined the flashlight beam along the wet pavement. He held one hand over his eyes as the lashing rain blew in on the tail of the storm. The rain slapped him in the face as he rounded the corner to the source of the noise. Colefield held the flashlight up and pointed the beam toward the roof. A section of gutter had fallen loose – eight feet of aluminum dangling down, slamming back and forth against the wooden siding.

I can't do anything with that tonight, he thought.

When he reentered the building the electricity was back on. Colefield pushed the door closed against the heavy wind. Costa looked up from the email regarding tomorrow's return to the island.

"Were you going to send me this?"

"I didn't know you were involved when I started that email. Consider this your official invitation."

"OK. Good."

"Do you remember in high school when you tried to hide under the bleacher seats during a blackout?"

"Don't remind me. I spent a weekend picking chewing gum out of my hair."

"Don't you miss those days?"

"Are you crazy? I hated high school."

"I was referring to something else. When I found you under there I distracted you much the way we did tonight."

"Oh – well, don't make too much out of this. I guess the separation is messing me up more than I thought."

Colefield felt deflated by her comment.

"I've got to get a towel and dry off, and then you can bring me up-to-date on where the FBI is on this. What are they calling it, again?"

"The Scoutmaster Killer."

"Right." Colefield stepped into a side room and was removing a towel from his locker, when he heard the front door slam shut.

He hustled over to the window and slid back the curtain. He just caught a glimpse of the taillights of Agent Costa's sedan as she left the parking lot and headed west on Marine Drive.

Tam was unexpected, unpredictable, uninhibited and unavailable. Again.

12

The next morning Colefield was back at work by eight. He stood on the dock giving the patrol boat the once over, climbed inside and glanced at the engine compartment. He flipped on a switch inside the cabin and checked the running lights. He stuck his head back outside and caught a brief glimpse of the sun poking its faint face through the scattered clouds, relieved the sky didn't promise rain.

The river still had a strong current from last night's storm. Mud and flotsam would clog the river in spots but at least there were no white caps forming. The ride to Sauvie Island would be calmer than it had been on the day they'd found Timmy's riddled body.

According to the Sunday weather report, the severe weather pattern from the previous night had blown over and was now dumping twelve inches of snow in the Cascades. Half of the city had been without electricity the previous evening due to downed power lines. The Eastside had only experienced a brief power outage which he had no trouble remembering. Had it been more than just a wild unpredictable moment with Tam?

As he began to disembark from the boat, heavy footsteps started down the ramp toward him. He turned as Bart and Weaver appeared. They were dressed head to foot in standard black tactical gear. Ready for a day on the river.

Bart was the first to speak. "Hey, Colefield, you change your cologne again? Office smells like a whorehouse." Bart had a big grin on his face. "You know anything about that?"

Tam's perfume!

"I must have spilled some of my aftershave in the locker room."

Colefield tried to brush it off but no one was buying it.

"Tell Jill she needs to cut back on the sweet stuff," Weaver said. "Or the Lieutenant will have your ass in a sling."

A twinge of guilt crept in but he kept a straight face.

"I went through the pre-check. Everything looks shipshape. Someone throw me my gear."

Bart reached for it just as Agent Costa came bobbing down the ramp, dressed for a day on the water. Even in foul weather gear, she could turn heads. All smiles and eager to help she reached for Colefield's bag.

"I'll get it," she said cheerfully, full of spunk. "Hello, deputies. Mind if I tag along?"

Bart and Weaver glanced back at Colefield. He was as surprised as they were to see Tam after last night's exit. Bart spoke up first. "Good to see you again, Ma'am. Deputy Colefield didn't mention you'd be joining us."

"He didn't?" she said smiling. "We discussed it last night."

The men worked to control their expressions as they put two and two together.

"Toss me your gear and climb aboard Agent Costa."

She passed her bag of equipment over the transom, grabbed Colefield's outstretched hand and climbed aboard. Colefield set her tote down by his leg and then helped the deputies with their equipment. Once the boat was loaded, Colefield took the helm. He fired up the engine allowing it to idle for a few minutes.

"Did someone think to carry down an extra air tank?" he asked the men.

Bart pointed toward a forward storage locker. "Stowed. Along with the evidence kit and tow line. I also threw in a spare dive suit should you need it."

Weaver took the stern line, Bart the bowline. Costa stowed the remaining gear in a dry location inside one of the compartments astern. When it came to water or boats she acted like an old deckhand.

Bart gave the nose a push-off and climbed aboard. Colefield

rolled back the throttle and the boat's engine came to life, pushing the bow through the stiff current.

While the two deputies stowed the lines and starboard bumpers, Costa slipped inside the cabin and stood beside Colefield. She remained quiet, looking out through the misty windshield toward the expanse of water.

Colefield turned and looked at her. "Why'd you run off last night?"

"I think right now our energies would be better spent finding Timmy's murderer."

Colefield looked her in the eye. "OK. Since we're moving on we are searching Anita's place to see if they returned yesterday. On the way there I want to check out possible beaches where the killer could have come ashore. Bart and I found a second trail from the crime scene which we are also revisiting today."

"Leading where?"

"Back down to the river. I believe the boy came ashore by boat."

Costa nodded. "We're on the same page. I hiked around a bit yesterday and I believe the boy could have arrived by boat."

"There was a boat at the house yesterday, and I'd like to check it out for hull marks or anything that would indicate it was used to drop him off." Colefield said. "He could have been shot by whoever delivered him. I figure if we can find that boat, we might be one step closer to finding the killer. But I'd like to take another look around the riverbank to be sure."

Costa switched gears. "Bart told me this is his first homicide investigation."

"Yeah. He's a little green, but he'll do fine."

"I hope so." Costa hesitated a moment and then took a deep breath. "You've read the files. As you know, I've been working a series of cases over the last three years, all involving children between the ages of ten and fifteen. At first they were thought to be accidental deaths. But a pattern emerged…"

"There was a case in Astoria three years ago involving a boy found crushed under a log along the beach. They found a single letter "C" inscribed in the sand next to his hand. I thought he was trying to write something – leave a clue. Because of the placement of the body and the incoming tide, it is possible there was more to the message before he was found. Or it could have just been a coincidence. That's what everyone figured at the time. Local authorities interviewed his friend who was playing on the beach with him earlier, thinking he put it there. He denied it. Still, they didn't suspect foul play. The death was ruled accidental. Beachcombing that day was heavy because of an International Scout convention in town which at the time didn't mean anything.

A year later on the same day, a girl's body was found just north of here on the railroad tracks. She'd been struck by a freight train. The engineer didn't know he'd run over her until we traced the evidence back to one of his rail cars. Her body had been drug along the tracks for miles before it finally dislodged. She has never been identified. The interesting thing was that we found the letter "U" written on a piece of paper pinned to her backpack when it was recovered where we believe she planned to jump the train. The ME's Office ruled it an accidental death. The thirteen year old was a runaway, and she had no identification on her or in her backpack. The theory was she made a miscalculation as she tried jumping onto an open boxcar."

"And no one ever listed her as a missing person?"

"No."

"And no connection to a Scout Master?"

"The girl was wearing a Girl Scout shirt, so I filed it away as a piece of information that needed to be revisited."

"Look, kids dress up in uniforms all the time."

"That's what the press said." Costa glanced at her notebook. "Did you know that Scarbough used to be a Scout Master?"

"Yes. You're not trying to tie him to these killings are you?"

"I do believe he is involved somehow," she said. "Look I wasn't certain how I felt about either death until this summer when they discovered the hiker."

"I remember that."

"His death occurred on the same day. A fourteen-year-old Boy Scout. Supposedly, he fell off a rocky embankment while on a hiking outing with his troop. Nothing out of the ordinary there, other than we found the letter "L" written on the palm of his right hand."

"He could have written it himself."

"He was right handed, so he would have written it on his left palm."

"So you think somebody else put it there?"

"That's the theory."

"Could mean anything. Or nothing."

"In all three of these cases there was a time lapse between when the death occurred and when the body was actually reported to the police. In the hiking incident they thought the boy had gone ahead. So it was almost an hour before the Scout Master turned back to look for him. I thought the Scout Master was guilty. I grilled him over and over."

"Scarbough?"

"No." Costa furrowed her brow. "We didn't have enough evidence to make an arrest." She heaved a long sigh before continuing. "Now we're to present day and Timmy's case. Bear with me for a moment. The boy, also a boy scout, was shot while supposedly hunting. Without the symbol written on his vest, I wouldn't have made a direct connection. There was a lag between the death and discovery, but the day is different. The perpetrator could be upping the tempo."

Colefield thought about it. "So the killer is leaving some kind of message with each body?"

Costa nodded. "Or clue. Serial killers tend to gloat over their skill."

As the patrol boat reached speed and noisily banged through the rough water, further conversation became impossible. Costa moved onto the bow just as the boat roared under the I-5 Bridge, spooking a gaggle of birds from the rusted steel beams.

Up ahead the narrow railroad bridge came into view. Costa turned and pointed out the retired naval ship moored next to the former luxurious Thunderbird Hotel, which was now just a vacant shell – one of endless abandoned buildings left to decay by the river's edge. At least the Sea Scouts were restoring the old naval ship. A few of them were aboard in white uniforms, painting the upper deck. Colefield had seen a group of them working on the boat off and on since the spring. A couple of the boys stopped painting and waved. The Admiral's daughter saluted back.

Colefield kept his hands on the wheel and tried to remain focused on the open river. From time to time his eyes drifted toward the woman who stood at watch, enjoying the way her long chestnut hair caught the breeze.

The same old youthful feelings stirred, but were quickly replaced by his torn feelings for Jill. Was he going to throw that away? After she cooled off, Jill might come back around. Wasn't she just testing his resolve? What were the odds of being dumped by a woman who he could see spending his future with, only to be pursued by another who arrived from his past?

He put them at a million-to-one that Tam would show up and get assigned to the same case. Or that he would have a run-in with old man Scarbough. Or that Jill would jettison him because of a ski trip. Maybe old Harv had been right. Maybe it was karma.

Off his port bow the patrol boat neared the houseboat community along the western end of Marine Drive. Colefield eased back on the throttle and glanced toward shore at the colorful homes linked together like a string of mismatched beads.

Just ahead he could see the sweeping bend where the converging waters of the Willamette and the Columbia rivers met. It was an epic vista of which he never tired. The current grew swift there. It churned and rolled with mysterious whitecaps boiling to the surface like a great cauldron in the comingling waters.

Bart stuck his head inside the cabin. "Are we heading to the eastside of the island first?"

"Thought I'd backtrack. See if we missed anything Friday."

The river made a sort of "Y" shape as it converged. The Columbia continued to bend north while the Willamette joined in from the south. Colefield eased back the throttle, made a course change to the south, and crossed the current at an angle to avoid chopping through the rough whitecaps. On deck, Costa jumped back as the bow dipped down in a rolling wave. She nearly made it before the frigid water crashed over and sprayed down.

She made a dash for the dry cabin. Once inside she brushed water from the front of her windbreaker.

"That couldn't be avoided." Colefield was grinning from ear to ear.

"Pay back for last night, right?"

Chuckling, Colefield increased throttle to power through the last of the stiff current. From there they traveled a short jaunt upriver on the Willamette, leaving the mighty Columbia in their wake. Weaver pointed out the opening to the Multnomah Channel. No more than a few boat lengths wide and just a mere finger of water, the channel would steer them to Sauvie Island.

He kept to the center, following the markers before they entered the narrow strait, passing several boat repair yards and more houseboats scattered along the riverbank. In the distance, the Sauvie Island Bridge emerged, its rusted arches outlined on the horizon.

"I like the Scout Master theory. But it will be hell on the organization if that turns out to be the case."

"Were any Boy Scouts on the island last week?" Costa asked. "I haven't been able to reach anyone at the local office."

"I don't know. It's easy enough to knock on their door. They're right downtown near the Federal Building. I think Scarbough is long retired from that."

"He isn't – I checked that much out."

Colefield turned and focused on the helm. His mind was churning.

Costa continued. "We need to interview the kid's stepbrother and sister, the father and stepfather, the grandparents and the boy's friends. Hopefully we can round a few of them up today."

"We can try. Aside from the grandfather, everybody else is in the wind. The mother was incapacitated by alcohol and didn't even know the kid was staying with her, and the rest of the family hasn't been located." Colefield paused. "You were serious last night?"

"About what?"

"The case. We're teaming up on this?"

"We'll make a formidable team."

Colefield raised an eyebrow. "This case is already shaping up to be one big clusterfuck. I think you just want someone besides you the FBI can blame when it all goes to shit."

13

The patrol boat killed its engine and glided toward land. Bart hopped out and waded ashore. Costa tossed him the bowline. Bart tied it off and then held the boat steady while the rest of the passengers climbed out.

Colefield followed Costa along the riverbank. The two deputies stayed behind and began to search in opposite directions.

Fifty feet from the shore, Colefield pointed out where he'd found the cigar butt. Costa wasn't impressed. She had her own opinions about the killer.

"I've got my killer pegged as a non-smoker."

Colefield looked at her. "Hank Scarbough smokes."

"Scarbough has no motive."

"None that we know of yet."

"OK. If not the old man, how about Dave, his son? He fit your profile?"

"My bet is on another Scout leader. Could even be a church figure who attends school functions."

For the better part of a half-hour the officers studied the muddy bank looking for tangible evidence that the boy had come ashore there. They found empty beer cans, fishing tackle, plastic water bottles, potato chip wrappers, plastic bags and more trash. Bart found a dead carp lodged in the weeds. But in the end, nothing conclusive or helpful was discovered.

They packed up and moved upriver and did it all over again with the same result.

Colefield said it was time to motor to the Eastside of the island and search Anita's place for signs the family had returned. They agreed it made the most sense since dispatch hadn't been able to send a patrol car out that morning. Everyone was tied up with an injury accident on the St. Helens Highway.

Colefield reported in and told dispatch their whereabouts and where they were headed. After the crew was back aboard, the patrol boat eased into the swift water and made its way north along the narrow Channel.

"Do you still own a boat, Jason?"

"I did for a while. Then I sort of lost interest. I sold the *Misspent Youth* to a young couple just starting out in boating."

"Do you miss it?" Costa searched his face. He wondered if she was referring to the boat or the many happy hours they had spent sailing it together.

"Sometimes." Colefield smiled. "Montgomery moors a Boston Whaler at the marina. When it is running, I borrow it. For now it takes care of my wanderlust."

As the boat rounded the Point, Colefield nodded toward shore. There was a large farmhouse with several outbuildings, a few pieces of farm equipment and a red barn surrounded by miles of plowed fields. The property was bordered by woods, mostly oak and elm trees.

He shouted over the engine. "Scarbough's place."

"Let's come back here after we search the mother's house," Costa said.

Colefield nodded and spun the wheel.

He remembered those fields well. Back when he used to tear across them on his dirt bike. Back then the fields seemed endless and symbolized freedom. Staring at them now he felt no stirring of those feelings. Perhaps his ability to see freedom in an open field had faded with his "misspent youth".

A foggy mist began to form over the island as the boat chopped over the water.

Inside the cabin, Costa appeared to be crossing items off in her notebook. Colefield checked the GPS and depth sounder, focusing on the reduced visibility and keeping an eye out for debris in the water. While keeping watch for other boaters, Weaver and Bart were conversing in low voices on deck about college sports.

As the patrol boat made a small course change Colefield remembered that up ahead the river entered a water fowl hunting area. With at least four hunter's blinds along the riverbank and two wooded areas, it was popular with hunters who liked to burrow in and use the trees for cover.

Just ahead a flock of ducks glided over the treetops and descended toward a calm section of the river. As they landed, gunshots shattered the silence.

Instinctively, Colefield cranked the wheel one-eighty, making a sweeping pass to see where the shots were coming from. Everyone aboard took cover until Colefield pointed out a string of decoys floating near the riverbank. A boy and his father, both holding shotguns, stepped out of a hunter's blind to examine their kill in the water.

Colefield flipped on his siren and flashing lights to get their attention. He held the microphone to his mouth. "Stand down! We're making a pass!"

Costa looked at Colefield and then back at her notebook.

Colefield turned off the siren and lights and motored by. The boy and his father waved sheepishly. The father waded down into the shallow water to retrieve one of the mallards the pair had shot.

The fog thickened. Visibility lessened. Colefield glanced at the screen of the radar and didn't see any obstructions heading his direction. He remained on course.

"I don't remember there being fog in Portland." Costa stood and looked out the windshield.

"Did you forget about the rain too?" Colefield reflected on how selective memory could be. You recall conversations clearly that might have been only in your head. One's sworn truth could be a lie or something you wanted to be true so hard you actually believed it happened.

Costa broke into his head. "Want to wager no one's home?"

"I'd say the odds are 50/50." Colefield turned serious. "Why don't you head out on the bow with the deputies? We're getting close. I'm going to kill the engine and glide in."

Costa perked up. "Finally – it's show time!" She closed her notebook and headed out.

Colefield's expression turned serious. He palmed the notebook, backed off on the throttle and pointed the nose of the boat toward land. Moss hung from the oaks lining the bank, scratching the dodger of the wheelhouse as they slowed and neared shore. According to his calculations, the house was just around the next bend where the trees grew denser and the riverbank narrowed. Bracing the notebook on the wheel, he pressed it open. It revealed page after page of letter combinations using the letters CUL, as well as sayings using the letters in combination with the infinity symbol. He didn't know what he'd expected to find, but something more substantive than word games. He tossed it back down as silence swallowed the sound of the sputtering engine as it breathed the last of its fuel.

They glided silently toward the small private dock. The boat that had been there the day before was gone. Colefield's mind quickly ran the list of those capable of driving the boat. He concluded that the entire Scarbough clan and most of the residents of the island could have commandeered the skiff.

The deputies and Costa jumped ashore. Colefield gave them a moment to spread out and surround the house while he secured the lines.

Like before, the blinds were drawn at the rear of the house. The same old rusty swing set sat frozen in time. Bart and Weaver stepped over broken toys scattered about the back yard while Costa took cover behind an old pump house on the far side of the property. The deputies were flanked on opposite corners facing the back door with guns drawn. Colefield crept to the front of the house to check the driveway for vehicles.

As he started to peer around the corner he heard sounds of a scuffle. He stepped back and raised his Glock, pointing it toward the sound. He had his finger near the trigger as he peered around the corner.

Down the driveway a fight was underway. A seagull was struggling to release his dinner from the grip of an enormous river rat. The ducks Penny had discarded the day before were a prize worth fighting over to the island wildlife.

He lowered his weapon and waived Costa over.

"Nothing parked in the driveway but a couple of dead ducks," Colefield whispered. "I'm heading around back to start the sweep. You secure the front door in case someone makes a run for it?"

The deputies were waiting for Colefield when he approached them in back. "Costa's got the front covered. You ready?"

The men nodded. Colefield cautiously stepped up on the back porch and reached for the knob. The door was partially open already. He gave it a quick shove. Bart and Weaver stormed inside while Colefield took up the rear right behind the men.

The deputies cleared each room. The house appeared unoccupied. Colefield went over to the front door and opened it, signaling to Costa that it was safe to come inside.

"How can you raise kids in a place like this?" Weaver commented, glancing around at the filth.

"Have they been back?" Costa holstered her weapon and looked at Colefield.

"Doesn't look like it." He hated that the girl was not here. He had hoped for the best but it looked like any chance of finding her quickly was long gone.

Bart checked out the kitchen, staring at the crusted dishes and dried blood in the sink. He seemed to be counting the bread scraps down on the floor.

"Bart, check the cupboards and refrigerator for weapons. This is the only room Detective Redden and I didn't search."

Colefield heard the refrigerator door open as he headed outside. After a long moment, Bart ran by him out the front door and stooped over, gagging.

"Nothing in the frig except a putrid quart of curdled milk and some rotting food." He spit on the ground, shaking the stink from his sinuses.

Weaver and Colefield exited the house just in time to see the seagull win the tug of war and take flight with what was left of one of the bloated carcass.

"This island creeps me out on so many levels." Weaver stared as the rat tore into the second bird.

Colefield closed the front door.

"Think it's gonna eat the whole thing?" Bart asked.

"Not before I retrieve some buckshot from it." Colefield pulled his buck knife and approached the rat holding onto his prize until the last moment before scurrying out of sight. Colefield held his breath as he dug the blade around in the meat, retrieving several pieces of shot. He bagged the evidence, cleaned his knife on the grass and rose to his feet.

"Fuck the duck." Costa headed toward the boat. "Let's go visit Hank Scarbough. I got a feeling he might know where to find everyone."

"You heard the lady, deputies. Climb aboard."

14

The large yellow farmhouse on the Point looked even more substantial as the patrol boat pulled up to its private dock. The property was bordered by cottonwoods and willows. Beyond that, vast acres of plowed fields looked like a mirage in the mist that finally seemed to be lifting on the western side of the island.

The deputies climbed out onto the dock followed by Costa. Colefield grabbed his binoculars from the helm and then joined the others ashore.

"Hold up a minute," Colefield said. He held the binoculars up to his eyes and scanned the area. Up by the main house a newer model white pickup truck and an old brown Buick sat in the drive. One of the outbuildings had its double doors open with farm equipment sitting inside. Next to it sat a big red barn with doors closed and padlocked. Beside it sat a semi-tractor trailer. Along the far edge of the property someone was using a John Deere tractor to mow tall grass along the shoulder of the private road leading to the estate. Colefield didn't recognize the driver but it was a boy, early teens with flaming red hair like his own. He looked back toward the others. "I don't see the dogs. You see them, Bart?"

The others stared out over the property. Bart pointed to the right side of the house. "Over there in the yard!"

Colefield turned in the general direction and adjusted the binoculars, zeroing in on the dogs.

The tractor made a short pass across the field and headed back toward the house. The deputies followed the tractor over to an outbuilding. The redheaded kid glanced over, ignored them and drove the tractor inside and parked it. Afterward, he stepped back

102 - DOC MACOMBER

through the metal doors and pulled them closed. Colefield thought he caught a glimpse of the same yellow 4 x 4 he'd been chasing the day before parked inside. Before he could question the kid about it, the front door of the house opened. Scarbough was escorting a conservatively dressed Latina carrying a medical bag. They spoke briefly on the front porch before the woman climbed inside the old Buick parked in the drive and drove off. From the side yard, Scarbough's dogs began barking at the officers. It alerted the old farmer and he turned to see what the commotion was about. Spying the deputies snooping around the outbuildings, he pulled the front door closed and headed down the stoop toward them.

Before Scarbough reached the officers, the dogs ran up to greet him. He gave them a brisk petting before heading down to see what the deputies wanted, his dogs at his side.

Scarbough ordered the dogs to heel. Then he faced the officers and scratched his chin.

"Deputies. Ma'am," he said. "What is it you all want now?"

The redheaded boy started to leave.

"Hold up there, son," Colefield said. "Mr. Scarbough, we have a few questions for you. You've met Deputy Ryan and Agent Costa. This is Deputy Weaver. He's also with the River Patrol."

"Hello again, Miss Costa." They all shook hands. Then he turned and signaled that it was okay for the boy to join them. The boy walked over and stood to the right of Scarbough, as erect as a pine tree. "This is my grandson, Jeb. Jeb these are the officers I was telling you about."

Jeb shook everyone's hand like a perfect gentleman. The boy had an iron grip and similar Irish features like Scarbough.

"You aren't here to tour my farm," Scarbough continued. "So, what can I do for you?"

Colefield studied the man's steely expression. "Sir on Friday, you indicated that you didn't know the dead boy. That's not completely true, is it?"

Scarbough thought about his response. He glanced over at his grandson and then back at the officers. "No. I reckon you're right.

You can speak in front of my grandson. He knows about Timmy."

"Why did you withhold information?"

"Until I got the call from the ME's Office, I wasn't certain it was my step-grandson. When I tried to speak to her earlier in the day, Anita was higher than a kite and not making much sense. She swore her boy was fine. I figured it was best if I tried to track down my son to put him on the trail but I didn't know his whereabouts either. She kept going on about these ducks. So I thought I'd sit on it overnight. Then Ms. Costa called me and said my daughter-in-law needed my help."

"Sir, where are your son and daughter-in-law now?"

"My boy's out of control again. I got him locked up until he sobers up. No telling what kind of trouble he'd get into in his condition. Better I lock him up before the law does. Don't you think, Deputy?"

"How did you find him when nobody else could?" Colefield asked.

"He drove straight here with Penny."

Costa broke in. "And you didn't think to tell me this when we were at the ME's last night?"

"It was an overwhelming day."

"We've expended hundreds of man hours and thousands of dollars chasing shadows, while the entire family was with you the whole time."

"My apologies. As I said, I've had a lot on my mind these past couple of days."

"Where is Dave now?"

"Behind you in that red barn over there."

"There's a warrant out for his arrest."

"On what charges?"

"Assault."

"All that's been taken care of."

"What do you mean, sir?"

"I straightened it all out."

"Where is Anita?" Costa asked. "I'll need to confirm that she is not pressing charges."

Scarbough turned and pointed back at the house to an upstairs window on the east-facing side. "My daughter-in-law is inside the house. She's just been examined by a doctor who lives on the island. Apparently, the poor child is suffering panic attacks and is very dehydrated and depressed. She needs bed rest for a few days. She's been given a sedative to allow her to sleep."

"What about your granddaughter, Penny?" Colefield asked.

"Afraid I was not as successful with her. She's run off again. I don't know where she is."

"Did your son hurt her?"

"No, sir. Not to my knowledge. She looked fine last time I saw her."

"When was that?"

Scarbough thought it over. "Late yesterday."

Colefield looked at the boy. "What do you know about Penny?"

"She ran off while grandfather was helping Agent Costa."

"Do you know where your sister is, Jeb?"

"No, sir."

Colefield turned and looked back at Scarbough.

"You told Jeb about his stepbrother?"

Scarbough nodded.

"So you were at the house with Timmy on Wednesday?" Colefield asked the boy.

"His grandparents dumped him off that night on their way to Reno. We hung out. We got our hunting gear together because on Thursday we thought dad was supposed to take us hunting. But he never showed. And I didn't see him again until he turned up yesterday with Penny."

Colefield looked at Scarbough and then at the boy, thinking. The story sounded rehearsed.

"How do you think your stepbrother ended up dead?" Costa asked.

Scarbough interrupted. "The boy's answered your questions, Agent Costa. Go easy on him now. As I understand it, you've been asking some pretty tough questions of my granddaughter, too. You managed to turn her against her father and that's not proper. She's just a child. She doesn't need to be hauled down to a tavern to identify her drunken daddy or be escorted to a police station to identify a corpse. It's a very confusing time in her life. She needs looking out for, just as her older brother here does."

Colefield began fuming under the collar. "Sir, where is the girl? I need to be assured she is safe."

"As I said, Penny ran off. I have several people on the island looking for her. They're quite capable of locating Penny if she's still in the area. And, as I also said, her stepmother is safe. Just as soon as my son is well enough, the family will be reunited and this whole matter can be cleared up."

Colefield looked at Costa. "Does your son Dave own a fiberglass boat with an outboard?"

"No. That boat was a gift to my grandson here."

"Do you think the girl took off in it?"

"Why? Is my boat gone?" Jeb asked.

"It is."

He frowned at Colefield.

Scarbough glanced down toward the dock. "Then you should be looking for her on the river, shouldn't you?"

"You are interfering with our investigation, sir," Bart interjected.

"Why young man, that almost sounds like a threat."

Colefield held up his thumb and index finger making a small gap. "I'm this close to arresting you for obstruction." Colefield looked him straight in the eye. "Open the barn!"

"You have a warrant?"

"I can get one in less than an hour. We can stand around out here waiting or you can cooperate and we'll be on our way."

Scarbough stared him down, his expression stern and unflinching. After a moment his eyes lit up with recognition. "We've met before haven't we, Deputy? You've grown into a man, but that insolent timbre in your voice hasn't changed a bit. You're that brat who lived on the other side of the island, aren't you? That kid who kept trespassing on my property and destroying my crops with his motorbike? Good thing your parents had the good sense to move...."

Colefield swallowed and willed his voice to stay neutral. "The barn, sir. We need to look inside it. Now!" He nodded to the deputies, who stepped back and kept an eye on the old farmer. "Agent Costa, will you go check on the daughter-in-law inside the house. Take Bart and Jeb with you."

"Hey, now!" Scarbough huffed. "Nobody gave you the right to enter my house."

"Your grandson will escort us. Won't you, son?"

Jeb looked at his granddaddy for approval.

Scarbough gave in. "All right! All right! Go check for yourself," he said and then paused. "Jeb, take the dogs and chain them up in the side yard. Deputy Colefield, I'd like you to follow me. Deputy Weaver, you're free to join us. You won't need your damned guns, my boy's not capable of causing any trouble."

Colefield wondered what that meant.

15

As Scarbough unlocked and slid the heavy barn door open, the strong stench of manure wafted out. Colefield's eyes teared. He wiped them dry and peered inside. Jagged slivers of sunlight wormed in through the rafters and windows, partially blocked by farm machinery. The pole beams were filled with cobwebs. Dried straw strewn about the dirt floor looked like it'd ignite at the faintest spark. As they followed Scarbough inside the ground crunched underfoot.

On one side of the barn three horse stalls stood open. The horses had been released into the pasture for the day but the stalls smelled rank and needed cleaning – fresh piles of manure, empty food and water troughs. On the other side was a large corral that, according to Scarbough, in its day had held a dozen or more prized pigs. A small door in back was boarded over with two-by-fours. Against a far wall, gunny sacks of seed and bales of hay were stacked floor to ceiling. More bales of hay were stacked in the overhead loft.

A groaning sound came from inside the former pig pen. There was a wooden gate that was closed and locked. He'd missed it at first, but as they moved in closer, through the narrow slots he could see that someone was inside. Curled up on a Pendleton blanket on the floor was the same man he'd seen the day before. Same firm jaw, same unshaven face. His coveralls were rolled under his head. He lay in a fetal position shivering and looked to be having a nightmare.

In the corner sat a metal bucket with bright urine in the bottom. A gallon-size coffee can with what looked like drinking water with a metal cup rested on a ledge on the opposite wall.

A heavy chain had been fastened around the man's right ankle. The chain trailed through the hay on the floor to where it was secured to a heavy metal ring bolted to the wall. There was about six feet of loose chain. The man could move around to a point.

The deputies stepped up to the gate for a closer look.

"He's still sleeping it off," Scarbough said.

"You have him shackled like an animal. I'm not certain that is even legal." Deputy Weaver sounded incredulous.

"It is if I have his consent. And I do. This is not the first time we've been through this together."

"I'll need to speak with him. Wake him up," Colefield said.

Scarbough didn't appreciate the Deputy's harsh tone. He appeared to think about it for a long moment and then took a bucket resting on the floor by a water barrel, dunked it down, pulled it out and carried it over to the gate. He opened the door and went inside, sloshing water along the floor. After he topped off the coffee can – the man's water supply – he picked up the bucket of urine and carried it back through the gate.

"You ever dumped another man's urine, Deputy?"

"Are you going to wake him or am I?"

Scarbough walked off.

Colefield had run out of patience. He looked at Weaver and then entered the corral. He stared down at the drunk on the floor and nudged his leg a few times. The man didn't budge. It took several more kicks but the physical contact seemed to be working. The man stirred awake, flailing his arm out like he was swatting away imaginary bats. He looked angry and dangerous.

"What the hell asshole," he grumbled, and rolled upright, glaring at his attacker. "Who the hell are you?"

"Where's the girl?"

"What girl?"

"Penny. The tavern yesterday – you took off with your daughter – is it coming back now?"

The man rubbed his greasy hair.

"I'm waiting, Dave!"

"I don't know where she is. Where's my daddy?"

"Dumping your piss. Good job for him. Did you kill your stepson?"

"What are you talking about?"

"He's dead. Why'd you shoot him?"

"I didn't shoot him."

"That's not what your wife said."

"My wife is a pain in the ass."

"You're a fine pair. Why'd you kill the kid?"

"I didn't kill him."

"You went hunting with him on Thursday."

"I haven't hunted in weeks."

"That's not what your daughter said."

"She's a liar. She's getting back at me."

"For what?"

"Stuff."

"What stuff?"

"Parent stuff."

"You're a model parent all right. Look, we know someone went hunting because we found two dead ducks in your kitchen sink. They didn't just fly in on their own. Someone had to put them there. Your wife said you shot them. She refused to pluck 'em and you popped her."

"She's a drunk. She makes stuff up."

"Like the bruises on her face?"

Scarbough returned with the empty bucket in hand. "That's enough for now, Deputy. My son will cooperate fully when he has his faculties back. Right now, he needs rest. If you don't allow this, I will have to assume it's what a lawyer would consider harassment."

"I'm not through here," Colefield said. "Where do you keep your shotguns, Dave?"

Dave Scarbough rubbed his eyes and looked confused. "I didn't kill no kid."

"You wouldn't remember if you did."

"Deputy! That's enough!" Scarbough snapped.

"Mr. Scarbough, unless your son has an alibi for the day the boy was shot, I'm going to arrest him on suspicion of murder. I'm also going to book him for assault."

"My son was driving a semi-tractor trailer to Eastern Oregon all week. There's no way he shot the boy. He's been making deliveries for the farm."

The news deflated Deputy Weaver but not Colefield. Someone was lying.

"That right, Dave?"

Dave Scarbough nodded. "I got back home Friday afternoon. Got into it with Anita, who was raving and blind drunk. Then Penny started giving me lip too, so I took off, and ended up at Bert's Tavern."

"I'll need proof you were out of town at the time of the murder."

Scarbough interrupted. "I've got bills of lading, DOT documents, fuel receipts and more. I'll even supply you with the names of the clients he delivered the farm equipment to if necessary."

"Oh, at the very least, sir."

Deputy Weaver questioned the man. "You asked Mr. Scarbough to chain you up?"

The man nodded. "I got an alcohol problem."

"There are facilities that deal with alcohol dependency issues."

Mr. Scarbough was losing patience with the deputies. "We've tried everything from Witch Hazel to Acupuncture. It runs in the family. I myself had to seek help back in the day. A doctor friend of mine suggested we try this approach. It may seem barbaric to a city boy but it's a common practice in some countries. After he's dried out I'll put him to work again."

"That what you're doing for the wife, too? Helping her?"

"Her situation is just as complicated."

"This mess has ties to you and you're trying to keep a lid on it. But I assure you, the truth will come out. I need to see those documents now."

The men entered the kitchen just as the other officers were

about to leave. They all stopped and looked at each other. Bart looked bored. The boy looked as if he'd been through this sort of thing a hundred times. Costa put her notebook away.

"You're wasting your time if you go upstairs. The wife is on heavy sedatives. She's out. Will be for hours, I presume."

"No girl?"

"No girl. We checked every room."

Jeb looked over at his grandfather. "I'm going to take Dad some food."

"Don't bother, son. I've seen that look before. Give him another hour or so."

"You finished with the husband?" she asked.

"Just finishing up."

"Deputy," he said to Colefield, "Follow me. I have those documents in my office."

"What documents?" Costa asked.

"He says the father has an alibi."

"Jeb, take the dogs the leftover bones from last night's dinner," Scarbough directed.

Colefield said, "Bart, keep an eye on him."

As Scarbough led them through the center of the house to get to the office in back, Colefield was surprised by the opulent furnishings. His furniture had buttery leather upholstery and appeared to be made from imported Brazilian hardwoods. He had art on the walls that looked to be authentic Nineteenth Century paintings. Before now the impression he had of Scarbough had not included a house filled with tasteful treasures. Perhaps his wife had been the influence. Colefield couldn't remember a thing about her.

Standing in his home Colefield had to admit his childhood impressions of the man may have been inaccurate. Could his present impression also be distorted? The line between memory and truth morphed again.

Scarbough seemed to enjoy the look on Colefield's face as he led them down the hall to an office at the back of the house. The room was set up with a big oak desk in the center. Behind it were large double windows that looked out toward the river. Oak shelving, floor to ceiling, lined the walls. A small library of books, 4H and Scout Master Trophies and Awards lined two shelves. Colefield stopped by the book shelves which housed row upon row of first-edition hardcover books.

Scarbough said. "I just need a moment to pull out the documents from my desk."

The old man dug through the bottom drawers of his desk until he found what he was looking for. He pulled out a file folder and held it up. "There it is," he said to Colefield. Costa did not wait for permission. She moved in, took the folder and opened it. Colefield came up from behind and together they studied the documents.

Inside were shipping and trucking documents that corresponded to what Scarbough had told him.

Colefield looked Scarbough in the eye. "OK. So where do you want to go from here?"

"I don't know if I understand exactly, Deputy."

"Your son assaulted his wife and daughter. We can't overlook this."

"Have you proof?"

"We saw the bruises on Anita's face. I witnessed his rough treatment of his daughter."

"It's just the drunken talk of a woman who suffers from a bipolar condition and an adolescent who needs discipline in her life. As I understand it she was out of control. Her father did what was necessary at the time."

"Just like you did with me? You remember that too, don't you?"

"One has nothing to do with the other. You were trespassing and had been warned several times. I needed to get your attention. And I did."

"Maybe you needed to get Timmy's attention the same way."

"I didn't shoot Timmy." Scarbough sighed.

"Colefield," Costa cut in. "These documents confirm that Dave Scarbough was not in the vicinity on the day of the boy's death."

"It's a little too neat for me."

Scarbough looked to Agent Costa for rational thinking. "Would Deputy Weaver care to see the documents?"

Weaver stepped up and glanced at the documents, then to Colefield with doubt in his eyes.

"That settles it," Scarbough announced. "Continue on with your investigation elsewhere. Do you understand, Deputy?"

Before he could answer, Costa grabbed his arm. "Mr. Scarbough. We follow the evidence. I will not be arresting your son today based on your documentation. However, I am taking your grandson, Jeb, downtown for a proper interview. He will be under my personal protection and I have already contacted a representative from Child Welfare Services to meet us. It is our hope that he can shed some light on who might have wanted to harm Timmy. Brothers talk and share things. Based on our discussions with Jeb, we will be in touch. You can count on it. We still need to interview your son and daughter-in-law. I am sure you would want them to help in any way possible. If you attempt to impede this investigation, I will have you arrested on obstruction. Are we clear?"

"Crystal clear, Agent Costa." Scarbough's face was stone, his tone deadly.

"If you'd like to say goodbye to your grandson, join us outside."

Without a further word, they all marched through the living room and out the front door.

"How does an educated guy with a beautiful estate like this chain up his son in a pigsty?" Weaver said to Costa.

"Or let his family live in squalor?" Costa added.

Jeb was throwing a football to Bart in the front yard and didn't notice his grandfather's expression as the group approached.

"The kid's got a great arm," Bart said, catching a pass.

"Deputy Colefield!" Jeb shouted. "Deputy Ryan told me you played college ball. Give me your best shot."

Costa and Weaver gave Colefield a warning look as Bart handed the ball to his partner.

"OK kid," he said. "I'm gonna throw you a pass so hot it will set your hair on fire." And with that Colefield cocked his arm and unleashed his best pigskin missile.

16

A s the patrol boat shoved off from the dock, Colefield
jumped aboard at the last minute and joined Costa, who
was talking on her cell outside the pilot house. Bart had
the helm. Deputy Weaver was gazing back with an odd expression
at the Scarbough barn. Scarbough's grandson, Jeb, had planted
himself at the helm, shoulder-to-shoulder with Bart, picking his
brain about every knob, gauge and control. Bart was doing his best
to answer the boy's many questions, clearly enjoying the teachable
moment and not paying attention to the heavy current that was
pushing hard on the stern, nosing the boat back toward shore.
Weaver snapped out of his funk and shouted at Bart. Surprised,
Bart looked up, reached out and grabbed the wheel and throttle at
the same time. He pulled the throttle back a notch and straightened
out the bow.

Costa signed off on her cell call. "Child Services will meet us
at the marina."

"We could do this at my office." Colefield was thinking out
loud. "Save time. After that you could have Child Services escort
while you drop him back off with his grandfather. It'd be great if
we could hold him overnight – give us more time. But CS won't let
that happen. We'll be lucky if they let us get in ten words."

"We need more time." Costa frowned. "This kid's too smart.
He's already got Bart wrapped around his little finger. He'll try the
same with you or me."

Sure enough, Bart was chattering like a monkey with the
Scarbough boy, pointing out this gadget or that, drawn in by the
boy's enthusiasm.

"Unlike his sister, he knows how to manipulate and charm,"

Costa said. "But there's something about him that kind of creeps me out." Costa shrugged. "Something is just off about him. I want to find out what it is."

"Once Child Services gets ahold of him, our hands are pretty much tied. If we're going to find out anything, it's now or never."

Costa appeared to be thinking it over. "It may not be admissible if he does tell us something of value. A lawyer could say it was coercion."

"I'm just saying … if the boy is anything like his grandfather, playing it by the book will get us nowhere."

"Scarbough really shot you?" Costa asked.

"Yes. Nearly took my head off." Colefield pointed to his scarred cheek. "He doesn't think the rules apply to him. And most of the time they don't."

Costa nodded. "You never mentioned it when we were dating. In fact when I mentioned your cheek one time you told me you hurt yourself shaving."

"I think I said something about having a close shave."

Colefield's reply didn't generate even the hint of a smile from Costa.

"Shall we do it together or separately?"

"You're in charge of this case." Colefield knew the idea of not waiting to find out what the boy might be sitting on had her intrigued. And thinking.

"Good cop? Or bad cop?" he asked.

"What do you think?"

Colefield followed Costa into the pilot house and stood directly behind Bart while Costa circled around to the right side of the two men and faced Jeb. Colefield leaned forward and whispered something into the Deputy's ear. Bart stepped back from the wheel.

The young deputy told the boy that they'd continue the lesson later. "See you later."

"Alligator," Jeb replied with a wide grin as Bart exited the wheelhouse, closing the door behind him.

As soon as the Deputy was gone, Costa squared her shoulders

and frowned over at the smiling boy.

"Look, Jeb, we know you and Timmy went hunting that day. Just tell us what happened."

Jeb didn't flinch. "I didn't go hunting with Timmy. I said that already. We were planning to but dad never showed. Then Timmy said he wanted to stay in and hang with Penny. So we called it off and I got ready to split in the boat. Then he shows up all dressed up to go hunting."

"Did he have a gun with him?"

"No."

"Why do you think he changed his mind?"

"Timmy said Penny's stupid boyfriend showed up at the last minute."

"Where'd you go?" Colefield asked.

"I motored over by the Point, dropped Timmy ashore and left. He said he just wanted to go flush birds."

"And?"

"I took the boat out for a spin. I went back later for him and I couldn't find him anywhere. I motored up and down the Channel looking. It was starting to get dark so I came back home, thinking maybe he had wandered back on his own."

"You hear any gun shots?" Costa asked.

"Plenty of them. It's hunting season."

"If you didn't go hunting, how do you explain the ducks?"

"What ducks?"

"The ducks we found in the sink when we showed up at the house."

"I shot those."

"So you two did go hunting?"

"No. I shot them from the boat after dropping him off."

"We're gonna need to examine that gun," Colefield said.

"It's at my grandfather's house," Jeb replied helpfully.

"So how does it make you feel that someone killed your stepbrother on your watch?" Costa asked.

Jeb's face slammed shut.

Colefield glanced down at the boy's hands. Jeb was flicking his thumb back and forth. The joint was either stiff or he got a thrill out of popping it in and out of its socket. What this suggested was anyone's guess, but it wasn't insignificant.

"Hey!" Colefield winked at Costa and then looked back at the boy. "You want to try your hand at the helm?"

Jeb grinned. "Sure."

Colefield stepped aside and turned over the controls.

"You really think he's capable of driving this boat?" Costa huffed.

Colefield said. "He's been captain of his own boat many times." He then looked over at Jeb. "This is just a larger version of your grandfather's skiff, right? You've probably driven boats since you were in diapers."

"It's not his boat, it's mine. He gave it to me."

"You're sure he didn't give it to both you boys?" Costa prodded.

"You heard him yourself. He told you the boat belonged to me."

"But your grandfather took a shine to Timmy, didn't he?"

"Where'd you hear that?"

"Penny."

"Penny liked Timmy because he'd listen to her crap. She's always talking shit." Jeb looked to Colefield. "You know what I'm talking about. You met her."

"So you didn't get along with your stepbrother?" Costa stared with steely eyes.

"I never said we didn't get along. We just didn't have much in common. He was a lot younger than me and he wasn't looking for a big brother."

"Penny said you were jealous of her relationship with him. And you resented that he got to live with his grandparents and away from all the Anita and Dave drama."

"Jealous? I could leave any time I wanted to and stay with my own grandfather at his estate, not some little shitwater shack."

Colefield reached out and bumped the throttle up a notch.

The boat rose up out of the water, the bow climbing up onto a breaking wave, planing over its surface like a knife smoothing the frothy filling of a freshly made soufflé.

"Look, we just want to hear your side of it, without your family hanging around. I figured you'd prefer talking in private."

"Ok. But what about telling my granddad you would be questioning me in front of Children Family Services?"

"We'll do a formal interview with them," Colefield said. "Right now we're just talking."

"Tell us a little about your relationship with Timmy," Costa asked. "What sorts of things did you do together? Hunting? Fishing? Did you ever let him pilot your boat when you were out together?"

"No. He wasn't a natural at those things like I was."

"What do you mean a 'natural'?"

"In Alaska, before we moved to Oregon, I used to go out commercial fishing with my dad."

"And?"

"I was a kid who did all kinds of dangerous stuff. My dad said it came naturally to me."

"Like what?"

"In the beginning they let me ride along and pilot the boat sometimes. Then the guys gave me a baseball bat and showed me how to kill fish. Where to club the head. When we hooked a shark they taught me how to use a .22 to shoot it in the water. I was only seven or eight at the time, but I got really good at it."

Colefield admitted to himself that he too had been taught to kill – first by his father, then the Navy and finally the Sheriff's Department. So in some respects, he and the kid were not so different. Yet there was a difference.

He remembered his own experience as a youth when he tried to club a Ling cod he caught by Haystack Rock, off the Pacific coast. He had to beat it senseless to kill it. But there was no joy in it for him. And he couldn't eat it after seeing it die and feeling his own blood lust. Unlike Jeb he wasn't a 'natural' at killing, though the line that divided them might be a fine one indeed.

Colefield eased back on the throttle. "That's pretty impressive."

Costa perked up. "So you smashed a few fish heads. Something that probably gave the guys who had already spent a lifetime at sea a cheap thrill." Costa shifted gears. "What about when your parents divorced? Were you still living in Alaska then?"

"Juneau. Penny and I were both born in Juneau."

Costa went out on a limb. "Is Juneau where your mother committed suicide?"

Jeb's face reddened. "No. Mom had moved to Anchorage after she and my dad split up. That's where she died. Afterward, we moved back to Oregon and stayed with my grandfather until dad found work. For a while he talked about going back. I knew it was just a pipe dream. He couldn't go back there. None of us could after all that had happened." Jeb hung his head. "Then he met Anita."

"Are you talking about the accident?" Costa continued.

"It didn't have to happen." Little beads of sweat broke out on the boy's forehead.

"Penny mentioned something about the accident while I was driving her to the other side of the island," Costa said. "Since I had time at the office yesterday, I dug up the accident report and investigation. I haven't shared this with my colleague yet so I hope you don't mind if I get him up to speed on this."

Colefield turned and stared at Costa as if he'd been blindsided. It wasn't an act.

"Your mother was a bus driver. Had been for several years. One day she was bringing you and some Boy Scouts back from a jamboree. You got rowdy as kids do. Your mom turned to tell everyone to settle down just as someone threw a paper airplane. It struck her in the eye. She lost control of the bus and drove off an embankment. Three children died on the scene and a number of others sustained injuries. Your mother was seriously injured as well and was airlifted to a hospital. You were unhurt and left behind to fend for yourself."

"I didn't know where they were taking her. Everybody was screaming and crying." Jeb's thumb jerked furiously.

Costa continued. "After the dust settled, there were some questions about what really happened that day. The paper airplane was never found. The kids' stories seemed conflicting at best."

"It wasn't her fault."

"I never said it was," Costa replied.

"Penny wasn't there. I was. The kid who did it, his dad was a hotshot attorney and sued the School District. They put the blame on mom. She couldn't take it." Jeb turned toward Colefield looking for something.

"Your dad must have taken the suicide hard. Felt guilty about the divorce and all. That's probably contributed to his drinking problem." Colefield empathized with the kid. "I suspect that's why Penny acts out like she does. She's got no female role model."

Costa grabbed the ball. "You on the other hand, are a model citizen. No record of any kind. It appears that you excel at whatever you do, despite what happens to the rest of your family."

Jeb's eyes narrowed. He returned his attention to the controls. "What's this switch do?" he asked Colefield. Without waiting for an answer he flipped it. Suddenly the boat crested the river. It rose as though an enormous hand pushed the hull up out of the water, freeing it from space and time. The jarring movement knocked Costa off balance but she regained her footing by clutching onto a handrail. Jeb smirked.

"Looks like you figured it out on your own." Colefield let out a little sigh and glanced over at Costa. "They're called trim tabs," Colefield went on to explain. "They control the height of the bow. How it rides over the waves. They have to be adjusted just right in order to have a smooth ride."

Jeb nodded. "Like the difference between sinking and swimming. One wrong move and you're dead."

Colefield reached out and flipped the switch in the opposite direction. The bow began to sink into the water, rather than ride above it, and the boat began to slow down.

Costa swallowed hard. "If we're finished with the carnival ride try telling us one more time about the day Timmy went missing."

"I told you. I split. When I came home, Anita was plowed again. Penny was screwing her lame boyfriend. So I didn't hang around. I threw the birds in the sink and left to stay with my grandfather."

"How'd you get there?" Costa asked. "You didn't take your boat."

"I drove an old tractor that was at our place."

"Why?"

"It was getting dark and I thought I might see Timmy walking home."

Costa shook her head like she didn't believe a word the boy was saying.

It wasn't Colefield's turn but he stepped in anyway. "Are you sure you are telling us everything?"

"Believe what you want. What I know is that your girlfriend is deliberately trying to piss me off."

Colefield reacted, but Jeb was watching Costa whose face revealed nothing.

"Nice try," she said. Her lack of response ignited Jeb.

"Why should I feel remorse for a stepbrother I barely knew? He didn't even live with us. He never listened to me. And look what happened...."

"Listened to you, how?" Colefield asked.

"What?"

"You said he never listened to you. What do you mean?"

"Just that he was hard-headed. Look, I tried to show him things. Teach him, you know, but he would rather play with Penny than learn anything from a big brother."

Colefield sensed something else was at the heart of the matter. But it would have to wait. He added it to the growing list of questions.

"Did Timmy have his own gun?" Costa asked

"A Winchester. Twelve gauge."

Colefield was still musing on the fact that the kid had picked up on Tam and him. The kid was way more observant than he had anticipated.

"We didn't find a gun with the body. What do you think happened to it?" Costa asked.

The boy's face remained calm. "I already told you. Timmy just went to flush birds. He didn't have his gun."

"Where on the island did you and Timmy usually hunt?"

"West and East sides."

"You use the blinds or field hunt?"

"It depended on the type of bird we were hunting."

"So both of you were pretty knowledgeable hunters and knew what you were doing?"

"I consider myself a good hunter and an expert marksman," he said with a gleam in his eye. "Like most everything I do, I'm good at it."

Colefield figured the kid would break down by now. All they needed to do was twist his story back on him and the kid, if he was lying, would stumble. But so far, the only stumbling was between him and Costa.

Costa grew impatient. "Tell us more about Juneau after the accident. What was your home life like?"

The boy's index finger twitched. "My mother was in a wheelchair. She couldn't use her legs. She lost her job. My parents started fighting all the time. But mom always loved me. Every day when I left for school, she'd say 'See you later.' And I'd say 'Alligator'. After they divorced and she moved away, I'd pretend she was still there in the mornings saying it when I left for school." Jeb hung his head. "Then one day, my dad told me she was dead. That she'd killed herself. After that I couldn't pretend anymore."

That explained the beaming look Jeb gave Bart when he said "See you later," Colefield mused. He too had been more close to his mom than his dad.

"You and Penny have any problems readjusting when your father remarried?"

"For a while it was OK. Anita got dad to think about something other than death. But it didn't last. One day I came home and Anita was crying and dad was drunk and screaming at her. Later I found out she'd been pregnant and had lost the baby. Dad blamed her. Things were never the same after that."

That fit what Colefield had heard from Tom Farmer. "How did you feel about the baby?"

"I didn't feel anything. I didn't even know about it before it was over."

"How about when you found out you would have Timmy as a stepbrother?"

"It didn't really matter one way or the other. Timmy didn't come around that often. Either we did stuff together or we didn't. I happen to like hunting and fishing and boats. Like I said Timmy was more into video games and chick stuff. He hung with Penny more than me. You should talk to her about it."

"We'd love to do that," Costa said.

"You think she took your boat?" Colefield asked.

"Probably. She knew where I kept a spare key onboard."

"Was there anyone on the island that might have wanted to harm Timmy?" Costa looked Jeb in the eye.

"Why? He was just a kid."

"Maybe Penny's boyfriend got jealous." Colefield prodded. "I've met him. He seems capable."

"He's a punk. He has trouble tying his own shoelaces."

"You sure?" Costa cut in, staring directly at the boy, then down at his nervous twitch. Jeb cupped his hand, which hid his jumpy digit. "If you're trying to analyze why my finger shakes, I dislocated it on a camping trip. It's still screwed up. Maybe if you lock me up, Agent Costa, I can get a cute nurse in Juvie to look at it."

"No one is going to lock you up," Colefield said. "We're just trying to gather all the information we can and make sense of this tragedy. If you prefer we end it here, we can. It's your choice."

Jeb looked right at Colefield. "Timmy was immature, spoiled, a momma's boy, and..."

Before he could finish, Deputy Weaver pulled open the pilot house door and reminded Colefield about the log debris ahead and the unexposed dolphins along the southern portion of the Columbia.

Colefield moved Jeb aside and regained control of the helm. Costa was staring out the cabin window at the snowcapped peak of Mount Hood in the distance and the gloomy storm clouds blowing in from the south.

"I knew there were sea lions up here, but dolphins?" Costa queried. Colefield wondered what the Admiral's daughter was up to.

Colefield explained. "Dolphins are trunks or logs that protrude out of the water or lay right under the surface like a booby trap. By the time you see them, it's too late."

Jeb spoke up, with a smug look on his face. "Hey maybe Timmy got caught by a land dolphin."

"What do you mean?" Costa asked.

"Maybe he flushed out a killer instead of a quail."

17

onday morning Colefield left the houseboat later than usual. He stopped to knock on Montgomery's door. A hand scrawled note posted there read: "Enter at Your Own Risk!"

Colefield poked his head in the door. "Bill! It's Jason! Can I come in?"

"Up here old boy! In the Penthouse!"

Colefield stepped inside.

As usual, the place was in general chaos. He ignored the piles of trash and papers, shifted a few clothing items from the bottom of the spiral staircase and climbed to the second level. That is where Montgomery slept and stored his vast collection of military knives, sniper rifles, handguns and classic 70's pornography. A wooden hot tub sat off the bedroom in a private bath that had a large stained-glass window with a private view of the Willamette River. In the back part of the bedroom was where Montgomery had a complete workshop for reloading ammo, cleaning guns and manifesting general mayhem. He found Montgomery sitting at his bench beside stacks of ammo boxes, shells and rifle stocks. NRA caps and shooting vests were strewn about everywhere there wasn't a box of bullets, collectable bayonets, swords, or other war memorabilia.

Montgomery slid back on his stool and lifted his magnifying hood. "I'm about to crack your golden goose egg."

"Great. I could use some good news."

"We both could. You notice that the dredge work started down at the north end of the dock?"

"I did."

"You call Ms. Sally?"

"I did. Her daughter will be in town using the loft."

"So you're going to share a bed?"

"No, Bill. Sally said I'm out of luck."

"You fucked?"

"Where are your hearing aids?"

Montgomery searched his bench for the brown case, extracted a bulky ancient hearing aid and popped it in the ear closest to Colefield. "I suggest you start buttering up that bartender of yours because it's time to fly the coop."

"I'm renting a hotel room."

"You're not planning on deducting that from the rent?"

"I might. In the meantime, what'd you find out about the shotgun shell?"

Montgomery dropped his hood and slid over to his bench. "It's a reload. Lines on the casing indicate it has been reloaded several times. And as you can see from the longer brass head, it's referred to as a high brass. You can get a hotter powder charge using more metal. According to my criteria, what you have here is your standard BB shot, which is typical for game birds. Here's the catch my boy, it's not steel shot but lead. Lead is a big No—No. As you may or may not know, you cannot legally hunt game birds with lead shot on certain State and Federal refuges. These areas have what is called a Toxic Shot Restriction. Non-toxic shot must be used when hunting waterfowl. No exceptions. Either your hunter was ignorant of the law or comingled his shells by accident. All the same, you should drop the hammer on him, Bucko. He's giving us hunters a bad rap!"

"Lead, eh?"

"Old Leadbelly himself."

Colefield retrieved his bag of shot taken from the duck carcass at Dave and Anita's house. "Could you take a look these pellets? I need to know – lead or steel? These are supposedly from the stepbrother's gun.

Montgomery slid them under his microscope.

"Steel shot. Legal shot." The news deflated Colefield, who had begun to like Jeb for the shooting.

"Scarbough Senior doesn't strike me as a guy who would accidently comingle shells. So maybe he wasn't hunting ducks with that gun after all?"

"Or maybe it wasn't his gun, old boy? Maybe he found it in the field, recognized the owner and confiscated it."

"We have it in evidence. I'll check it out."

"Anything else?"

"I could go on how lead is heavier, faster, and travels farther. It's superior. Kills cleaner. Birds don't suffer as much. Is that enough?"

"You're the pro, you tell me."

"Thank you. It's important to be known for something other than drinking rum to excess."

"What about the make of the reloader? Any luck there?"

"Oh, yes. Whoever reloaded this shell used a standard Lock-N-Load classic. A single stage press. Retails for about the cost of a quality bottle of single malt at your local retail outlet. Probably get it on-line for less. They are so simple to load a girl could use one."

Montgomery was old school and believed as a true chauvinist that women belonged in the kitchen cooking and not in the field killing.

"Can you narrow down the manufacturer?"

"Not with any precision. Sorry. My Jarhead skills take me only so far."

Montgomery scooped the pieces into a plastic bag, zipped it closed and turned the evidence over to him. "Good luck with this case. By the way, how's it going?"

"It's murky."

"Death is tricky business."

"It's still cool if I use your car?"

"Consider it yours until it isn't."

"See you around. And thanks!"

"Out by day after tomorrow. OK?"

"That's an affirmative."

"*Adios bravado de'* Colefield. Go forth. Be bold. Kill all the pukes!"

18

The old Federal Building still housed a small division of the FBI among other federal agencies and was located downtown on Second Street. He took in the surrounding view, mostly office buildings and renovated condominiums. Just down the road was Waterfront Park, a large outdoor concert space that overlooked the Willamette River.

Colefield parked Montgomery's beater downtown, got out and headed toward the main entrance. On the way, he pulled out his new cell phone, a purchase he made that morning. Supposedly all his old information was transferred from his old pile of parts, but he'd have to check that out later.

He checked in with the Security Desk in the lobby and took the elevator to the Ninth floor.

A narrow corridor lead toward glass doors marked with bold lettering: Federal Bureau of Investigation. Through the window he could see a conservatively clad receptionist behind a large faux maple desk looking bored. Above the door was a video camera that followed his movements. His photograph had probably popped up on some computer screen with his stats next to it. He stated his intention to the receptionist, put his hand on the door and waited to be buzzed in.

The woman told him to wait for a moment while she made a call.

Eventually, Costa appeared through a side door, wearing an equally conservative gray suit. She skipped any type of formal greeting.

"Come in," she said, tipping her head toward the open door.

Agent's Costa office was small and contained your usual

government dull-gray desk and filing cabinets. The carpet smelled like petroleum. On the wall behind her was a fading picture of J. Edgar Hoover. The view out her window was of the back of another building.

"I'll be a minute, Jason. I'm just finishing up." Costa left.

He wandered about the office. He stopped at the bookshelf in the corner, removed a technical book on Forensic Science Investigation and skimmed through it before shelving it beside a stack of law books. He wandered over to the window but the lack of a view depressed him. He glanced at a few citations on the wall. None belonged to Costa. He stopped at her desk and picked up a framed photograph. This one actually had a connection to her. It was a photograph of her posing on a sandy beach somewhere in the tropics. She wore a skimpy swimsuit. Her arm was around a man Colefield assumed was her soon-to-be ex.

"Keep your hands off my stuff." Colefield hadn't heard her come into the office. She took the photograph back and put it down on her desk. "Have a seat."

"Who's the guy?"

"You know who. Now sit down."

Why is the ex's picture on her desk?

Colefield wanted to ask her that, but instead said: "I need for you to check on the type of pellets that were used to kill Timmy."

"What exactly are you looking for?"

"The shell I took from Scarbough's gun contained lead shot. Never used for hunting waterfowl legally. I suppose Scarbough could have used it on grouse on his private land. But that's pushing it … since the majority of the island's federally protected. Clay targets, yes. Birds, very unlikely."

Costa perked up. "I'd love to tie him to the shooting." She picked up the phone, then hesitated, flashing steely eyes. "I didn't notice that a shell had been logged into evidence last week..."

Colefield shrugged it off. "I'll have to ask Bart about that. Probably just a paperwork glitch."

"You never did like doing things by the book. I hope you know what you're doing." Costa dialed. He waited until she hung up.

"We'll have results by tomorrow morning."

"It would have taken me three weeks to get a result. Nice to have FBI credentials."

Costa smirked, removed her overcoat from a rack behind her desk and put it on.

"Ready?" she said, turning to face him.

They took a different elevator to the basement which led out to a private parking garage. Costa's sedan sat at the far end. She marched toward the car with purpose. Colefield followed close behind in the wake of her freshly washed hair. That night in the locker room it had smelled the same. It caused him to smile. Yet he didn't feel particularly like sharing the thought.

"What'd you do last night after we got back?" she asked, breaking the silence.

"Worked."

"Why didn't you call? We could have gone out to dinner. Or something..."

"Or something?"

Costa ignored the implication.

"Where does Timmy's dad work again?"

"DeMarco Manufacturing in Beaverton. He's the production manager."

"Who called who?" Colefield asked.

"We made the notification, but he already knew."

"But he didn't contact the police?" Colefield was incredulous.

"He said something about how he wanted to discuss it with his wife first...."

"Unbelievable. Planning damage control?" Colefield shook his head. "That poor kid."

"Wait. It gets better," Costa continued. "I finally tracked down the boy's grandparents. We conducted an extensive interview via Skype. They claimed to be devastated by the news, but had no knowledge of who would want their grandchild dead. They stated that Anita and Dave were fine parents, but that Timmy needed a more stable environment than they could provide because of the challenges of raising Penny, who they claim had gone wild."

"They are implicating Penny?" Colefield couldn't believe it. "When are they going to be available for a personal interview? And I need to get inside their home as soon as possible."

"They agreed to a search of their home, which is ongoing even as we speak. Then they asked if it was really necessary for them to return right away since it was their first vacation in a while, and with Timmy already dead, and no funeral planned, what was the harm if they finished their gambling junket with their friends?"

"Didn't anybody in this world care about that boy besides his stepsister?" Colefield rolled his eyes.

"Speaking of which, I called dispatch. Still no sign of the girl."

Costa drove as they headed west out of downtown and picked up Highway 26. Colefield stared up at the somber clouds forming over downtown, lost in a deep funk.

"What's on your mind?" Costa said out of the blue.

"I was thinking about where we went wrong on the interview with Jeb yesterday. And if he knows where Penny is."

"She'll turn up. When I was that age, I'd take off for days at a time and wouldn't tell a soul."

"I remember a few of those times. I'm glad I never locked my bedroom window. Even if you did run away from a strict upbringing and military structure to experience freedom you always knew you could go home. Penny's a wounded animal with no home or family to return to."

Costa flipped the blinker on to change lanes. Traffic grew heavier up by the Zoo Exit. Drivers merged left and right, all at the same time, some trying to avoid large potholes in the road.

"Why exactly did Scarbough shoot you with rock salt?"

"He had it in for kids with motorcycles."

"That's how you remember it?" she said. "He said you were a repeated trespasser and vandal."

"Maybe both statements are true," Colefield admitted.

"Even with us you remember things differently."

"What are you talking about?" Colefield turned toward Costa.

"You thought I dumped you because of college. That was never true. I broke up because you did the one thing that I couldn't handle. You joined the Navy." She glanced toward Colefield's shocked face. "I had spent my whole life as a Navy brat. I didn't want to spend the rest of it as a Navy wife."

As Colefield's eyes widened, a spot of sunlight broke through the clouds and rays of bending light reflected through the windshield. A shiny silver star pressed upon her forehead.

"You could have mentioned this before."

"It wouldn't have changed anything. We both had futures that diverged."

He thought about that for a moment. She was right.

"All I ever wanted was to do something important with my life. The FBI gave me that. It helped me grow up. Then it all just started falling apart. First the agency started downsizing and we lost some very good people. I put my job before my husband. No surprise the marriage went south."

"We are more alike than I thought," Colefield said. "You asked why I wasn't married? I've been accused of putting my job first innumerable times."

She was going to miss the exit. "You'll need to get over in the other lane and take the next right."

"Why doesn't this cheap piece of shit have a GPS?"

He cracked a smile but it didn't last. "Are you going through with the divorce?"

"Funny you should ask that. After all these years, I feel like maybe we don't get a do-over in life. Something tells me I'm too late to fix my mistakes."

Colefield wondered if she was talking about her marriage or their relationship.

"There it is, just ahead on the right," he called out.

The sedan turned into the parking lot of a big blue concrete building with bright yellow trim. A giant tub of butter, dropped down in the middle of an asphalt slab, semi-tractor trailers poking out from each side of the building like gills on a steelhead.

Costa pulled into a visitors parking space and turned off the motor.

She turned and faced him. "Look. I want you to let me handle this. You were once a great listener. Would you do that for me?"

"I'm not making any promises."

"This man just lost a son. He doesn't need a suspicious hard-ass coming down on him. I think you are too close emotionally to this case."

"Everyone that had contact with the boy is a suspect."

"Just let me handle it."

Like the FBI, this facility had its own Reception area but with coffee and donuts for its guests. Colefield grabbed a cup of black coffee, dumped in a pile of sugar and fake creamer and grabbed the last glazed donut in the box. Costa skipped the snacks, spoke with the receptionist and then walked over to sit down beside Colefield. She checked her cell phone for messages.

It was a short wait. Colefield was knocking donut crumbs from his lips when an athletic looking man in his thirties wearing blue coveralls arrived in the waiting area and greeted them. The man wore a hair net and little plastic booties over his shoes. After introductions were made, he handed them each a hair net and pair of shoe covers.

"We have to cross the main floor to reach my office," he explained. "We're in the middle of a new production run. We're required to suit up."

Costa began to tuck her hair up under the hair net. "I want to say how sorry I am about your son, Mr. Dodson."

The man glanced over at the receptionist who was all ears. "Let's continue this discussion in my office, shall we?"

He and Costa followed the man through a double door and inside the restricted area.

The clean area was the size of a small football field, a maze of white-booty worker bees buzzing about like minions in a futuristic film. Turning knobs, punching buttons, cranking valves, climbing ladders to take product samples from inside enormous volcano shaped stainless steel vats. Colefield had read in the reception area that this corporation created over a dozen different oil and butter products, each containing a variety of creamy artery-hardening transfats.

They entered a large office that Jim Dodson shared with the supervisor of maintenance, a short, dark-haired man named Ben Ross. He rose from his desk holding a cup of coffee and excused himself from the room.

"Sit down. Please," Dodson said, and closed the office door behind his co-worker.

Colefield glanced around. The room had the same sterilized feel of the restricted area. No personal objects with the exception of a Notre Dame coffee cup sitting on Mr. Dodson's pre-fab desk in the corner.

"You play in college?" Colefield asked with curiosity at they moved toward chairs. Costa sat in a chair closest to the desk. She quickly turned and gave Colefield a look. A reminder that she was taking lead on this interview.

The man glanced down at his empty cup. "I had high hopes of playing baseball for the University of Washington, but it didn't work out."

"Don't tell me: you threw your arm out during training camp?"

"No. I wrecked my Harley and ruined my elbow in the process. Ended any chance of playing again."

"Mr. Dodson, again my apologies for not getting to you earlier," Costa said. "We hoped we'd be coming to you with some better news. We were wondering if you could start from the beginning. Perhaps give us an account of when you last saw your boy. Anything you remember that might be of help to us..."

"Well, officers, that would have been a week or two before Christmas."

"You didn't visit your son after that?"

"No, Ma'am. I'm remarried and raising five girls. It keeps me pretty busy." He paused. "I have no information as to who could have done this. Have you checked with his teachers at school?"

"We're looking into that next," Colefield said.

"What about his grandparents? What did they tell you?"

"They are as shocked by this as you are, I can assure you."

"That's not what I asked, Agent Costa."

"As you may or may not know, they're out of town. I conducted an extensive interview by Skype with them and they weren't able to provide us with any useful information."

Mr. Dodson picked up a pencil from his desk and began tapping it on the desk top. Colefield sat up straight. Dodson appeared more distracted than upset.

"How did you get along with the stepfather?" Costa asked.

"I've never gotten along with him. He's a real son-of-a-bitch."

"How so?" Colefield asked.

"It stems from a fight we had years earlier. Old history. But we all do it, don't we?"

"Do what?" Colefield asked.

"Hold grudges."

"You fought over what, sir?" Colefield ignored Costa's burning glare fired his direction.

"I caught him kissing Anita in the parking lot of a tavern. Up until then, I thought our marriage was good. I called him out and we exchanged punches. Nothing came of it beyond a few bruises. Anita broke it up. We divorced shortly after that. She went on to marry the SOB anyway."

"Where was your boy at the time?"

"With Anita's folks for the weekend."

"Are these the same grandparents who raised him?"

"Yes. Clarence and Hazel. They're good people. They must be really torn up over this."

You'd be surprised.

"Why didn't Anita raise him?"

"Our marriage and then her marriage to Dave were rocky. So many fights and splits ... his whole life the only stability Timmy ever knew was with his grandparents. They practically raised him from an infant. Even back before our marriage hit the skids when he was still in diapers we left him with them. We worked opposing shifts. She'd stop by after work to see him for an hour or so. I'd see him on weekends. Then I went to work for the Woodburn Police Department. Things sort of went south between us and we divorced not long after that."

"How long after your divorce did she remarry?"

"Two months."

"Ouch."

"They had been seeing each other while we were still together. I'm sure of it."

"OK. Let's focus on the boy now. Did he have many friends?"

"A few."

"Did he ever go hunting with them?"

"As far as I know, just with BB guns," he said. "He had a buddy named Kyle who lives in California now. They used to go shooting together. He might hang out with some of the neighborhood boys but I couldn't tell you anything about them."

"You ever take Timmy hunting?"

"No."

"What about the grandfather?" Colefield asked.

"His grandparents are not all that keen on him hunting. No handguns or shotguns that I know of. In his day the guy hunted deer and elk, but he was mostly into fishing. He did shoot a nice six-point buck that was mounted and hung on the wall in their hallway. He never expressed an interest in teaching Timmy how to shoot. I was going to do that, but..."

"... but you're a busy guy," Colefield interrupted.

Costa cleared her throat and frowned at Colefield.

"Did the grandparents lock up the guns they owned?"

"Not that I know of, but you're on the wrong track looking at those people. Dave had an armory of guns and is a violent guy. If it was me, that's where I'd start my investigation."

"We did," Colefield said. "He has an alibi for the time in question."

"What about his son, Jeb?"

"The boy admits dropping him off along the riverbank and claims he went back to pick him up, but couldn't find him."

"What about Dave's dad, Hank Scarbough? He found the body. Could he be covering up for someone?

"He is a person of interest in the case, but we have nothing specific to tie him to the murder yet and he has not made Dave or Anita available for questioning," Costa said.

"What about the Sea Scout Master?"

"Timmy was a Sea Scout?"

"Timmy went to a few of their outings. I've never met the man." Dodson dropped his head into his hands. "Just throwing out everything I can think of."

Colefield flexed his fingers. "Where can we find this person?"

"Anita should know."

"She's not in any shape to share information at the moment."

"Oh?"

"She's sedated," Costa said.

"Is that what they're calling it now? Well, she's extremely talented at staying 'sedated'."

Costa leaned forward in her seat. "We'll check it out."

"Go talk to his friends at school. Somebody should know something that could help."

"We're headed there next."

Silence filled the room. The interview was over.

"If you think of anything, feel free to call Deputy Colefield or myself. We appreciate you taking the time to talk with us."

Colefield stood, but didn't offer to shake hands. Costa stood next to hand Timmy's father a business card.

Colefield laid his card down on the desk and then turned and started out the door without waiting for Costa to join him. He made no apologies.

Costa caught up to him out in the Reception Area. Colefield was struggling with one of the elastic booties caught on the toe of his shoe.

"Well, that was a waste of time," Costa said, slipping off her hair net.

"The father moved on years ago. He didn't even see his son at Christmas and probably missed his birthdays. He didn't call the FBI and hadn't even bothered to call the grandparents after learning of Timmy's death." Colefield ripped the bootie free.

"I'm beginning to share your opinion that nobody even cared enough about this boy to shoot him."

"Death by Apathy. That's a first."

19

It was déjà vu all over again. The last time Colefield strolled the hallways of junior high was when he was a student. Even then he didn't like being there especially didn't like sitting in the Principal's office, but that's where he now found himself, plunked down on a chair made for a child. Costa sat on an adult chair across from him, grinning at what Colefield imagined was a ludicrous scene. He toughed it out...

Principal Reagan hung up the telephone. "Now where were we, Deputy?"

"You received the news that Timmy Dodson has been murdered?"

"Yes. It's tragic."

"We'd like to speak with a few of Timmy's classmates if we may."

"Let's see..." Principal Reagan glanced at her watch. "They'll be on a lunch break in ten minutes. I believe that would be the most appropriate time to engage with the children. They'll be in the cafeteria or outside among the food trucks. Some of the students throw Frisbees on the football field. You might have luck there as well."

"One other thing, I understand his stepsister, Penny Scarbough, attends this school. Do you know if she showed up for classes today?"

"As a matter of fact, her name was added to the Non-Attendance Roster. This makes the sixth missed day this year. I'm afraid if the girl does not start attending classes, we will be forced to expel her."

Colefield tried to stand but his ass was stuck in the chair. "Due

140

to the circumstances regarding the death of her brother, you might want to cut her some slack."

Colefield fought his way out of the chair and stood.

"It's not up to me. We have Federal and State guidelines we must follow," she said. "Regarding the girl's absenteeism, there is very little leeway in what we can and cannot do."

"Exceptions can be made, Ms. Reagan," Colefield said. "Everyone makes them."

The principal sat back in her chair and stared disconcertedly at the deputy and then turned her attention toward Costa. "I hope you plan on conducting the interviews with the children, Detective."

"The deputy is just worried about the girl, ma'am, as is the FBI." Costa opened her notebook. "Now what can you tell us about the boy?"

She glanced down at the open file on her desk that her secretary had delivered earlier. "Let's see here. From what I can tell, Timmy was an average student. His grades reflect this. His attendance was good, but several of his former teachers indicated that his motivation needed improvement. Also, his math scores were quite low, but he seemed to be excelling in the Industrial Arts."

"What about his classmates?" Colefield interrupted. "Did he have any squabbles with them?"

"Squabbles? Let me see here, no … wait, yes, there does seem to be a notation that he had a disagreement with a fellow student about one month ago. Yes, I see that we notified the parents. No wait, I see here that he lives with his grandparents. Yes, we contacted his grandmother, a Mrs. Wells, and discussed the matter. It appears there have been no further issues with the boy or any of his other classmates since."

"What was the fight about?" Costa asked.

"Let's see. Well, let me read this comment from his Homeroom teacher. It appears that it was over a harsh comment the other boy made."

"And?"

"The boy made fun of Timmy's lisp."

"Was he receiving any special attention for this?" Costa asked.

"Yes. We caught it early. With some additional work, we would have been able to correct the impediment without permanent consequences."

Principal Reagan glanced down at her desk, re-checking the information.

"Anything else, ma'am?" Colefield asked.

"He came to school with a bruise on his face a couple of weeks ago."

"When a student comes to school with a bruised face, do you take them aside and ask them about it?"

"We always make a point of addressing it."

"Did you speak with Timmy Dodson about his face?"

"We did ask him about it, but he said it was an accident that happened at home." The principal studied the file. "There doesn't seem to be any follow-up discussion about it in his file."

She closed the folder. "He had only been with us since September. I see here that he moved to this school district in July of 2012. Or, I should say, the district partitioned. Some of the kids that attended West Jesuit Junior High last year are now attending Parish Junior High. This was a budgetary decision affecting many students and families. School districts expand and shrink due to population statistics. If one district feels it is bearing too much of the financial responsibility, school districts get restructured. An arbitrary line is created."

The hyperbole was getting a little deep for Colefield's taste. He checked his watch and glanced at Costa.

Principal Reagan wasn't prepared to end the discussion just yet. But Costa stood and the woman went along with the officer's wishes.

"The children should be exiting the classrooms any moment now. Please be gentle with them. They are fragile at this age. Timmy's death has been hard on the student body. Many of them just learned of it this morning."

"We won't water-board anyone," Colefield said. "We're just here to see if Timmy's friends can help."

"Very well then," she said. "I'll escort you."

"That won't be necessary," Costa volunteered. "If you could make us a quick list of his friends – we'll mingle our way through. Thank you again for seeing us on such short notice. If we have further questions, we'll be in touch."

The principal jotted some names down on a piece of paper and then handed it to Costa.

Colefield nodded and then led the way out of the Principal's office.

Standing in the hallway, Colefield turned to Costa. "You laid it on pretty thick in there."

"Sure I did, Deputy Rogue. It's my job. Got any other questions?"

Colefield shook his head and headed toward the Exit sign ahead.

Outside, the weather was marginal at best, a cross between dreary and dismal. A brisk breeze had kicked up since they arrived. The teenagers didn't seem to mind in the least as they filed outside, their skirts, shirts and coats flipping about in the wind. It seemed that very few wanted to lunch in the cafeteria. The excitement was happening outside. Small groups huddled around the food trucks and around the back of the school at a row of picnic benches, munching on junk food. Across the football field, in a secluded culvert far enough away from the Principal's watchful eye is where the bad kids hung. Smoked or did whatever. Ten or twelve had gathered there.

Costa studied the list. There were six names written out. She quickly tore the paper into strips and handed three names to Colefield. "You take the boys and I'll check out the girls," she said.

"Sure. I'll meet you over by the Gymnasium when we're through."

Costa headed toward a group of students hanging around a food cart that had just pulled up out on the street. Colefield tagged along behind.

She stopped, annoyed. "What are you doing?"

"I'm hungry."

"You take the smokers across the field. Go!"

His stomach growled in protest as he turned and headed toward the miscreants.

The group of kids, huddled around the culvert in their leather jackets and jeans, turned. Several dropped their cigarettes or joints and stomped them out on the concrete.

"I'm not here to bust anyone," Colefield called out to the group. "Just relax. I'm a Deputy with the Multnomah County River Patrol. I need to ask you a few questions about Timmy Dodson."

Colefield stopped a few feet away and looked for the person most in charge.

No one was volunteering any information, so he pointed to a stocky kid wearing a leather jacket with a chain wallet. "You there. Were you a friend of Timmy's?"

"No, man," the kid fired back. "None of us hung with the little dude."

"None of you?"

Colefield unrumpled his list of names. "Anybody here named Tom? How about Chris?"

"Randy?"

A shy kid in a yellow ski jacket stepped forward, staring at the ground. "We didn't hang, but I knew him. He was into boats and stuff."

"Go on…"

Colefield stepped toward the kid but did his best not to intimidate unless it was necessary. The kid in the leather jacket stood between them. He had something to prove, a lit cigarette dangling from his lips. Coalfield needed to be proactive so he reached out, snatched the cigarette and flipped it into the sky above the kid's head.

The group scattered similar to the way crowds do during a political rally when tear gas is shot off. The cigarette tumbled over the ground, landed in a puddle of water and sizzled out.

The kid folded and stepped aside so Colefield could get by. He stopped in front of the shy kid who was clearly frightened.

Colefield took him by the shoulder and led him off to talk in private. Out of earshot of the others, the boy seemed more relaxed.

"You a real cop?"

"I'm a real cop, Randy."

The kid had some kind of allergy. He kept sniffling. He needed a Kleenex, but he'd just have to man up and spit it out or swallow it.

"It's real bad to hear about Timmy. I liked him."

"Yeah, you got a screwed-up family too?"

Kid nodded. "Who doesn't?"

The kid had a point, but he was at that age where he probably thought all adults were screwed up.

"What can you tell me about Timmy?"

"Just that he hung with us but didn't smoke. He was mostly a loner. I never seen him—"

"You never saw him, you meant to say."

"He never hung out with anybody in particular."

"You said that. What else?"

"He came to school with a black eye last month."

"Who gave him the black eye?"

"He didn't tell me but I overheard him in the can make a comment that his stepbrother beat the crap out of him."

"You mean Jeb Scarbough?"

"Yeah, that's right."

"Did he say why he hit him?"

"They got in a fight over his stepsister."

"Over what?"

"Beats me, dude, but they hung out sometimes."

"Penny and Timmy?"

"Yeah."

"Out here?"

"Yeah – Penny smokes. Timmy and her talked."

"What about?"

"Stuff. It was bad for him, you know. Jeb was jealous."

"Jealous of whom? Penny and Timmy?"

The kid shrugged. "Like Timmy liked hanging with chicks and it pissed Jeb off."

"Was Timmy scared of his stepdad?"

"Yeah. He'd get drunk and beat him. His mom was a screw job too, but he was more scared of his stepbrother."

"Did you meet Jeb?"

"Nah ... but I've heard stories that he's pretty mean."

"What stories?"

"You know, stuff that goes around school."

"Have any specifics?"

"Like he went camping one time and a kid died."

Colefield grew very serious. "Say that again."

"He was on a hiking trip this summer. One of the kids fell off a cliff and died. Timmy thought his stepbrother had something to do with it."

"Did he have proof?"

"No. Just a gut feeling."

"Was he with him on the trip?"

"Yeah."

"Did he tell anyone else?"

"Probably just Penny."

The kid looked over his shoulder. The others were smoking again and staring.

"Can I go now?"

"What's your last name, Randy?"

"Brant."

"Don't mention what we talked about to your friends, all right?"

"OK."

"You're a good kid. Find some new friends to hang with."

The kid reluctantly walked back over and rejoined the group. The kid in the leather jacket kept his eye on Colefield as he crossed the field.

* * *

The next two kids had nothing new to add to the discussion other than Timmy was an outsider who wasn't attached to any peer group. Apparently he wasn't bad enough to hang with the troublemakers, and not chill enough to hang with the cool kids.

Colefield found Costa waiting at the back of the Gymnasium, a mustard-colored brick building with graffiti on the walls. Using the building as a windbreak, she was in the middle of jotting something down in her notebook, then crossing it out, her head shaking in frustration.

"I think we have a suspect."

She stopped writing and looked up. "You're serious?"

He nodded. "Remember that hiker that fell off the cliff last summer?"

"Yeah, sure."

"Well, I think I just breathed new life into your case. Do you have a list of the kids that were on the hiking trip?"

"Back at the office."

"Do you remember talking to Jeb Scarbough?" She thought about it.

"Think hard. It's important we make a connection. Was he there?"

"I'd like to say I know the names and faces of every one of those boys I interviewed that day but I just don't."

"What about Timmy Dodson?"

"What about him?"

"The kid I talked to said he was there that day."

"You're sure?"

"The kid's sure."

"I think I would have remembered him."

"If Jeb and Timmy were on that hiking trip last summer, Timmy might have seen something he wasn't supposed to.

Recently, he came to school with a black eye. Perhaps that was the first warning to keep his mouth shut. The second warning could have been more serious."

"When I get back to the office, I'll double-check my notes. We'll go from there."

"Did you find out anything yet?"

"Just that I'm glad I'm not a teenager anymore."

They exchanged a look. A few students wandered off around the far side of the building. That left the two of them alone.

He didn't need reminding that their very first kiss was out behind a gymnasium. Did she remember it as vividly as he had?

"Remember what we used to do behind the gym?" he asked.

"Don't flatter yourself." Costa laughed. "I think you pretended to be a lousy kisser, just so you could practice."

20

The following morning, Colefield waited outside the FBI Building leaning against the hood of Montgomery's derelict wreck. Two female joggers in their twenties sprinted by in Nike shorts and tank tops when Costa finally showed up. She hopped up on the hood beside him and gave him a quick smile.

"See something you like?"

Colefield kept it to himself. "Have any luck?"

"If that kid is telling the truth that Timmy and Jeb were on the same hiking trip, then we have some more digging to do."

"I've been sitting here thinking about why the boy would lie. There's no reason he would. If he says Timmy and his stepbrother were there then I believe him."

"OK – so we go on the assumption both boys were hiking that day and not part of the Boy Scout group. I want to play the devil's advocate here. If the stepbrother did kill the Boy Scout, if my theory is accurate about the other cases, then I'll need to place him at each crime scene."

"Can you?"

"There have been no witnesses, so besides his brother, there is no one to ID him."

"What about the pellets?"

"The forensic department identified them as lead shot. They're still trying to make a match to the shotgun."

"Scarbough was lying when he said he was bird hunting with that gun." Colefield absently scratched his scar. Costa took note.

"Oh, hey, I brought breakfast for you."

Resting on the hood next to Colefield was a brown paper bag

that contained something that was leaking grease stains through the bottom of the sack.

He reached inside it and removed two fat, juicy burritos. He handed one to Costa and kept the other for himself. "My treat."

She held the smelly burrito like it was road kill. "Is it gluten free?"

"Really – Tam?"

"I've got allergies aggravated by wheat products." She handed the burrito back to him. Colefield didn't skip a beat. He put the burrito back into the sack and removed a small plastic container of hot sauce. He tore it open and dribbled it over his breakfast.

"You want something else?" he asked, eager to dig in.

"I'm going across the street to the Deli. You want to hang or come with?"

"I'll hang."

She strolled across the street and entered a Delicatessen on the next block. Halfway through his breakfast, his cell phone rang.

He pulled it out of his jacket pocket, trying his best not to get the buttons fouled with the sticky hot sauce on his fingertips. "Hello?"

It was a woman's voice on the other end of the line. "Mr. Colefield?"

"You got him. What can I do for you?"

"This is Sally Ashley ... Mr. Montgomery's friend. Do you remember me?"

"Sure. You had the loft."

"That's correct. At the time of our conversation I said my daughter was coming to town to visit. Well, that has changed. My daughter's girl is too sick to travel so if you'd still like to use the condo for a few weeks while they dredge the moorage, it's available."

"That'd be great. When can I pick up a key?"

"Where are you now?"

"I'm downtown, near the Waterfront, sitting on the hood of a car eating a very messy burrito."

"That is probably something you shouldn't tell your future landlady. You do agree to pay for anything you damage?"

"I'm not as messy as it might sound. I was in the Navy. They harp on tidiness."

"So was my husband. I wouldn't say he was all that clean though."

Colefield licked a drop of hot sauce teetering on the edge of his burrito that was about to fall off and splat on his leg. "Where would you like to meet?"

"Could you possibly meet me – say in an hour? You could come by the loft."

"Shoot me the address."

As she rattled it off Colefield balanced the burrito on his leg. Grabbing a pen from his pocket, he took down the information on the only non-oily corner of the brown paper sack.

He said he'd see her soon and hung up.

Colefield was preoccupied with his thoughts when Costa returned. She placed a plastic container of green salad on the hood. "I'm going be civilized and eat this up in the office later. I need to get caught up on some Emails and review the list of scouts on the trip in which the boy died. You got enough things to do on your own?"

"I've got to go look at a loft and then head to work.

"You're moving?"

"Temporarily. I'll fill you in later."

"Shall we plan on meeting … say around Happy Hour?"

"It depends. Are you willing to help me move some stuff from the houseboat in exchange for a libation?"

"I'd usually do about anything not to drink alone," she said. "But helping you move is pushing it."

"I'll call you later. After I figure out if this loft is going to work out."

"In the meantime, I'll research our chief suspect."

Costa started to walk away and then stopped. She gestured toward the corner of her mouth. "You missed a spot."

* * *

The Pearl District is an area that encompasses some of the priciest real estate in Portland. It is located just north of downtown. Expensive high-rises, French boutiques, art supply shops, galleries, brewpubs, fine dining restaurants and a vast selection of historic warehouses-to-lofts conversions. You can get drunk in a martini bar, watch live theatre in a historic old armory, get a college degree from a renowned art school, take a cooking class, practice yoga, work out in a private gym with a personal trainer swinging kettle bells or buy most any street drug you can imagine two blocks East of the area. It supplies the best and the worst Portland has to offer.

The loft that Sally Ashley owned was in a building known as the Gregory, a twelve-floor, sand-colored brick building near NW 11th and Glisan in the heart of the Pearl. A Pizza Schmizza was on one corner of the building, next to a drop-off child care center, allowing people from the suburbs to stash their rowdy kids in a protected environment for a few hours while enjoying fine dining in the neighborhood.

Colefield was not much of a loft person, but it would be convenient, he reasoned. There's a lot to be said about convenience.

Sally Ashley was in her seventies but held her age well. She wore designer clothes and lots of flashy jewelry. Her fingers were sprinkled with diamonds. Her arms were weighed down with bracelets of jingly gold. She had on a fitted skirt and a white lace shirt, open at the neck. Her figure was trim. Her skin tanned. Her chest well-endowed. Her eyes and neck were as tight as a twenty-year-old. Expensive heels clicked over the marble floor as she approached the main entrance. Her eyes smiled at Colefield as they exchanged brief introductions.

"You're right on time," Sally said, glancing down at her Rolex. "What do you think of the area?"

"It'll do, Ms. Ashley."

"Call me Sally."

"All right, Sally. Thanks for calling me back. I was beginning to think I was going to have to push an inner tube out in the middle of the Willamette and sit this thing out."

"Yes, William told me you were being stubborn about moving."

"It's just a time issue. I've been wrapped up in a homicide investigation that has me running all over the place."

"I see. So you're a policeman?"

Colefield just nodded. "Shall we go inside and see this terrific place of yours?"

21

Every once in a while things go your way, Colefield mused as he drove back toward the River Patrol Headquarters on Marine Drive, the keys to Sally Ashley's loft safely in hand.

The inside of her place was like a stage set, full of stylish knickknacks and modern art to muse on, impeccable throughout, right down to the perfectly matched dishes and color coordinated towels in the opulent bathroom. The loft boasted every conceivable amenity, including a spectacular view. He could see two bridges and a tail section of the Willamette River winding its way north. A six-hundred thousand dollar elegant home in the sky with a great view and a weekly cleaning service.

But hey, the homeless can't be choosy.

Since the Sea Scouts were located less than a mile from his office, he decided to follow up on the lead Timmy's father had given him.

The turnoff for the clubhouse came up sooner than he had expected and he nearly missed it. At the last moment, he made a sharp left hand turn into the dirt drive. The tires skidded as the car came to a stop at the marina.

At the end sat a wooden headquarters building. A Coast Guard vessel sat idle at the south end of the dock along with several personal watercraft, rocking back and forth in the light breeze. There were a dozen or so boat houses chained along the western edge of the dock and an old decommissioned tug tied to the northern end.

Colefield climbed out and strode toward where a group of teenagers huddled around a short, chubby man in his sixties, wearing a polo shirt and tan shorts. The troop broke up and the kids divided up into pairs, making their way toward eight or nine sailboats. In groups of two they climbed aboard their assigned craft, donned life vests and prepped sails.

A redheaded boy down at the end glanced back at Colefield. He couldn't be certain but he would have sworn it was Jeb Scarbough who climbed into the boat and took over the helm.

The teens were practiced sailors. They wasted no time in firing up the small outboards, untying bow lines, and shoving off from the dock. The boats funneled onto the river in single file. Only one boat was left behind. That appeared to be the Scout Leader's. He ran along the dock barking orders until the last boat had left the moorage.

Before the commander's small boat had a chance to join them, Colefield snagged the bowline and reeled the boat back toward the dock.

"Hey, sir!" The man looked outraged. "What's this?"

Colefield flashed his badge. "I'm coming with you."

The man pointed to a forward storage locker. "Life vests are in there. They may not be your size…"

Colefield climbed aboard, rocking the boat back and forth. After he sat down in the bow, he lifted the lid on the forward compartment. He tried a vest on for size but it was too small to fit around his large shoulders. He put it back and tried a second. It fit, but was still tight. He managed to get the straps fastened.

"So now that you've commandeered my boat, what is it I can do for you, Deputy?" The man fidgeted with his own inflatable life vest and then readjusted his cap.

"I'd like you to catch up with the kids."

"Yes, all right. Anyone in particular? Or are you arresting them all?"

"Was that Jeb Scarbough in the lead boat?"

"Yes. He's a fine lad and a good sailor to boot. What's the nature of your business with the boy?"

"I'll fill you in on the ride."

The man at the helm reached out and attempted to pull-start

the outboard engine. It sputtered and coughed. A puff of blue smoke floated skyward. He pulled a second time, and a third, and a fourth. He took a little break, winded, and then messed with the choke lever. All the while, the other boats motored out of view.

"I know a thing ot two about outboards. Let me try!" Colefield volunteered.

"I have been operating these engines for years. Just sit tight. It will start … you'll see!"

The man pulled the cord one more time. The little two-horse engine sputtered to life, swallowing them in a blue plume.

"Giddy up!" Colefield shouted.

At the mouth of the entrance to the Columbia, calm water ended. At that point they left behind the protective waters of the moorage. Whitecaps crashed over the bow as the boats merged with the stiff current head-on. Heavy water splashed over the gunwales, soaking Colefield's pant legs. The icy cold water sent shivers down to his toes.

By now the other boaters were sailing down the middle of the river, mains up, jibs flying in the wind. The young sailors tightened lines and trimmed sails. Their tiny boats tipped sideways and soared through the water like the hulls were on a sheet of blue ice. The wind slapped at Colefield, making his eyes water. He swiped a wet sleeve across his face and focused on the lead.

Colefield pointed. "Is that Jeb's boat?"

The man glanced ahead. "Yes sir. Is this about his stepbrother's death?"

"It is connected. I want to ask him about a hiking trip he and Timmy took last summer."

"You must be referring to our Beacon Rock trip last August?"

Colefield's face brightened momentarily. "Yeah. The one where the kid died."

"That was just dreadful. He was not one of ours, you understand. Anyway, yes I organized the trip. We sailed upriver in August and camped at Beacon Point Campground. That poor boy falling to his death. What a tragedy."

"Did you talk to the police that day?"

"Well, no. We were not with that hiking group per se."

"But you were in the vicinity?"

"Yes."

"Did you or any of the scouts see anything unusual that day?"

"If I had I would have reported it."

"Let me ask you another question. Has your group ever taken a trip to the coast?"

The man made a quick course adjustment with the tiller, rolled on the throttle while he thought it over. "We make yearly trips to the coast. It's part of our coastal sailing program. We spend three days going over techniques that have been taught in the classroom throughout the year. We touch on celestial navigation, coastal sailing, tide tables, calculate how current affects charting. We practice sea survival skills. It is a very busy and exciting time for the boys and girls. I must say, it is one of my favorite parts of the program."

"Do you happen to remember the dates of your last coastal trip?"

"It was sometime in August, if I remember correctly. We try to coordinate it with the annual Scout Master Convention held there at the same time. Since the scout convention was cancelled this past August, we opted to sail to Beacon Rock trip instead."

Colefield fell silent, thinking about Costa's profile of the killer. This man fit the description. A leader, forceful, and surrounded by young boys. He didn't seem the least bit nervous answering Colefield's questions. Yet, he could still be hiding something.

Colefield pulled out his cell and punched in Costa's number. After the third ring, her phone went to voice mail. He left a brief message and then hung up, stuffing his phone back inside his jacket.

"Let's hoist the sails, shall we? Start with the main line to your left there."

Colefield frowned. "I've sailed before –"

The man looked surprised. "In that case, hoist away, Deputy."

Colefield grabbed onto the main line, held it tight and began pulling on the rope until the sail shot up. Then he hoisted the jib. Quickly, he tied off the line. When the rush of wind hit the sails, the little boat heeled, almost taking on water. Colefield clutched the side rail, steadied himself while the boat shot ahead, water gushing against the hull so close you could reach out and stick your toe in it. At one point in his life, this had all been so very exhilarating.

The other boats kept their pace upriver. Colefield's boat started gaining ground. One by one it passed up the slower boats. The Scout Master signaled for the other sailors to allow him by. As they neared the lead boat, the red-headed boy stole the jib line away from his skinny boat mate and re-trimmed the headsail in order to gain speed.

"We're losing them!" Colefield shouted.

"They have half the weight we do. He probably thinks we're racing!"

As a last attempt, Colefield waved his arms to get their attention. The other boy in the boat glanced back at them. A concerned expression painted his face. He shouted at his boat mate. Then Jeb did something that Colefield would later find so calculating. He reached around and unfastened the boy's life jacket, and before the kid knew what happened, tossed it aside.

Then, without warning, the tiny boat turned into the wind, bow first, the tiller flung hard right. The sails slackened until the boat made its full turn. The boom swung to the opposite side, and the sails filled with wind again. The sudden movement of the turn jostled Jeb's mate and he lost balance and was unable to get out of the way of the swinging boom in time. The impact knocked the boy backwards over the rail and he plunged into the swift river.

The other boats were moving at high speeds, swerving to alter their courses when Jeb's boat made the 180-degree turn straight into their path. Two of the boats veered to miss him, but ended up colliding, sending a second scout into the icy river. Colefield grabbed the tiller from the Scout Master and yanked it sideways, steering the boat toward the boys.

The scout without the life vest sank quickly below the surface. The boy might have been unconscious from the impact with the boom.

Suddenly, the boy's head broke the surface. He was coughing, gagging, and spitting river water.

"I'm going in!" Colefield shouted.

He plunged into the frigid water and swam toward the drowning boy. He reached him, hooked his soggy sleeve, kicked hard, and swam backwards. The boy fought with the deputy, but was no match for Colefield's powerful legs. Colefield dragged the boy through the water to the Scout Master's boat, which was now hove-to in the wind, idle, and poised for a well-rehearsed recovery.

The other boats were dangerously close to running into each other. The boat with Jeb aboard zeroed in on the second kid, splashing about in his life vest. Colefield caught a glimpse of the boat about to make contact when to his surprise Jeb dropped the sails and glided to within a meter of the struggling boy. As the boat drew down, Jeb leaned over the bow, hooked the boy's arm and pulled him aboard the swaying boat.

Colefield couldn't believe his eyes. He reached the Scout Master's boat. With the other man leaning out toward him they hefted the barely conscious boy's body up inside. Exhausted, Colefield knew he couldn't survive long in the cold water. Hypothermia would paralyze his limbs. Already the cold clawed at his arms and legs, an evil monster stronger than any man. But his weight would be too much for the Scout Master's boat now. Staying much longer in the water was a sure death sentence. He spotted a third boat, slightly larger than the rest, with two small boys frantically waving at him.

He kicked onward. The boat slowly floated toward him.

The scouts were shaking with fear. Colefield talked them down. In a calm voice he told them each what to do.

He hefted his chest up on the stern, while the boys steadied the bow. He muscled his way aboard like a cranky seal, his boots and jeans clinging and heavy as dumbbells tied around his ankles.

Now, out of breath but safely aboard, shivering and exhausted, he sat upright and glanced back over his shoulder. "Is everyone out of the water?" he asked.

The boys nodded.

He searched the other boats, in particular for Jeb. Jeb, the brave sailor, was tending to the shivering boy he'd pulled from the water. Jeb couldn't have counted on the second sailor falling overboard. Had he wanted to save his boat mate for show?

He reached inside his wet pocket. His hand sloshed back and forth against his cell – a soaked rock against his side now. "Either of you have a phone?"

Before the scouts could answer, the Scout Master shouted from his boat. "He's breathing! I'll call for an ambulance to meet us at the marina!"

"Have them dispatch the River Patrol. They'll know what to do."

Within minutes, the familiar aluminum patrol boat charged through the water toward them.

22

Bart's eyes widened in surprise as the patrol boat idled down to a throaty purr and glided alongside the sailboat. Colefield sat hunched over the bow of the small craft, his sodden clothes giving the appearance of wet concrete.

It was Weaver who spoke first. "What are you doing here, Red?"

"Working the case." Colefield offered a pathetic frozen smile.

"How many more are there?" The experienced deputy grasped Colefield's arm and pulled him aboard.

Colefield pointed out the two injured boys as the Scout Master's boat approached. While he hooked the bow line, the other deputy leaned down and lifted the shivering boy from the sailboat and carried him inside the main cabin.

Bart noted the bluing skin and shallow breathing as he stripped the boy's clothing, wrapped him in a wool blanket and moved him next to the propane heater. Bart examined the bloody cut on the boy's forehead and applied a clean dressing to the wound while Weaver helped Colefield secure the second boat.

Jeb's passenger was trembling and unstable on his feet but otherwise unhurt. As Colefield guided the second boy in, Weaver told the Scout Master they would handle transportation of the injured boys and that an ambulance would meet them at the marina. The Scout Master looked toward the wheelhouse and then back at the scouts, unsure what to do.

Colefield emerged from the cabin, staring hard at the conflicted Scout Master. "Keep it together. We've got this handled." He glanced at the scared boys bouncing on the water. "Your troops need you."

Nodding to Colefield, the Scout Master turned and waved to the boys.

"They'll be fine. Now follow me, sailors. There's hot chocolate waiting for us back at the clubhouse." And with that he hoisted his boat's sails and began leading his flock back home.

Weaver signaled to Bart to take the helm as they moved back inside. Colefield walked up to the first boy whose eyes now hovered at half-mast. "How're you feeling?"

"OK, I guess. What happened?"

"You took a tumble after a boom hit you in the head." Colefield kept his voice calm.

The second boy jumped to his feet. "Red saved my life."

Was he referring to him?

"Son, I…" And then it dawned on him that the Scarbough boy was red-headed and probably had the same nickname. "Jeb? I guess he did now, didn't he? You were both lucky today."

Weaver turned toward them. "You three were lucky, you mean. With the winter runoff, this river is a glacial graveyard."

Based on the numbness creeping through Colefield's bones, no one needed to point that out to him. "I need to change out of these wet clothes. We still carry a spare set aboard?"

Weaver nodded. "And we'll need to debrief the boys and interview Jeb Scarbough back at the clubhouse."

"Their parents should be present for this," Bart chimed in.

"Our moms will be there to pick us up." The second boy spoke up. "Except for Jeb. His grandpa gets him."

The first boy stirred. "You're not going to arrest Jeb, are you mister?"

"Nobody's going to get arrested." Colefield fingered water from his ear and concentrated on stripping off his sodden shoes. "We just have to make an official report."

Ten minutes later, as a KGW-NEWS helicopter circled overhead, the river patrol boat pulled up to the marina and tied off. Two paramedics approached as the waiting ambulance's lights pulsed a scarlet heartbeat on the water.

Colefield stood by as the men came aboard and performed a preliminary examination.

"We're taking them both with us," one of them said. "The contusion needs immediate attention. And both boys show signs of hypothermia." The paramedic stared at the soaked clothes on the floor, then at Colefield's wet hair and runny nose. "Deputy, I need to take a look at you as well."

"I'm fine." Colefield waved him off.

The paramedic raised an eyebrow.

"Look, after we complete our report, I'll get checked out." Colefield followed them to the ambulance where the Scout Master stood guard as the boys were loaded inside. He had recovered his persona as the man-in-charge.

"I'm meeting their parents at the hospital and I'd appreciate it if you would stay here until all the boys are picked up." The Scout Master climbed inside the ambulance. "There's hot cider and cocoa in the clubhouse."

"I'll take care of it. I'll be sending a deputy over to the hospital to interview all of you there." Colefield then told the boys the ride to the hospital would be a blast, winking at the driver, who gave him a thumbs-up. Colefield stepped away as the back door swung closed. Within seconds the ambulance was spitting gravel as it exited the lot, siren screaming.

Colefield rejoined Bart and Weaver. "Hobo, I'm gonna need you to head to the hospital to collect statements from the boys and Scout Master." Colefield looked around at the excited scouts, parents and curious gawkers who were watching the activity from the sidelines. "Have you seen the Scarbough boy?"

"He went inside the clubhouse with his grandfather and a reporter," Bart offered.

"Alone? With a reporter?" Colefield realized he hadn't briefed his squad on his thoughts about this afternoon's "accidents". He turned to the milling crowd and shouted.

"OK everybody, the excitement's over. I'm going to need all the scouts and parents to join us inside for hot cider and cocoa. To the rest of you, have a good day."

Colefield led the way up the narrow flight of steps leading to the clubhouse as Bart brought up the rear.

The interior had a large open space with old furnishings and a nautical theme. The wood floors creaked as Colefield moved deeper inside. He made out some fresh wet footprints, leading to a separate room.

"Jeb! You in here?" Colefield shouted. "I need to go over a few things about what happened today."

He followed the prints toward the open door of the room. Old maps and historic whaling pictures from the Northwest caught his eye along the walls. Spread out on a large round table in the center of the room was a marine chart of the Columbia River. There were pencil marks where the boys had been practicing navigation techniques.

Jeb was leaning over the map, pointing out specific spots to his grandfather and a reporter. They looked up when Colefield's long shadow blocked the light to the map as he entered the room.

"Jeb has been telling us about how you two saved those boys on the river today." The reporter extended his hand. "Would you mind standing together by the map for a photo?"

Colefield was beyond shocked. The last thing he expected was to be hailed as a hero with a potential psychopath.

"Please, officer. It would mean a lot to the boy, especially in light of his recent loss." Senior Scarbough turned to the reporter. "His brother was recently found dead. Possible hunting accident."

The reporter, sensing a bigger story, made a quick phone call to his stringer at the television affiliate.

Could he have been wrong? Colefield listened with a police officer's ear as Jeb described trying to save his friend from yellow jackets by jerking his boat mate's life vest away, just as the wind changed and the boom knocked him into the frigid water. It was plausible, but it looked premeditated to him. He couldn't prove it, but he thought Jeb targeted the boy on purpose. Maybe save him to throw suspicion elsewhere? Could a boy really be that calculating?

He couldn't have anticipated the second scout falling into the river. Lucky break for Jeb – who came out of this smelling like a rose.

So while Bart made cocoa and took notes at the clubhouse, and Weaver retrieved statements from the boys and Scout Master at the hospital, Colefield smiled woodenly for the camera. The evening edition of the paper would show a large man with matted red hair in an ill-fitting shirt, with his arm around a beaming boy that could have passed for his own son.

* * *

Back at headquarters, Colefield was telling his story to the Lieutenant before he left for a luncheon meeting. His boss stepped out of his office, jacket in hand, heading for the door.

"The kid's as slippery as a brook trout."

"I'm late – Colefield. Fill me in later. Re-interview the boy tomorrow."

"I'll head back out to the island first thing."

"Just make sure you do it by the book. Even if he is a potential suspect, he's just a kid."

"He's not just a kid. He's a dangerous, unpredictable killer."

"All the more reason to be careful. Take one of the other deputies with you. Better yet, take Agent Costa. Bring the kid back in for questioning. If anyone pitches you shit, call Children's Services. In the meantime, check out the Sea Scout connection."

"If I'm right, we can place Jeb at three out of four scenes."

"Not so fast, Colefield. Think this through before you jump to conclusions. Could have been Senior Scarbough or even Timmy. He was bullied, a loner ... he might have been responsible for more than we know. This could be far more complicated than we first thought."

"You're now talking about multiple killers?"

"I'm just saying. Do your homework and tie it up nice and neat. Find a connection between the kid and the girl scout." The Lieutenant looked at his watch. "Shit. I'm late. The Mayor is uptight over the increase in our response times. Says they are substandard. He overlooks the fact that ninety percent of our 'recoveries' are dead as soon as they hit the water."

"Roger that."

"I'm just glad no one drowned today. You did all right, Colefield, saving that kid."

"Use it for leverage with the Mayor."

After the Lieutenant left, Colefield sat down at his desk and stared toward the river. The coastal range stood out against a leaden sky. The Interstate Bridge was lifting, stopping commuter traffic along the I-5 corridor while a barge passed under the steel beams. There was more activity across the river on the Washington side but Colefield couldn't focus. It had been a long day and it still wasn't over. Not for him. But it could have been over for good.

He couldn't wrap his head around the day's events, even though he had experienced it firsthand when Jeb had turned him into a pawn for the media. Or had he? Colefield rubbed his temple.

He played back Jeb's earlier reminiscences about killing fish. Maybe the first strike with a club didn't always do it, but only made the fish flop madly on the deck. How many times had the boy just missed killing the fish in order to torture it first?

Could Jeb's killing tendencies have brought on the smile he thought he witnessed today as his boat mate plunged into the frigid river?

A cold splintering pain ran through his body, an aftershock of being subjected to the icy river. Every muscle seemed to ache; every joint throbbed, almost like the bends that he got during training as a Navy diver. He closed his eyes, took in deep breaths, and blew them out slowly.

He got up and checked his watch. He had to get moving. Because as minutes ticked by he was seriously losing his motivation.

A half hour later, he walked down to the moorage, relieved to be home, even if it was only for an hour. Maybe a cold beer and short nap would help. Then he caught sight of the enormous dredge churning at the end of his marina and it made some metaphorical sense.

Time was running out...

23

Late into the night, Colefield figured, workers would be disconnecting plumbing and electrical from the now deserted row of houseboats. By noon tomorrow half of them would be moved thirty feet back into the main channel of the river while sand was dredged from beneath their slips – a hell of a project, if you asked him. To uproot an entire community of floating homes just to scoop sand seemed insane.

Colefield checked his mailbox and stepped up onto the creaky dock, spooking a scruffy calico that scurried away toward Montgomery's kingdom. The cat didn't belong to Montgomery or anyone else for that matter. He was one of the feral cats that lived on the moorage. Colefield hadn't even considered what would happen to the animals and waterfowl that also called the moorage home. Seemed nothing was safe from the disruption.

He dumped his mail on the counter, reminding himself to put in an address change with the Post Office first thing tomorrow. Crossing his bedroom, he pulled a huge military duffle down out of the closet. He carried it to the bed and began emptying his drawers. He snapped up the Ziploc with the dismantled shotgun shell and buckshot inside and put it into his side pocket.

Afterwards, he placed the bag by the door, took a long last look around to see if he'd forgotten anything. He felt like an orphan, but then so was the old pirate Montgomery, Penny, and even Calico Jack – the stranded cat he'd name after another famous pirate, Jack Ratham.

Shit, you named the cat?

He knew what he had to do. With all the enthusiasm of a

man about to be executed, he rummaged around in his closet until he found his mesh gym bag and headed toward the kitchen. When he was finally ready to go, he closed the door and went to say farewell to his landlord.

Crouched down in a pile of buoys a few feet away, two green eyes watched his every move. "I got something for you buddy." Colefield squatted down and studied the cat's face. Jack too had a scar on his grizzled muzzle. He placed an open can of tuna inside the gym bag. "Stay put. I'll be right back."

He knocked on Montgomery's door. A voice thundered from inside. "Enter!"

Twisting the brass knob, he stepped inside. "It's Jason!"

"Just the scoundrel I wanted to see."

He closed the door and entered the galley. The son had built a wheelchair ramp last year after Montgomery took a few spills on his stairs, each time dislocating his bad hip. Colefield marched up the ramp like he was entering his former commanding officer's chamber and plopped down on a wobbly stool, about as stable as a matchstick.

Montgomery sat across from him at the kitchen table. He had on a pair of greasy reading glasses and before him spread out everywhere were crumpled up, marked up, newspapers. Somewhere under the pile was the holy grail of them all – the Sunday New York Times.

Montgomery put down his pen. "So, you've won the heart of my former tart, I hear…"

"She took pity on me, though it will take some getting used to. The place is a bit wussy."

"Rat pussy?"

"Wussy."

"We'll see?"

Colefield held up his hand in defeat. He spied Montgomery's hearing aid laying on an ad for an upcoming gun show and handed it to him.

Sighing, Montgomery screwed it into his ear.

Colefield tried again. "Where you camping out?"

"I'm heading North. My son Dennis has asked me to bunk in with him in Alaska. I hear once you go Eskimo, you never go back." Montgomery's face grew contemplative.

"Would you look in on the place, old boy? Make sure they don't forget to move the old dame back. I'd hate to find her floating downriver."

"Will do. Oh, can I borrow your telephone. I destroyed another cell in the drink today."

"Good place for a cell phone." Montgomery's hearing prevented any real conversations via mobile device. Reception on the river was tough on a good day, what with the commercial flights overhead and powerboats roaring by.

"Help yourself. You know where it is."

Colefield got up from the table and used the landline in Bill's private office to make a call. He kept it short and then rejoined Montgomery in the galley.

"Need a lift to the airport?"

"I've got a cab coming in thirty minutes. Thanks for the offer."

"You still OK with me using your car?"

"I'll add it to your rent next month."

He grinned and then picked up his pen to scribble something down on the newspaper. "So how's the case coming?"

"I don't know yet."

"Did the shotgun shell provide you with any leads?"

"I've got it in my suitcase. My friend at the FBI has confirmed the pellets found in the dead boy were lead. Thought I'd revisit that piece of evidence later in the week. For now, I've got a little redhead I need to track down."

"Never did trust a redhead. But come to think of it, I never trusted a blonde or brunette either. Stay with your hunches. Hunches always seem to lead us to our victories."

Colefield held out his hand, offering to shake. "Take care of yourself up North. See you when you get back."

"If I find a keeper in the tundra, I'll send a telegram."

* * *

A couple hours later, Colefield sat back in his new unfamiliar surroundings trying to acclimate. The leather sofa was a little too short for him to stretch out on and the pillows were all too puffy. And the place smelled a little sweet. But he had a killer view, and he enjoyed the house plants scattered about the place, as long as he didn't have to water them. The big screen TV impressed him the most.

He sunk back into the cushions, scrolling through the channels, with the mute button on. It'd been an emotionally and physically exhausting day. He'd found himself in deep water, literally. And he managed to climb to safety. And it was causing him frustration that he couldn't drive out to the island, knock down Scarbough Senior's door, and haul them both off. But he'd promised Tam he would wait it out until morning. And he had to admit he was in no condition to even get undressed, much less track down and arrest a serial killer.

His stomach growled, signaling the fact he hadn't eaten since lunch. He got up, went into the kitchen and opened the refrigerator. He had packed up the perishable goods from the houseboat. He took a quick inventory: an unopened cube of Tillamook butter, a half-gallon of Almond milk, a couple containers of Greek Yogurt, a jar of Jiffy's peanut butter, a small bottle of Tabasco sauce, several brown eggs, an open package of maple bacon and a welcoming bottle of champagne, courtesy of Sally Ashley.

He closed the right side door and opened the left side freezer compartment. It was an even sorrier sight. A half-eaten carton of Ben & Jerry's sat on the top shelf. Underneath that sat a package of frozen hamburger, a box of frozen spinach, and a package of chicken thighs. The other three shelves sat empty.

He opened the cupboards and took in all the fancy plates and glassware. Everything matched. The silverware drawer was the same. Every matching fork, spoon and knife appeared to be brand new. The pots and pans showed no hint of use. No greasy smudge marks, no stains, no scratches. The walls, the pottery, the throw rugs and furniture seemed to exactly match, color for color. Everything in the room had a proper place. The orderliness was getting to him.

About then, someone knocked at the door. Wondering if he could "rise to the occasion" he walked over and opened it.

Tonight Costa had followed his lead and dressed down. The tight dress had been replaced by an Oregon Ducks sweatshirt. Instead of stiletto heels, scuffed cowboy boots peeked from beneath her boot cut jeans. Why did this woman look good in everything she wore? Her ebony eyes shone. When she smiled at him, even her teeth sparkled. She held out a bottle of chilled champagne in one hand and a large bag of rice in the other.

"Happy housewarming." she said.

"Champagne. I'm flattered," he said and actually meant it.

"Don't be," Costa laughed. "It was on sale, and it was lighter to carry than a six-pack."

"I understand the champagne, but what's the rice for?"

"Do you want your new cell phone to suffer an untimely death by apathy?"

"What?"

She ignored the question and wandered through the loft, checking out the bathroom, the king-size bed, marble counters and expensive furniture and shaking her head in amazement. She immediately wandered over and gazed out the large windows at the terrific view of the city. "This is an awesome place. But it must be driving you insane. It's got a woman's touch."

Colefield deadpanned. "It'll do."

"I know about a dozen people that would kill for a place like this. How's the bed?"

Before he could answer, Costa had flopped down on the mattress and ran her hand over the silk comforter. "Not bad. I could certainly curl up here for the night."

"You want champagne first?"

"Sure, why not."

She hopped up and wandered back toward the kitchen counter and eventually sat down on a barstool. "Hell, I even like the way this cushion feels."

"They came from a place called 'Design within Reach', if you're interested. The store is in the Pearl. My new landlady told me all about this place before she handed over the keys."

"And how long will you be here?"

"If it's more than three weeks, I'll probably feel a need to buy a new wardrobe."

"Nice."

She glanced around once more and then began to nervously tap her heel on the barstool. As if appearing on cue, Jack wound between her legs, purring up a storm and putting on a show.

"Where'd you come from?" She absently scratched his head.

"He's just another castaway I am providing safe harbor for."

"It must be your day to save people." She tore open the top of the rice sack. "Where's your cell phone?"

Colefield reached into a cardboard box containing the shell, his baggie of phone parts from the tavern and his water soaked cell. She grabbed it and shoved it deeply into the bag.

"They teach you that in the FBI?"

"Should be good as new by tomorrow." She smiled at Colefield and then stared at her empty glass. "Can we talk about the case first?"

She frowned. "When I'm properly lubricated."

"It's a good thing my landlady left another bottle for us." He handed her a glass of champagne and toasted. "Well ... here's to lubrication."

Costa threw back the champagne and held her empty glass out wanting a refill. Colefield detected something. An unsettled look maybe.

"I signed my divorce papers today."

Colefield gulped from his glass, then hopped up and poured

her a refill. "Here's to two displaced orphans adrift on the sea of life." They clanked glasses.

"Got anything to munch on?"

"Just a stick of butter."

"I've never heard it called that before."

"My appetizer selection is limited."

"Let's order in a pizza from downstairs. They have a yummy Hawaiian pizza that is gluten free and vegan."

"How good can it be without pepperoni?"

"You'll see, you old carnivore."

"We'll have to use your phone."

Costa's eyes softened. "You saved a child today and nearly died doing it."

Colefield tried to shrug it off but even that slight movement caused him to wince in pain.

"Let's run you a hot bath. It does wonders for aches and pains." She headed toward the bathroom. "Besides this tub is big enough for both of us to swim in.

Colefield picked up Costa's cell phone. "How hungry are you?"

"Famished."

*   *   *

An hour later, soaking in steaming water up to his shoulders, Colefield passed the last piece of pizza to Costa who opened wide and bit it off straight from his outstretched hand. An empty champagne bottle bobbed on the water, having been replaced by Sally's bottle.

It was Costa who broke the mood and began discussing the case. "I did some research on the outings and both Timmy and Jeb were there. Still no link to the girl scout."

"It's funny," Colefield added, "but I went to the marina to investigate the Scout Master and left there convinced Jeb is our killer."

"It is too early to tell," Costa said. "It could still be an older father figure." She set her glass down. "I always said the last killing was out of synch … maybe because somebody else did it."

"Like who?" Colefield asked. "You think Timmy killed them all, and then Jeb or Scarbough killed him?"

"I'm not ready to discount any combination."

"I don't believe Timmy was a killer." Colefield was emphatic in his defense of the child. "And his body was marked with a symbol so he has to be part of the package."

"Nothing completely lines up on this case," Costa admitted.

"How you coming on the letters?"

"These letters are a signature of some kind. I've tried every word that starts with CUL in every language."

"Or maybe they were initials for a name, maybe something to do with his mother's death. But what does the infinity symbol have to do with it?" Colefield asked. "What if the letters and symbol are a code for an entirely new alphabet?"

"I've thought of that too," Costa said. "That's why I'm bringing in an expert to run different programs to decipher what it could mean."

"Find the message; find the killer?"

Costa nodded. "It's some of our only tangible evidence."

"Surviving my trip into the drink gave me a new look at the Scarbough kid up close. I saw him deliberately try to kill a child right in front of me, but then after hearing his explanation, I disbelieved what I saw and knew to be true."

Costa changed gears. "The media's run with the Sea Scout rescue. It's all over the news. And commentators are remarking on the striking physical resemblance between you two."

"Cop as Batman, boy killer as Robin?" Colefield mused.

"Whatever the reason, it's not good to see you connected with a potential suspect." Costa's face turned serious. "This is going to put some pressure on us."

"What's new about that? What worries me is his sister. She's still off the radar."

Costa thought a moment. "If Timmy confided in Penny about

his suspicion regarding the hiker who fell, Jeb would have every reason to eliminate her as a witness as well.

24

Sunlight and sirens poured in the large windows shortly after sunrise the next morning. Since he hadn't thought to close the blinds the previous night, Colefield was now paying the price. He rolled over and through bloodshot eyes searched for something to cover his face. He grabbed a decorative bolster by the bed and laid it across his forehead. He would later learn that the sirens were due to a pile up on I-405 during the morning commute.

As Colefield lay in bed making an assessment of his aches and pains, Tam moaned under the covers beside him. *Tam!* How often had he dreamed of waking up with her in a soft bed after a romantic evening? He hadn't factored into his naïve scenario the encroachment of reality.

"How much did we drink last night?" Her eyes scrunched down as she shielded them from the light.

"A bottle of champagne apiece."

"It's so bright in here I feel like I'm under a police spotlight," Costa grumbled, grabbed a pillow and covered her face. "And it sounds like we're in the middle of the freeway."

The half-a-million dollar loft-in-the-sky was alive with sound. Colefield laid back and soon identified garbage trucks banging around, tractor-trailers grinding gears as they left the main post office on Hoyt, commingling with the general rumble of traffic on Glisan – a cacophony unconducive to easing into a conscious state.

Costa threw back the covers and sat up. "Time to catch us a child killer."

Colefield climbed out of bed and headed for the coffee pot, which wasn't there. Seems Ms. Ashley didn't have the caffeine vice. He pulled on some jeans, a T-shirt and sneakers and then headed for the door.

"I'm hitting Starbucks. What would you like?"

"A double latte with four raw sugars, please."

By the time he made it back with two large containers of coffee and bagels, Costa had made it out of bed and dressed. Her eyes were bloodshot but there was life coming back into them.

He sat the coffees on the counter next to the sack of rice. "There're bagels in the sack and butter in the fridge. I'm gonna hit the head."

She let out a moan and rose to her feet just as his water-soaked phone sprang back to life.

* * *

They decided to drive separate cars out to the Island. Colefield stopped by the office to pick up Bart, but the younger officer was tied up with Deputy Weaver at a boating accident. Budget cuts had furloughed Tony until the end of the month. That left just the Lieutenant who had his weekly Wednesday morning meeting with the City Commissioner scheduled in an hour.

"By the book, Colefield!" the Lieutenant said, as he headed out of the office carrying his Kevlar vest. "By the way, you look like shit today. Let's hope your FBI agent is in better shape."

Tam was at least sharp enough to hand him his phone as he left the loft this morning, something he'd completed spaced on. The thought no sooner entered his mind than his phone chirped that he's missed a message. He climbed into the patrol car and punched buttons. He had three phone messages and a text. He listened to the phone messages first.

"Red? It's Jill. I just saw the news. Are you all right? I went by your houseboat and left a note, but looks like you might already be gone. And I don't know where to find you. Look I'm sorry about the other night. Please call me, OK?"

Colefield's face flushed. He hit the next message.

"Hey now I'm starting to worry. If you don't want to talk to me,

just leave a message telling me you are OK?"

He held his breath as he pushed the next one, made at 3 a.m.

"All your buddies have been in the bar and they say you're fine, so I'm guessing you just don't want to talk to me, or maybe I was right before and you are just too busy being a cop to be a boyfriend."

And just like that Jill had broken up with him. Again. His shoulders slumped as he checked his text. It was from Bart and had just come in.

TIED ^@ AKCDENT. WIL B N TUCH.

He got the gist of the message. Someday he'd have to have Bart fully decipher his text talk. He put the phone back in his pocket and started the engine. What other job affected you in so many ways as police work? He mused on the conflict between the job and his personal life as he drove through heavy traffic to the Island. Before this case, he had considered himself independent and strong, but now he realized his soul harbored an angry and hurt boy who still reacted against painful memories. The realization that he'd met people that by the sheer act of rebelling against them had set the tone for his life was mind blowing. He now clearly saw that last night's illusory *tête-à-tête* with Tam, while pleasant, wasn't real. They had both hidden behind champagne and carefully choreographed conversation in an effort to recreate their earlier and forever lost times together.

They met at the Island store. This time Colefield spotted her sedan in the lot. He parked alongside the building and climbed out of his patrol car. Agent Costa had her window down breathing in the fresh air as he opened the passenger door.

"This time I got the coffee." Costa handed Colefield a steaming cup of salvation.

"Let's make a plan."

Colefield donned a pair of dark sunglasses and his "take no prisoners" attitude as they pulled out of the parking lot.

"You interview the parents and I'll have another go at the grandfather." Costa was back on the FBI horse. "Based on the results of those interviews, we'll have another talk with Jeb."

"Sounds good to me," Colefield nodded. "What's our angle on this?"

"I have no idea," Costa admitted. "Fishing expedition. Let's see what surfaces."

The Scarbough farm was over the next hill. Sirens approached from behind. Colefield craned around in the passenger seat.

Costa had been watching the activity in her rear view mirror. "Paramedics," she pointed out, and began to pull the car to the side of the road to allow the emergency vehicle to pass.

The red truck raced by and headed toward the Point.

"There is only one farm out this far. Step on it!" Colefield said.

The sedan pulled back onto the narrow road and sped off. Over the next ridge the Scarbough farm came into view.

The red emergency vehicle had pulled up to the front of the house and the paramedics were already inside when the sedan pulled into the driveway. The two jumped out of the car and headed up the front steps. Since the door was ajar they pushed it open and went inside.

The living room was filled with daylight sifting in through lacy curtains. An open paperback was resting on the dining room table along with a pair of reading glasses. Colefield caught a whiff of fresh coffee brewing in the kitchen. There didn't appear to be anyone around downstairs.

There were voices upstairs. He nodded to Costa to lead the way.

The bedroom door was open. Across the room two paramedics were performing CPR on someone lying in bed. Colefield drew closer. It was Mr. Scarbough's daughter-in-law, Anita. The dead boy's mother.

Scarbough was standing back from the bed watching. After a few more moments, the paramedics stopped pumping on the woman's chest and stepped back from the bed, shaking their heads.

"We're sorry sir. She's gone."

They gathered up their emergency kits and headed for the door. Colefield stopped them. "What happened?"

"Appears to be an overdose," one of them said. "We'll make the call to the Medical Examiner's Office." Colefield stepped aside so the paramedics could leave.

Costa stepped up to the bed, looked down at the dead woman and glanced at the night stand where a brown prescription bottle rested on its side, its white cap beside it.

She took a pen from her pocket, plucked up the prescription bottle and studied the label. "Seconal," she turned and said to Colefield. "Prescription is for 40 pills. Bottle's empty." She looked toward the haggard man. "The script is in your name, Mr. Scarbough."

Scarbough nodded. "I had some issues sleeping awhile back. They were in my medicine cabinet. She must have found them."

"Where's Jeb?" Costa asked.

"He's out looking for his dad."

"Isn't Dave locked up in the barn?" Colefield asked.

"He's gone."

"When?"

"When I woke up this morning."

"Maybe Jeb let him loose."

"Don't believe so. His truck was gone and Jeb was still in bed." The man's hands were shaking.

"Is Jeb on foot?"

"No. He took his skiff."

"When did he find his boat?"

"Yesterday morning, he checked the grandparents' house for Penny and it was tied to the dock."

"And Penny?"

"Still no sign of her."

"If the boat is still on the island, then odds are so is she," Costa jumped into the conversation.

"Any idea where Dave might go?" Colefield asked.

"Tavern, probably."

"How'd he get free?" Colefield knew he had to have help.

"He's stronger than a bull, but there's no way he broke that chain. Someone let him loose. The key was on a hook by the door. Maybe Anita did it. She was up and around yesterday. She asked to see him. I wouldn't allow it, but she knew where he was."

"When was the doctor last here?" Colefield asked.

"She was by yesterday morning and we decided not to sedate Anita anymore. That's why she was out of bed."

"When do you think she got the pills?" Costa asked.

"I went to the grocery store about 4pm. I was gone about an hour. That's the only time I've been off the radar."

"Was Jeb here alone with them?" Costa asked.

"Yes."

Colefield and Costa exchanged glances.

"Does Jeb have a cell phone?"

"He did, but told me he lost it in the river yesterday."

"So there's no way to reach him or track him….." Colefield didn't like where this was heading.

"I'm calling this in. We need to bring in some help to process this scene," Colefield said.

Colefield stepped out of the room and called his office from his resurrected cell phone. It took some doing, but he reached Bart by text. His young partner assured him that he and Weaver would be at the farm within the hour. Colefield made a couple more calls, checked his watch and returned to the bedroom.

Scarbough took a seat across the room by the window. Costa was pacing.

"I got them," he said to her. "They're on their way."

"Jason, I think we ought to leave now before the boy has a chance to hook up with the dad or his sister."

Colefield shook his head. "Leave for where? We'd just be chasing our tail. I put an APB out on Dave's car. That will be easier to spot than Jeb's boat."

She didn't like it but went along with it. "Jeb could have given Anita the pills and sprung his dad last night. Dave could be miles from here by now," Costa agreed.

"Mr. Scarbough I'm going to need you to remain here until

the ME arrives," Colefield said.

Scarbough nodded. By the sagging jawline and blackened circles around his eyes, caring for these broken relatives of his had extracted a heavy toll.

"Stay with him. I'm going to check the barn," Colefield said.

"Watch out for my dogs," Scarbough called as Colefield headed out the door.

Once outside the house, Colefield followed a dirt path toward the barn, keeping an eye out for the Labs. Not a whimper or a bark came from the side yard where they had been chained up before. They didn't appear to be on the loose in the field either. Had they been locked inside the barn by mistake? Maybe Jeb took them with him. Colefield mused they were probably pretty good trackers.

As he pulled open the barn door, he kept his hands up in a defensive posture. As his eyes got used to the dim interior he relaxed and moved toward the back of the barn to the former pig pen.

It was empty. The hay was still on the ground where the man had slept. The bucket by the wall had some old urine in it. The tin of water was half-full. The big chain attached to the wall snaked across the floor but the end that had been locked to a metal cuff around Dave Scarbough's ankle was lying on the ground.

As he turned to leave he noticed a piece of fabric clinging to the gate latch. Colefield unsnagged the thin material from the wooden post, put it in his pocket.

He circled back behind the barn on his return to the house and found a small workshop. A table in the corner had some spent shells and reloading supplies. He walked over and took a closer look at the reloader. It was a single stage Lock-N-Load classic, just like the one Montgomery had described.

The bedroom door was wide open. Costa was sitting in a chair opposite Scarbough. "Find anything on the body?" Colefield asked.

"No signature letter anywhere on Anita that I can find without disturbing the scene."

Colefield nodded. "Well I found something in the barn." He removed the piece of cloth, walked over to Anita's body and searched her nightgown. Down near the hem the garment was missing a section of material. Colefield compared the piece of torn cloth against the piece missing on the gown. It was a perfect match.

"She was in the barn."

"The chain that had been used on your son had been unlocked. I found this piece of material snagged on the gate. She was inside the pen. I suspect she's the one that let him loose."

Scarbough just stared across the room, the life sucked out of him.

Colefield looked over at Scarbough. "Your dogs are gone too."

"My Sarah and Sadie are gone? Is that what you said?"

"Yes sir." Colefield was somehow touched by hearing him say their names. "Do you think Jeb or Dave took them?"

The old man was done talking for now. He turned and stared at the wall.

Colefield moved to the window. Down in the driveway a ME's van pulled up to the house and parked. Two men climbed out and approached the front door.

"Agent Costa, could you go downstairs and let the ME know we're up here."

Costa nodded and headed to the front door.

As soon as she left the room, Scarbough mumbled aloud. "I saw it."

Colefield moved to the window. "What?"

Scarbough looked vacant. "The shooting."

"You saw Timmy get shot?"

"No. I heard the shots. I saw something fall out in the field. So I got my dogs and went down there. On the way I heard an outboard motor fire up in the channel."

Colefield could hear the others downstairs. He had to hurry. "So you discovered Timmy's body when?"

"The day before I called it in."

"And he was already dead?"

"I told you that. Then I found my shotgun tossed in the bushes halfway to the river. Only one person could have done that. I had to think about it – what I was going to do. Jeb was my great hope for the family. A miracle really that he survived his tumultuous upbringing."

"You should have called the authorities."

"I suppose I should have. Instead, I just smoked a cigar along the riverbank. Soon enough, I figured, one of us would have to face a firing squad."

Scarbough glanced over at the dead woman on the bed before facing him again. "What are the odds that Jeb would lose two different mothers to suicide?"

"We're not 100% sure if this is a suicide," Colefield replied.

Scarbough processed Colefield's comment, then turned to him. "You knew I was lying about something. When you took that shell of mine, I knew I had a fifty-fifty chance you'd figure it out."

"It wasn't legal bird shot. You weren't hunting game that day."

"You're right, Deputy. I spent the entire day and night with that gun by my side." Scarbough looked him dead in the eye. "Because I thought I might be next."

Before Colefield had time to digest the grandfather's most recent statement, Costa arrived with the men in white from the ME's office.

It was all too much for Scarbough to handle. He started shaking. "I can't watch them take another member of my family away."

"No problem." Colefield pulled out his handcuffs and hooked Scarbough's limp wrists together as he read him his Miranda Rights, surprised to discover that the long anticipated scenario did not give him the satisfaction he had expected.

Colefield turned to Costa. "Could you escort Mr. Scarbough to your car? And make arrangements for him to be taken downtown and booked?"

"On what charge?" Costa asked.

"Obstruction, conspiracy and as a suspect in the death of Timothy Dodson."

25

The channel under the Sauvie Island Bridge was narrow and the current swift. The river patrol boat circled against the tide and floated toward the small dock. Bart was behind the helm and Weaver stood on the bow with a line in hand ready to throw it to Colefield standing ashore.

"Toss it!" Colefield caught the rope and tied it off. He held onto the boat's gunwale while the deputy climbed out and joined him on the dock. Behind them, Costa was waiting impatiently outside her car double parked in the lot.

"We confirmed the 4 X 4 is at the grandparent's home," Weaver said.

"Anything on the kid?"

"Not yet."

"What about the dogs?"

"There's an APB out on the Labradors now?" Weaver laughed.

"I think they might be with Dave," Colefield said. "Can't see Jeb taking the dogs in a boat and besides if Dave has the dogs they can't be used to track him."

"Or they could be running loose like dogs do," Bart said.

Bart hopped down into the wheelhouse and waved up at Costa, standing with her arms crossed and looking badass in her tactical gear. The agent didn't wave back.

"She looks ready to bite," Bart said.

"She's getting heat from her superiors."

"Like that's anything new." Weaver yawned.

"She's itching' to break this thing open." Colefield turned to Weaver. "You ready?"

"Shit! Bart I need the radio."

Bart leaned inside the wheelhouse, picked up the handheld off the chart table, and carried it over to Weaver.

Weaver turned it on then checked the dial. "Still channel 22?"

Colefield nodded, then turned, glanced back up the hill and gave a thumbs-up to Costa, still posing like a soldier on watch as Weaver joined her.

* * *

The plan was going to be simple. The house sat at the end of a houseboat moorage, providing adequate cover. They had studied the layout of the house and would hit it from the front and back simultaneously. There was just no telling what Dave would do. Colefield suspected he might flee via the water, so they'd better be prepared.

The winter chill started creeping through Colefield's bones as he moved outside the wheelhouse to get a better look with the binoculars. Just around the bend in the Channel, he could see houseboats coming into view. The road leading to the floating homes was different than the main road leading to Scappoose. He was sure Costa could find her way even without a working GPS.

Debris was heavy again on the river. It was just that time of year. Colefield pointed out a few stumps and limbs floating into the boat's path. Bart made small adjustments to dodge them. He was learning, his piloting skills improving all the time.

The first floating home came into view. A cedar-shingled shack with a swim platform. The curtains were pulled on the windows and Colefield suspected that the place was used as a weekend get-a-way. There were plenty of those units and a few were abandoned with Foreclosure signs posted. The vacant residences would make it easier on the deputies if they had to draw their weapons. Fewer civilians to worry about meant fewer potential casualties. As they crept through the murky lapping water, more activity could be seen on the river. Suspicious faces peered out bedroom windows.

For some reason, Colefield thought of Montgomery. How he

was faring in Alaska. Stuck at a hunting lodge on some private island surrounded by wealthy guests most of whom had never hunted a day in their lives, nor for that matter, actually seen a brown bear in the wild. Yet they still desired to shoot one. The need to kill was in all of us.

He would have to go check on Montgomery's castle after all this was over. See how the dredging was going.

Just as soon as it was all over....

Bart tapped on the wheelhouse window. Through the river mist on the windshield he was pointing at something ashore. Just ahead, at the end of the row of floating homes, the house came into view. Colefield picked up the binoculars. Through a kitchen window, he saw the two missing dogs barking and agitated.

Anxiety tugged at his gut, a feeling that didn't come very often. Just then the handheld crackled out static and a clear voice announced: "River Dog Two, calling River Dog One, over!"

Colefield pressed the transmit button on the side. "This is River Dog One, over!"

"The dogs are inside the premises with others unseen. Use caution. Wait for my signal, over."

"Roger that! We have eyes on the dogs as well. No one else visible riverside. Five minutes until in position, over."

Colefield clipped the radio to his vest. "Pull in just after the yellow floating home. I remember there's an empty slip we can use as cover. We can stay out of direct line of fire and work our way across the adjoining decks."

"OK boss!"

The boat glided in with its engines at a quiet idle. Colefield jumped out, tied off the bowline and steadied the boat while Bart strapped on his Kevlar vest.

Using the floating homes as cover the men stayed close to the walls. The gap between the decks was an easy jump if they timed it right. Ducking in behind a railing, Colefield peered ahead, keeping his eye on the sliding door opening onto the deck. Colefield pointed to his wristwatch and reached for his radio.

"River Dog One to River Dog Two, it's a go! Over!"

"Roger, River Dog One. See you on the other side. Out!"

Colefield clipped his radio to his vest. "Let's go!"

Just as the deputies started to roll out from behind the wall, Dave Scarbough stumbled through the sliding glass door onto the deck, clutching his belly. Blood oozed through his fingers. His pants were saturated. He fell to his knees and swayed close to the water's edge. The last time Colefield had seen Jeb's father, he was chained to the ground and drinking water from a trough in a pig pen. He would have placed even odds that things couldn't have gotten any worse for the guy.

Colefield couldn't risk stepping out into the open to help the injured man until he was certain it was clear. As he was weighing his options, the wounded man tumbled forward onto the deck.

"Jeb or Penny may be inside," Colefield whispered, his heart racing. It was now or never. "Stay low."

The men rolled out from behind the wall, tumbling across the deck and sprang to their feet in a defensive position. With Glock in hand, Colefield made a move toward the living room.

Costa stepped out through the open door with her gun drawn. "The dogs are chained up, but there's nobody else inside."

Bart was working on Dave while Weaver called for an air ambulance. It didn't look good. Colefield leaned close.

"Penny..." Dave uttered.

"Penny shot you?" Colefield asked.

"I'm so..." Dave released a long breath and lost consciousness.

"Why are we always five minutes too late on this case?" Colefield said and returned inside. "So what happened in here?"

"Looks like Penny was hiding out here when Dave arrived. Her stuff is all over the place. The shot took place here in the living room after a struggle." Costa indicated a turned over table. "We haven't found a weapon."

"The dogs were tied up, so at least they haven't contaminated the scene."

"Dave mentioned Penny by name before he lost consciousness.

Do we think she shot Dave?" Colefield was thinking out loud.

"If she did, why didn't she take off in the 4 x 4?" Costa asked.

"Maybe she didn't need the car. Maybe she left by boat," Colefield said.

"If Jeb arrived by boat. Maybe he came to kill Penny and Dad got between them and took the hit."

"Or he came here to kill Dave and Penny witnessed it and either ran away on foot or he took her with him."

Christ, what a mess...

"Until we get more from Dave, we don't even know if Jeb or Penny were directly involved in this shooting," Colefield said. "A guy like Dave is bound to have enemies."

He heard the Lieutenant's words: "By the book, Colefield. By the book."

Colefield sighed. "Our best chance is to get a chopper out here and some extra patrolmen and seal up the island."

26

The search continued through the night. A chopper and a team of dogs were brought in, but the Sheriff's office had no luck locating the missing teenagers. River Patrol from both counties circled the island several times but found no trace of the small outboard. Colefield and Bart then joined the hunt on foot but it proved equally futile. Costa was having no luck either; nor were the two FBI agents that were called in to help out. Both of the Scarbough houses were searched. No kids – but a worn photo of Jeb's mom was found in his sailing gear. At Anita's house they found the gun safe open, which to Colefield meant that Scarbough junior had probably collected a weapon before he went to the houseboat. Or, it was not a stretch to consider Jeb had been the one who had opened the safe.

They searched the entire island. Dave never regained consciousness, but the doctors told Colefield that he died alcohol free, which might be scant comfort for Scarbough senior, who remained behind bars, still not talking, waiting on his lawyer for counsel.

Colefield had been trying to finish Dave's unfinished statement. Now he believed he wasn't trying to say 'I'm sorry", but rather "I'm sober."

And Colefield still had his own explaining to do.

Colefield walked out of the Lieutenant's office with a splitting headache. "Dead bodies and missing children draw attention, Colefield!"

"Yes, sir."

"I want your complete report before you leave here. Maybe we can still salvage something from this debacle."

The City rumbled like never before. The Mayor needed to place blame somewhere. Putting it all on the head of a supposedly heroic teenage boy – given the sketchy evidence and vague theories shared by the deputy and Costa, left little room for anything other than the Lieutenant to place Colefield on administrative leave until the case could be sorted out. The FBI also decided to bring in "fresh eyes", unceremoniously reassigning Costa. It was unfair but it had to be done, which is why he hadn't slept and had stayed at it all night working on his report until he was forced out the following morning.

By the time he reached the loft at nine-thirty the next morning he was in a foul mood, which didn't improve when Jack howled his discontent at his empty chow bowl and full cat box.

Every part of his body ached. He needed a long, hot bath and a stiff shot of something, which he now had, courtesy of Montgomery's rolling distillery parked in the garage. He found a flask in the glove box. Thank you, Bill.

Colefield twisted the top off and took a sniff. Smelled like booze. He threw back a slug. Tasted like booze.

He set the flask on the counter and stepped it up a notch for the rambunctious cat, feeding him canned tuna. Afterward, he hit the bed like a ton of bricks and fell into a deep sleep, filled with distorted images. First, it was a girl floating face down in the water followed by a headless corpse lying in the center of a pumpkin patch. The image that came next was a giant carp flicking a pierced tongue at him in jest as the big fish flopped about in the bed of his pickup truck. Just when he thought it was safe to close his eyes again, another nightmarish image would appear.

It was evening by the time he struggled awake and crawled from bed. He wandered over to the large windows, looked out at the city, and tried to concentrate on something other than his distorted thoughts.

The endless sparkle of lights did nothing to lift his sullen mood. He moved into the kitchen, turned on the faucet and stuck his parched lips down under the flow of cool water. He couldn't stand his own sour smell any longer and went in and took a long shower. Afterward, as he sat naked on the bed and tried to picture what the kid and the girl were doing, his cell phone chirped, signaling a text. Had to be Bart. He opened it up. All it said was "CUL8R". After mouthing different combinations, trying to decipher the message it came at him so hard he fell back against the wall. It wasn't an infinity symbol, it was an 8. It was text talk for "See you later".

"Alligator," Colefield said out loud, recalling Jeb's story about the saying and how he lost the ritual with his mother after her death. So he had replaced it with another ritual ... killing scouts on the same day every year. Colefield grabbed his notebook, flipping through it furiously. The deaths occurred on August 10th. It didn't jibe with the accident date, or her divorce. Or the date of her suicide. What could it mean? Reading through his interview notes with Jeb, he found it. It was the anniversary of the day she was found and the family was notified, three days after the time of death, a date that would only be significant to Jeb.

Colefield sat down. So he honored his mother each year by sacrificing a Scout in her honor. Until Timmy saw something he shouldn't have, and became another body on the funeral pyre. If Jeb was tying up loose ends, finding Penny took on a new urgency.

Had Jeb even taken her? Was she alive? Was the plan all along to kill his entire family and hide it behind a serial killer facade? But what could be the motive? His grandfather's estate? Another reason to get rid of Penny? Hadn't the old man said himself that Jeb was a miraculous blessing to him?

He dialed Tam's cellphone. And as usual, it went straight to voicemail. Again.

*   *   *

The days that followed, proved to be less eventful and more frustrating....

Despite having the answer to the puzzle and not being able to continue on the case, Colefield had been looking forward to the time off. Maybe he and Tam could take a few days to give them time to sort out the past and see if the future held promise. But to his chagrin, she had left town immediately without any real explanation, other than a voicemail that she needed to take care of some personal business. She provided no details but she didn't need to. Colefield knew where she was, but as time passed he wasn't sure what personal details she was wrapping up – her husband or him.

One afternoon he broke down and called Harvey to see if he was back in town and if they could hook up for a beer at Goose Hollow Tavern. Harvey had agreed. Yet all he could talk about was how much New York had changed since he'd been there last and how all his relatives still had the ability to piss him off. Then, he wanted to know if things had picked up where they had left off years ago with Tam. But Colefield didn't provide details. Not because he didn't want to, but because he didn't know. Since her last message there had been no calls, no texts, no messages of any kind. So instead he directed the conversation back to the Scarbough case and the motive behind the killings.

"I'm intrigued with your theory," Harvey said. "If you find me the kid, I'd love to discuss it with him."

With no new leads or information on the teenagers' whereabouts the case may have been a priority in Colefield's eyes, but it was only one of about a dozen others assigned Harvey, who thought it was cursed by Colefield's bad karma.

Harvey's newest case had to do with the murder of a young couple found shot in the head execution style in their apartment over in Southeast Portland, off Division Street. Harvey was going for the drug-deal-gone-bad angle. And so was his partner, Detective Redden, who, by the way, was not healing well from his injury and claimed he would never set foot on Sauvie Island again.

The day of their little mishap seemed like an eternity ago.

He missed his truck. And driving Montgomery's beater was wearing thin. Especially since the engine had developed another oil leak. Not only did he leave puddles wherever he went but he now had to contend with smoke pouring out from under the hood at every stoplight.

He must have had some guilt about letting Montgomery drive the rattletrap because one morning he had swung by a garage to get it checked out. After waiting nearly an hour for the technician to look at it, the mechanic just threw up his hands and said it wasn't worth the money to fix. Before leaving, Colefield managed to get him to tighten a loose water hose clamp, which stopped the smoking issue to a degree. He then drove to the marina to check on the houseboats and collect mail. While he was there, he learned from one of the workers that the project was behind schedule. Another week at least before they were letting anyone move back onto the moorage. He thought about pushing the issue and sneaking back home, figuring he could shower at the office, but it was so noisy with the herculean dredge operating day and night, he decided to just ride it out in the loft. What were a few more days in the city going to hurt?

He called Montgomery in Alaska and gave him the update. The old pirate took the news hard. He too was ready to come home. But the moorage walkways were unsafe and Colefield told him he was better off where he was until things were put back together. He reminded him that he didn't need to fall and dislocate his hip again.

"You're nagging like a wife," Montgomery said on the phone. "What's wrong?"

He explained that he'd been put on administrative leave and the time off was not turning out like he had expected.

"Never does," Montgomery said. With that, the phone went dead in his hand, Montgomery signing off with his usual abruptness.

As he was putting the phone down, it rang again. He answered it, thinking Montgomery had forgotten to tell him something. "What do you want you old fart?"

There was a long silence on the other end. Then a different man's voice said: "Is this Deputy Colefield?"

The voice sounded familiar but he couldn't place it. "Yes,

who's this?"

"Tom Farmer. I have your pickup truck repaired."

"Great! First good news I've had all week."

"The repair costs are higher than I quoted. Parts were hard to locate."

"Just give me the damage."

* * *

By the time he reached the Sauvie Island Bridge, Montgomery's car was on its last adventure. White smoke was blowing out from under the hood and funneling out the tailpipe. Colefield was too afraid to pull over and stop for fear the car would never start again. So he drove it toward the address that Tom Farmer had given him over the telephone. Along the winding road that bordered the channel and veered east toward the river, he spotted a flock of swans, and took this as a good omen, especially as he neared the Pumpkin Patch. He could still see the deep tracks in the shredded soil where his pickup truck had attempted to blaze a trail to the opposite side, and the long irrigation ditch that had abruptly ended the chase. There were fresh tracks he assumed had been made when the pickup truck had been towed from the field.

By the time he pulled into the driveway of the farmhouse, the engine was groaning and smoking so fiercely, he could barely see out the windshield. The garage was at the back of the property with a dirt road leading to it. After he drove past some farming machinery, Colefield could see his pickup parked outside the shop and pulled in beside it. As he climbed out from behind the wheel, some hissing and a plume of white smoke began to pour out from under Montgomery's beast. He could smell the familiar sweet scent of antifreeze. The fabled mythical fire-breathing dragon cloud forming above the car's hood had to be a ruptured radiator hose.

Colefield just left the keys in the ignition and went to track down the mechanic.

Tom Farmer strolled out of the garage wiping his dirty hands onto a red rag. He walked over to Montgomery's car and slowly lifted the hood. He stepped back as more steam poured out. The man fanned his hand back and forth over the front of the engine, examined the damage done, and then turned to Colefield.

"Can you save it?" Colefield asked.

"Can you leave it for a few days?"

"It would be good to get it out of my sight for a while." Colefield's frown slowly turned into a smile as he took a good look at his old pickup truck. He lifted the hood and admired the new rubber radiator hoses, a new fan belt, and Tom Farmer had put in new sparkplugs and a new distributor cap. He leaned close to the sparkling clean undercarriage and where the steering rod had been replaced. He closed the hood and climbed into the cab. The key was in the ignition. He turned it and the engine fired to life immediately, no hesitation whatsoever. He revved the engine several times and listened to the throaty exhaust purr.

Farmer came over to the door. "I went ahead and gave it a minor tune-up. Your distributor cap had a crack in it and your plugs were old. I replaced both your radiator hoses and your fan belt and put in some fresh oil and new anti-freeze. You should be good to go."

"Thanks, I appreciate it."

Colefield climbed out of the cab and paid the man in cash.

The man slid the bills into his wallet. "There's been plenty of commotion on the island lately," he said. "I've been seeing patrol cars cruise by. And they have an officer watching the Scarbough estate. They really think the grandson is connected to the deaths?"

"They believe he may have killed his father and kidnapped his sister. He's also a person of interest in the death of his step-mother and stepbrother."

"It's like the family is cursed." Farmer shook his head.

"If there is a hex on the family that would mean the whole thing is out of our hands already, and I can't go there."

"Well, God works in mysterious ways. He'll dish out his own sense of justice."

Colefield nodded though he doubted God had had much to do with this case.

Since he was out on the Island already, there would be no harm done in snooping around a bit before he headed back to Portland. He turned east out of Tom Farmer's property and headed along the river, following the winding road. Sometimes you just have to follow your gut. If word got back to his lieutenant that he'd been spotted on the island, he had a fistful of reasons for being there that had nothing to do with the case. Picking up his pickup truck and visiting his old homestead being two.

His first stop took him clear across the island to Anita's house. It seemed as deserted as the first day he had seen it. He got out of his pickup truck, examined the fresh car tracks in the drive, and then walked the perimeter, keeping his hand near his Glock. Nothing. At the back door the crime scene tape had not been disturbed. Colefield went over to the windows but the blinds were pulled and the windows locked. The house was secure and undisturbed. Next he checked around the small dock before returning to his pickup truck. Colefield sat thinking on the side of the road for ten minutes before he finally drove off.

His next trip was out to the Point, to Scarbough's estate. At least one patrol car was parked in the drive with an officer watching the house as he drove on by. The policeman had probably seen his truck. What would come of it, Colefield didn't give a rat's ass. He needed to see if the law was doing its job. It appeared that they were.

His final stop was down by the Pumpkin Patch. On a stretch of deserted road Colefield pressed the accelerator to the floor. The old truck was running the best it had in years thanks to Tom Farmer. He looked down at the speedometer as the needle climbed to the 80 mph mark before he lifted his foot off the accelerator and let the truck coast. Up ahead, about a quarter-mile, he slowed down to a crawl and turned into the dirt drive of his old homestead and parked. From the cab of his truck he had a view of the entire house.

The roof was in rough shape. A number of shingles had blown

off recently and the paint had become so faded you could barely tell that at one time it had been blue – a color his mother always associated with her childhood memories of Cape Cod. Tall spindly grass snaked up through cracks in the rotting porch. On the side of the house that he could see, broken glass glinted on the ground, where someone had broken out a window. The weed choked yard that surrounded the property hadn't been mowed in years. A real estate agent he dated for a short while before Jill had told him about a family and their plans to buy the place from a retired railroad worker. He'd lost his wife to cancer and moved in with his daughter in Scottsdale where he eventually died. He had left the house to his daughter who had no desire for fixing up the place and had no toleration for Oregon's rain-soaked weather. Instead, she allowed the house to rot away which was just fine with Colefield. Let the past be the past, he liked to say. Yet he couldn't free himself from stopping by the decaying property whenever he was in the area, and still reacting to events long gone from his life.

27

Since his parents had migrated from the Midwest where the threat of tornadoes was a common fact of life, his father had insisted on building a storm shelter at the back of the property. Nothing more than an underground bunker with dirt walls reinforced with stout lumber. When the Cold War period entered history, his father had started to store food there and added a 500-gallon storage tank that could hold enough water for the family to survive for a month if all hell broke out between the US and Russia.

Yet, the only time they should have used it, they didn't. When a severe windstorm hit the area on February 13th 1979, his entire bedroom wall had been torn off the house – a room that he shared with his younger brother, Kenny. Record winds had split a giant oak which came crashing down through the roof and onto their beds, narrowly missing him and crushing his brother's arm.

Colefield walked to the back of the house and stared at the ragged patch on the roof, and then at the dead severed oak, still rattling menacingly against the winter sky. He eyeballed the bedroom through the broken window. Vagrants had obviously made themselves at home inside, though he couldn't imagine most homeless folks bunking in 20 miles from any city services.

Unless they didn't want to be found...

He wondered if this house had been part of the search. As he turned toward his truck, his eyes spotted the lipstick tube among the shards of glass at his feet. He stooped and retrieved it with his shirt sleeve and removed the cap – a violet tongue glistened. He remembered his mother's lipstick taking on that shape after she swiped it back and forth on her closed lips day after day. But purple was not her color. So this is another place where Penny hid out. Maybe Jeb too. But where were they now?

He'd have to get a team out here to process this place for evidence and clues. He moved toward the storm shelter. It was locked, but someone had replaced the old rusted chain. It had been cut off and lay in a pile on the ground. A new heavier chain and modern lock had been attached in its place. A realtor had probably done it in case somebody wanted a look down below. Who knew where the original key was.

He approached the bunker and rattled the new chain. It was stout and secure. So was the door it safeguarded. His dad had spared no expense building the door to the bunker. Colefield figured old aged timber like this was probably worth some money in today's market, where recycling wood was a growing trend in remodeling. He leaned forward to inspect the timber. Shit, somebody had carved it up. Kids! He had to admit he'd carved his name in more than few trees in his day. He brushed the surface free of dirt and debris, revealing a ragged "R". His throat tightened. It was freshly carved. He kept rubbing the wood, but nothing else appeared. The final letter stared up at him. God, don't let him be too late again. He pounded on the door.

It was faint at first but what sounded like a cry came from inside the bunker. A young girl's voice, strained and very weak.

"Penny! It's Deputy Colefield!"

A moan crescendoed through the door.

"I have some tools in my truck. I'll be right back!"

Penny screamed an unearthly sound.

There was no time for tools. "Step back from the door. I'm going to shoot the lock off! You understand?"

He pulled out his Glock, pointed it at the padlock and pulled the trigger. His ears echoed and roared as the bullet broke the steel open like a cracked egg. Within seconds he had it pried off and the chain undone. He pulled back the heavy doors and a wave of decay rolled out into the light of day.

"Penny!"

He started down the stairs. With each step darkness grew like a wall around him. When he reached the bottom, he detected movement against the back wall. The darkness enveloped everything. He squatted down to allow more light to filter into the room. The floor undulated as squealing rats scattered and panicked.

"Penny?"

"Help me!" Penny's plaintive voice was a whisper.

"Come toward me, toward the light."

"I'm too weak. I won't make it."

"OK. Just stay where you are. I'll get you."

He tried to remember if there had been a lantern or candles in the bunker. But for the life of him, he couldn't. This was the only time he regretted not taking up smoking. At least then he would have had a match or a lighter. A tactical flashlight was part of his River Patrol uniform. But it did him no good now since the flashlight was attached to his Kevlar vest back at the office.

He allowed his eyes to adjust briefly and then moved forward until he sensed he was within arm's reach. And then she screamed again as she sacrificed another morsel of flesh to the scurrying vermin.

Colefield kicked wildly with his feet, then lunged forward and scooped her up into his arms.

He couldn't risk putting her down. She felt like spaghetti. Muscling up the flight of stairs toward daylight, the rats following them like some twisted Pied Piper scene.

He carried her to the bed of his truck and gently placed her on her side.

Her clothing was torn and dirty. Her lips cracked and split. The piercing was gone, replaced with a boil-like sore. She wore no shoes and her arms and legs bled from open wounds. Her feet were black with crusted blood. Rat bites, probably. Her nails were torn and the tips of her fingers raw as if she had been trying to dig herself to freedom. Her face nearly black with soot was unrecognizable as the youthful girl he had met a week ago. He desired to clean and bandage her, but was acutely aware that her entire person was a crime scene and needed to be properly processed.

The bright light overpowered her enlarged pupils. "I can't see…"

"Hold on!" Colefield blocked the sun with his arm.

It took her a moment to adjust from the darkness before she could fully focus. When she did, she still had a mole-like squint.

"It's darker in the cab."

He scooped her up again and after he placed her inside the cab on the bench seat, he stayed close by propping her up. She had a far-away expression, rolling her head from side to side, mumbling incoherently as he poured water over her cracked lips and down her throat.

He laid her head back and told her to close her eyes. Then he quietly closed the door, hurried to the driver's side climbed in behind the wheel and sped toward the Scarbough estate.

28

inding the missing girl alive was the lead story on the 5
o'clock news, coupled with the picture taken earlier of Jeb
and Colefield after the river rescue. But by the following
morning, bloggers and conspiracy nuts had begun their own
"investigations".

"*There's No Place Like Home*" was the headline on the front
page of *The Oregonian*, the following morning, which highlighted
the fact that Colefield was on administrative leave at the time
of the rescue, and that the missing girl was found on property
once owned by his family. *The Columbian* ran with the original
river rescue story, which included an interview with the Sea Scout
Master in which he detailed that his ship was commandeered by
Colefield and that his stalking of the Scarbough boy had set up the
entire near drowning event. *The Sellwood Bee* said that Colefield
was in the wind and missing from his moorage. *The Northwest
Examiner* wanted to run an article because for all practical
purposes he currently resided in the Pearl, however brief his stay
on the 9th floor might turn out to be. Everyone wanted a piece of
him – opinion was evenly divided. Colefield was either a reluctant
hero or a cunning out of control cop.

The FBI put up a steel wall and refused to discuss the case.
The Mayor was apoplectic when his name was mentioned in some
stories that he had pushed the officer to the breaking point in order
to have good PR for his upcoming primary.

Colefield bunkered down in the Pearl, with the blessed Sally
Ashley supplying food and succor. Jack the cat was the benefactor
of $5 a can "Rad Cat" cat food, which Sally fed her own felines.
Word was that Penny was conscious and improving daily, and that

she had been debriefed on the matter and was cooperating fully with the authorities. This of course only put more gasoline on the fire for the press, who were only too eager to follow any thread no matter how tiny. The headline *"No Shelter From The Storm"* detailed how the police were pressuring the still traumatized and vulnerable girl to bend the story their way.

While Portland burned through the juicy details, Colefield himself tried to make sense of it all. To lock her up on his old homestead – the very last place he would think to look had been brilliantly diabolical, Colefield thought. And if he hadn't gotten Tom Farmer's call to pick up his truck, she wouldn't have been found alive, and could have turned into dust before anyone opened the shelter door. If anyone ever did.

Jeb had been there with his grandfather when he recognized Colefield. It wasn't a big leap to figure out how the idea hatched. The matter of purchasing a new lock and chain had probably been the final piece of the puzzle. He'd called Harvey with that detail. If Jeb bought the lock, it was tangible evidence that he was directly implicated in the abduction and attempted murder of his sister.

The hunt was still on for Jeb Scarbough. He'd been missing in action ever since his father's escape and his mother's overdose. The press and public have short attention spans. After a week of ever decreasing headlines, and no new information, the tale finally ran out of rope.

The following Monday, Colefield was called back to work. The consequences of his actions while placed on administrative leave were still up in the air.

"Welcome back." The Lieutenant shook Colefield's hand. "If I had any brains at all, I'd be suspending you for disobeying my direct order to stay out of the case."

"Yes sir," Colefield replied.

"Now get out of my office and get back to work before I change my mind."

Colefield sat at his desk at the Columbia River Marine Patrol office, littered with stained phone messages and empty coffee cups, having become a de facto dumping ground in his absence. Bart and Weaver were out on a distress call when he arrived. A boater had gone aground near the eastern tip of Tomahawk Island. Not that unusual of a mishap given the shallow sand bar in that area. What made it pressing was that the boater had left his heart medication back at the marina and he was having chest pains. He needed his nitroglycerin pills and this required a tad more urgency.

When the men returned to the office, Colefield was still sitting at his desk making little piles of various notes and messages. He had not moved a finger to throw out the refuse.

Bart took off his jacket and slung it over the back of his chair while Weaver went into the shop to talk to the mechanic about a run-ability issue with the boat. A transmission cable, they thought, had gone out of adjustment making it difficult to shift into gear.

"Welcome back Red." Bart slapped Colefield on the back as he walked over to mess with the marine radio.

"You OK?" Bart asked.

"What?" Colefield stared at a note in his hand.

"I said, are you OK?"

"I'm just looking over my phone messages." He pointed to three piles stacked in front of him. "This large pile is people that want me finished, figuratively, literally or both."

Colefield shifted to the middle pile. "Now these folks are folks that want to help me."

"That's good right?" Bart enthused.

"Not really. These are the lawyers and other bottom feeders that always wash up to pick over a carcass."

Colefield held up two pieces of paper in the scant third pile. "This one is from my mom and dad telling me they love me and this one is from my crotchety landlord, telling me to 'shoot all the bastards'."

Colefield shook his head slowly. "When I look at this, it makes me realize that real friends are few and far between."

"We weren't allowed to contact you." Bart's face flushed.

"Officially," Colefield said.

"You're right. I should have called you but I didn't know what to say. We weren't allowed to discuss the case, and that was all anybody was talking about."

"It's OK, Bart. You know how lame I am? I was looking for a note from Jill or Tam."

Bart looked surprised. "Jill told me you blew her off."

"And Agent Costa was a married woman here on official business." Colefield felt like a complete schmuck. Shaking it off, he stood up and put his jacket on.

"Where are you going?" Bart asked.

"I need some fresh air. I'm going to fix the gutter. I'm tired of listening to it rattle." Colefield hit the door.

The wind had kicked up and the gutter was banging on the siding chipping the paint. It irked Colefield that none of the other deputies had made the repair while he was off duty.

The extension ladder was in its usual place leaning against the backside of the building under weeds. He pulled it out, carried it around to the front of the building, and stood it upright.

After retrieving a few tools and a pair of binoculars from the garage, he climbed up onto the roof. The shingles had slimy green gobs of mold sprouting up everywhere. It was a little tricky going but he managed to climb to the crest and take in the expansive view.

From this height he could see for miles. Looking through the binoculars he scanned the highway, the open field across the street, and then the parking lot of the Sextant Bar. He tried not to think about Jill but she was on his mind, what could he say?

About then a silver Mercedes pulled into the empty overflow parking lot of the Sextant and parked. There were two passengers inside. The driver was a handsome enough guy, with gold rimmed glasses and a smart polo shirt. The passenger, a slender blonde, was busy reaching behind the seat searching for her purse, Colefield presumed. When she was finished and turned back around, he dialed in the focus. His heart skipped a beat. It was Jill. A twinge of jealousy spanked him as his former date leaned across the seat and planted a kiss on the driver's lips. She smiled at him and then jumped out of the car, looking as happy as he'd ever seen her, prancing away like a filly.

He continued to spy through the binoculars. At the door to the tavern she stopped, glanced back toward the luxurious automobile and waved one last time. Then, as if she sensed she was being watched, she turned and looked directly up at him. Feeling busted and foolish, he waved at her. She ignored the gesture, turned and marched inside the back door of the restaurant.

His timing couldn't have been worse. Bad enough the press had called him a stalker, now Jill probably thought the same thing.

Colefield sat down and stared at the river as the Lieutenant's sedan pulled into the parking lot. The lieutenant got out from behind the wheel and stood looking up at Colefield.

"If you're a jumper the roof's too low."

"Funny."

"Am I going to need to call a shrink?"

"I'll let you know."

"Since you're up there, why don't you make yourself useful and fix the gutter."

"That's a good idea," Colefield nodded in agreement.

The Lieutenant frowned. "If you fall off of there make sure you land on your head."

* * *

Around quitting time, Weaver came up to Colefield, carrying his jacket.

"Hey, Red? Want to go get a beer down the street?"

Colefield who had been staring at a blank computer screen for the last twenty minutes, turned around. "The Sextant?"

"You got some other place in mind?"

"There's always Salty's."

"Are we dressed for that?"

"Change."

"Right," Weaver smirked. "You lost it?"

"Maybe..."

"C'mon! Man up and go get this thing with Jill over with."

"You guys don't know the half of it."

Bart came out of the Lieutenant's office sighing. "We have a Red Cross training exercise at 8am. The Lieutenant wanted me to remind you guys. And don't be late."

"Great," Weaver said. "You coming, Colefield?"

"I'm gonna take a pass."

"How 'bout you, Bart? Up for a few brewskies?"

"Sure."

The men couldn't get away from their depressed partner fast enough.

29

The next few days Colefield went on daily river patrols. He wrote tickets for expired tags, cited an obnoxious fisherman for not having the proper life jacket, and went through the motions. But he was detached, removed, and his mood was troubled. Penny had recovered enough to leave the hospital and he had appeared at a private hearing regarding her potential placement, courtesy of a counselor at the Outside In, a nonprofit agency for troubled youths, where he now volunteered.

The good news was Penny would recover physically. While hospitalized they had run pregnancy, HIV and Hep tests. She was in the clear on those and the report also noted that her skin was free of tattoos or other permanent marks. *Except the ones made from the rat bites...* Colefield would never forget the chasms in her legs.

Her memory of the events leading up to her discovery was ragged and telling. Colefield knew all about PTSD. If watching your father be gut shot in front of you by your brother wouldn't do it, being locked in a pitch black pit filled with rats certainly would. Colefield also knew a thing or two about guilt. The old *"it should have been me"* premise. Colefield had said that a thousand times with reference to his brother's arm being crushed under the tree. Penny might well feel the same way after watching her father, a man she had little respect for, step in front of her without ever wavering to save her life. The judge made a note to try to get her to a counselor Colefield recommended. After shaking hands with Penny's new foster parents, he walked away filled with doubt and hope.

Friday night, he gave in and went out with his colleagues for a beer at the Sextant. He was nervous to see Jill but it was time to confront the past.

To his surprise, Jill was not working that night. He'd worked himself up for the big moment, and all the wind was taken out of his sails when she was not behind the bar like he'd counted on. Two of her regular waitresses refused to serve him so word had gotten out. "Jason Colefield is an Asshole!"

Weaver and Bart bookended Colefield at a long table in the back of the restaurant. They toughed it out for nearly ten minutes before one of the waitresses broke ranks and served the table a round of beers. Colefield picked up his glass and studied it carefully to see if one of Jill's comrades had dropped in a pubic hair or something worse.

After he was pretty sure the contents were safe, he took a sip of beer but it was warmer than he liked and had a suspicious tart aftertaste, so he left the glass on the table and hung out while the other deputies drank theirs.

"Don't see Jill here," Bart said, after polishing off his drink. "You bummed, Red?"

"I had mentally geared up for it," Colefield acknowledged.

Weaver cracked his knuckles. "You got to get back in the saddle."

"Weaver's right, Red, you've been a moody prick lately."

"Well that won't happen in this bar any time soon. These waitresses hate me."

"Too bad Tony isn't here. He could cull a winner out of the herd for you," Weaver added helpfully.

Colefield stood up, pulled out a twenty and tossed it down on the table. "The next round's on me!"

"Where are you going?"

"Home."

"You didn't finish your beer." Weaver eyed his glass.

"I got something I gotta do." *Gotta feed the cat, trim my toenails, take a nap...*

Weaver reached over and replaced his empty glass with Colefield's full one.

"Later, dude!" Bart said.

Colefield headed toward the exit. He was feet from the door when Jill walked in strutting a new hair style and a new dress – a sexy jade number that looked stunning with her long tanned legs.

Their eyes locked. Jill's face flattened as she passed him by.

Then, almost as an afterthought, she stopped and turned back around. "Next time, deputy, try using a cell phone instead of a pair of binoculars." She turned her back on him and disappeared into the crowd.

Colefield stopped. "OK." he shouted back. Of course he wanted to see her again, whatever it took.

He made a move to go after her, but reconsidered. She'd entered enemy territory and he knew nothing good would come of a discussion tonight. The chance encounter had left him feeling hopeful.

Back at the River Patrol Headquarters, he sat in his old pickup in the deserted parking lot and stared at the dark river. He had a luxurious free condo downtown he could escape to, but he preferred the comfort of the cab of his old truck. He thought about sleeping there but that would be pushing what was tolerated. If the Lieutenant found him the following morning asleep inside his cab for certain the man would call in the shrinks.

He checked his cell phone for messages but there were none. This, too, shouldn't have bothered him but it did. He needed to hear from somebody, anybody, just to break him out of this deep funk that he'd fallen into. He pulled out his car keys and tried the ignition. The engine turned over but didn't fire. He tried it again, and then again. The engine turned over. That was all.

He found a flashlight behind the seat, climbed out, popped the hood and shined the beam down on the engine compartment. It was apparent soon enough what the problem was.

The wire from the ignition coil to the distributor was missing. One of the deputies had taken it as a joke apparently. Ha, ha…

He stomped down toward the office figuring the wire was probably lying on his desk in plain sight. Alan, the mechanic, had probably taken it because he'd been giving Colefield some shit lately about the way he had lost his humor. Alan didn't like it when someone lost their sense of humor. It was contagious, he said, and had to be fought against at all costs.

He went inside the building, turned on the lights, checked his desk, but didn't see the coil wire lying around anywhere. He checked the shop, nothing there either. Odd... The guys were really testing his patience this time.

Maybe they had set it in his tire wheel well. They had done that before, several years ago. He started to close the outside door to the building when a sloshing sound down by the boat ramp caught his attention.

He stared toward the river. Something shiny down in the water caught the light. The blast of light was swallowed by darkness. The night lights on the dock were on a timer that would strobe on and off every few minutes.

He walked down the ramp to the waterline. A small dinghy was tied to the dock, slapping about in the rough waves. He checked the bow for a registration number. It was Jeb Scarbough's ride. That explained the missing coil wire...

Cautiously, he stepped back. The cold breeze picked up. He was taking no chances this time. He quickly pulled out his pocket knife and sliced through the boat's fuel line. He put his knife away. He still had his Glock in a concealed shoulder holster; he took it out. That gave him some comfort as he set off to find the kid.

Without a light, he couldn't see but a few feet ahead of him. Shadows moved about in his mind like crabs scurrying along a dock. He checked the nearby boathouse, keeping low, his gun hand raised and shaking slightly. Best he could, he tried to steady his shooting hand. Certain the boathouse was empty he moved on, checked other areas where the boy might hide, but found nothing. He searched the Fire Department's storage and tanker. Again, nothing.

As the overheads flashed on again he hugged the buildings and searched the shadows, until a loud explosion echoed from the parking lot.

Orange flames licked the night sky. His mind whirled. His pickup truck! A raging fire had already begun to consume the cab and flames poured out the open driver's side window.

Fighting back the heat, he yanked open the driver's side door and swatted at the fire with his jacket. There was a jerry can resting on the passenger floorboard with a burning rag shoved in the top. Fuel had been dumped all over the seat and floorboards. Any moment the whole truck would explode. He had to move fast.

Colefield stepped back and shielded his face from the searing flames. There was a hose connected to an outside faucet nearby where the men washed off their muddy boots before entering the office.

He ran toward it, turned on the water, and rushed back over and began hosing down the cab, which was a total loss, but at least he'd saved the rest of the old girl.

An outboard motor fired up down at the dock. He turned just as the boat disappeared into the night.

Even in the moonless night, he was sure he could make out the jack-o-lantern smile of Jeb Scarbough....

And then the outboard sputtered, coughed, and conked out several hundred yards from shore. He could just make out the small dinghy floating down river with the boy frantically pulling on the starter rope.

He threw the hose to the ground and took off running.

30

About an eighth-mile from the River Patrol office, the dinghy floated ashore along a sandy river bank. In the distance he made out the white and red Sea Scout buildings. As he ran, the icy breeze gusting over the churning water, moist with fine debris, stung his cheeks. His eyes were still burning from the smoke. Colefield caught a glimpse of the kid baling from the boat and running overland toward the vacated buildings. He'd been here before, the memory painfully fresh in his mind.

He fumbled for his phone and tried Bart and then Weaver. *Pick up... Pick up...*

No answer. Had they seen his number and pressed Ignore? How could he blame them? He'd been an antisocial dick lately. He was taking no chances; he dialed again and requested police backup. *Just play it by the book...*

Winded from running, Colefield held up and rested momentarily taking in the view the misty yellow light cast on the stark wooden buildings. Three flood lights lit the entire compound. A small prison surrounded by water. He counted the small boats tied to the dock. No slip was empty. He was here. Somewhere in the midst of these buildings was a teenage murderer – the question, where?

His hands turned sweaty as he clutched his weapon. The kid had unwittingly tried to destroy the only thing that gave him comfort. Sure, it was just a pickup truck, but it was more than that. It was part of his history. Strong. Sturdy. Reliable. If the kid thought he could destroy that, he had another thing coming.

He approached the first building, tried the door. Locked. He moved on to the second and found it unlocked. His heart pounded. He yanked it open and jumped back. The door banged on its hinges. He crouched low and moved inside, swept his gun from side to side, the flashlight beam just above it, shining back and forth. Just a sliver of light entered through the windows near the ceiling, not enough to really see into the shadowy space. There was an old Tollycraft that sat still in the water and several rusting 55-gallon drums stacked against the walls. No sign of the kid though. He moved on to the next building.

The door there was unlocked but stuck in its frame. Old wood, even older hinges. He pried on it, but the door was not budging. He moved on to the fourth building.

That door was nailed closed. So he inspected alongside the buildings and moved to the opposite side of the dock. Only three buildings left.

The first two were a bust. There was only one remaining. What was Jeb planning this time?

His breathing was out of control, his heart racing. He tried to calm the rage he was feeling inside, but nothing worked. Memories of Timmy's chewed fingernails and destroyed face competed with the sight of Penny's mangled legs. How could Jeb's love for his mother transform him into someone who enjoyed torture and death?

The last door was hanging off its hinges. Concealing his body the best he could he shot forward and shined his light back and forth along the floor and walls. Primed to even the smallest sounds, he listened to the old building creak, the decrepit boards dry and rotten. A breeze blew in from somewhere and startled him.

He didn't dare step forward; he didn't trust the wood below his feet. The kid was in here. Inside this creaking black cavern the kid had the upper hand.

Suddenly, a whooshing sound came from above. He tried to dodge the rusted hoist that swung down out of the rafters and managed to avoid it, but the sudden motion caused the planking to give way underfoot. His right foot busted through a hole up to the knee. He was still on his feet, but had dropped his Glock which skidded across several boards before it came to rest out of reach.

He tried pulling himself free but his leg was caught on the lip of the broken oak. The pain was excruciating. *Fight through it.* Screaming like a banshee he jerked himself free.

Just as he was stable on his feet, the kid jumped from the rafters and landed feet first on his shoulders. They crashed to the floor. The kid was strong and fierce. He clawed and fought to reach Colefield's weapon.

Just in the nick of time, Colefield kicked his toe out and clipped the Glock handle and sent the barrel spinning out of the boy's reach. The kid clawed his eyes and dove for the gun.

Colefield fell back and landed on a broken two-by-four. As he struggled to get up the kid picked up the handgun and pointed it at Colefield.

Jeb grinned. "You've been in the papers a lot lately."

"Pretty clever, stashing Penny at my place." Colefield wrapped his hand around the broken two-by-four behind him. "Could have gone badly for me if somebody had found her later."

"I would have made sure that a clue would have appeared that helped with that."

"Why kill your sister?"

"Timmy wouldn't listen. He told Penny about the hiker I killed. She put two and two together."

"So she was going to be the end?" Colefield asked. "The final letter."

"Until you fucked it up by finding her alive." Jeb was getting fired up.

"Was the girl scout one of yours too?" Colefield figured he might want to brag a bit. He'd been holding it inside for a long time.

"I didn't mean to kill her."

"What?"

"I wasn't looking for anyone. I was cruising up the river on my mom's anniversary when I saw the girl. I wasn't planning on killing anyone else. I thought the first scout might have been enough for me."

"The boy at the coast?" Colefield wanted to keep him talking.

"Yeah," he said and spit some blood. "I'd written the message there, but the water washed it away."

Colefield remembered that only a "C" remained...

"Anyway she was camped along the river by the train tracks. I saw her from my boat. Told me she was a runaway and gonna ride the rails to Mexico."

"Where'd the shirt come from?" Colefield gauged the distance between them.

"It was a sign, man. She was wearing it. That's when I knew."

"Knew what?"

"She was sent to me that day. Nobody knew her or cared about her, but I did."

"You have a funny way of showing it. Everybody you care about seems to end up dead."

Jeb's face flattened. "Then I guess I care about you." He raised the gun, "See you later, Deputy."

Colefield swung the wood like a heavy club at the kid's torso. He landed a direct hit, knocking the air out of him as he fell to his knees. Yet, Jeb managed to hold onto the gun and stagger to his feet. Colefield threw the club at him, hitting him in the shoulder. This time the impact launched him backwards, gasping for air, dangerously close to the water's edge, teetering to remain on his feet.

The boy squeezed off a shot but the bullet went flying upward, into the rafters, splintering and raining down debris. Loose boards and rubble showered down as Jeb lost his footing and stumbled backward into the water.

Half blind and crippled he still tried to save the boy. Stretching out over the water Colefield attempted to grab Jeb's shirt collar as the he floundered about in the icy river. Kicking away from Colefield he moved into the current, only to get snagged onto something below the river's surface. Gagging, unable to keep his head above water the "dolphin" pulled him down. The boy clung on for his last breath, still fighting to free himself before he was flung into the main current. His pale arm sank slowly down into the jaws of the Columbia.

It happened within seconds.

Colefield didn't want it to end this way. He crawled over to the edge and stared into the void where the unforgiving river had sucked Jeb down.

*   *   *

By the time the fire department arrived, the smoldering interior and seared paint fumes were all that remained of the cab of his truck. Bart and Weaver came trotting down the street following the police sirens looking dumbstruck.

Colefield, bleeding and hobbling from the ordeal with the kid, just stood back and stared at the pickup. His clothes were soaking wet, his face streaked with perspiration and dirt. The cab resembled a burnt marshmallow after a raging campfire.

"Christ, what the hell happened?" Bart asked.

"Scarbough…"

"The kid did this?" Bart asked. "Where is he?"

Colefield didn't reply.

Weaver was stooped over catching his breath, breathing heavily after the run. "Why didn't the little shit torch it up while you were at the bar?"

Colefield thought it over. "Because he wanted me to see it burn."

Weaver puffed out between breaths. "He's really upped the ante now…"

"I think he's dead," Colefield said.

"Dead? Where?" Bart asked.

"He fell in at the Sea Scout building. Let's grab the sled."

"Christ, Colefield!" The two deputies exchanged knowing looks. "We didn't know you were in trouble."

"It wouldn't have mattered. There wasn't time for you to help. It was over in minutes."

The fire department gave the old truck a final once over and then called it a night. The shift commander walked over to speak with Colefield.

"Know who did this?"

"Yep."

"Fill me in."

"Later – I've got a body to find."

31

The dredging project down at the houseboat community of the Portland Rowing Club was winding up. Once again, against his better judgment, Colefield was driving Montgomery's old piece of shit with the trunk latch that wouldn't lock and the engine that let out a burp of black smoke every time he turned off the motor.

Standing in the center of an oil cloud, he opened the trunk, removed an armload of clothing and headed off toward the ramp.

He was carrying the last of it when a woman's voice called out from behind. He stopped dead in his tracks and adjusted his expression before he turned around.

Agent Tamara Costa was back, dressed in tight-fitting blue jeans, red cowboy boots, and a crisp white shirt. Her black leather jacket that he remembered she'd worn on one of their dates was slung over her shoulder. She smiled as she came toward him.

"I hear you've been busy," she said, stepping on tiptoes to plant a kiss on his cheek, leaving behind a trace of lipstick.

"Where you been, Tam?"

"Sorry, I thought I told you I was out of town."

"I left several messages." Colefield waited for her typical snappy comeback.

"I would have called you but I didn't know what to say."

"Well, here," he said, and handed her half of the stack of shirts on hangers. "While you figure it out, you can help me. I can't afford to lose another thing downriver today."

Costa laughed. "So it's finally over?"

"The evil thing known as the dredge has moved on. It's safe to come home."

"I was talking about the case."

Colefield breathed in the fresh cool air. The sky was overcast and gloomy, but at least it wasn't raining. They proceeded down the ramp together. The familiar heat of being near her flickered, but something had emotionally changed in him. He'd quit bargaining with fate about Tam. No more *"what if I had done this or said that to make her stay"*. Her unexplained absence and return only confirmed that there was nothing he could have done or said to hold onto the mercurial Admiral's daughter.

After they entered the houseboat and she put the shirts down on a sofa cluttered with boxes, she turned and stretched out a kink in her back. Colefield stared at her. She had lost a little weight, or had buffed up, or something. She was lean and fit and her skin had a golden glow.

"So where'd you go? Hawaii?"

"Mexico. Zihuatanejo and Ixtapa. We were gone a week."

"We?"

"My husband and I."

"I see." But he didn't. Probably never would. That realization caused him to shake his head and smile.

"Long way to go to sign divorce papers…" He wasn't going to make it easy for her.

"Yeah – that's why I'm here. I've got some news."

"You won the lottery?" He already knew what she was going to say the minute she used the word "husband".

"In a way … I'm not getting a divorce."

He moved to the fridge and pulled out two beers. He popped the tops and carried them back out into the living room and handed one to her. "Well, here's to reunions."

"Remember when I told you I didn't think we got a do-over in life, that I thought you couldn't go back and correct mistakes?"

"Yeah I remember. That was during the conversation where you told me you were glad for the divorce."

"Look. I'm as surprised as you are."

"I doubt that, but at the moment I'd drink to most anything."

He peered into her eyes. The old attraction was still there, but now it really felt "*old*", an affair rooted in the past with no promise of a future. Armed with this new clarity, he felt unburdened from the unsettling memory of losing her, and in doing so losing himself.

Right on schedule, Costa changed the conversation. "Congratulations on getting Jeb Scarbough for me."

"For you?" Colefield laughed. "Well OK, but we technically never 'got' him. We never recovered a body."

She set the half-finished beer down, reached out and touched his face. Her hands were cold. "I gotta run."

He walked her out the door and to the ramp leading to the parking lot. Several hundred yards away sat a black sedan with a man leaning against the driver's door, smoking a cigarette.

I think I'm owed a 'do-over' too. Before she could see it coming Colefield leaned in and kissed her goodbye. To his surprise, she didn't pull back. He tasted her sweet lips for the last time and let her go.

"Take it easy, Tam."

She ascended the steep ramp and climbed into the passenger side door of the sedan. For the pure orneriness of it – he waved goodbye to the hubby with his middle finger discretely extended.

32

The day after her visit, the distress call came in over the two-way radio. Colefield was sitting at his desk at River Patrol headquarters on Marine Drive repairing a seal on his dry suit when he slid his chair over and lifted the microphone to speak.

"This is Deputy Colefield of the Multnomah County River Patrol One. Over."

The voice was garbled and scared.

"Your voice broke up. Repeat. Over."

The microphone went dead. Colefield figured the caller would try again.

Having just left the restroom, and still fussing with his zipper, Bart ambled into the tiny office and paid no attention to the radio.

The woman's voice rattled aloud again. This time Colefield tried a different tactic.

"Calm down," Colefield said. "Just tell me where you are. Slow down. Yes. Yes..." Colefield jotted something down on paper. "Repeat again, please. Over."

He rechecked his scribbles. "Give us 30 minutes. Don't leave the area. River Patrol One out."

Bart sat down and removed a Power Bar from his lower desk drawer. "What was that about?"

"Someone spotted a body in the water."

"Where?"

"Down River, near Sauvie Island, just north of Collin's Beach."

Bart peeled the wrapper back on his protein bar and took a bite. Chewing, he asked: "Any idea who the floater is?"

"The woman sounded pretty hysterical. She couldn't ID it.

225

Her husband's operating the boat and circling the area to keep an eye on it. Details were sketchy at best. I'm going to take along my dive gear just in case."

"I'll round up Weaver. Does the boat have fuel?"

"I filled it yesterday. We should be good."

Ten minutes later, the men where down at the dock boarding the patrol boat. Deputy Weaver untied the lines and climbed aboard. Bart had control of the helm. Colefield was busy feeding the coordinates into the GPS as the boat glided out of the slip.

"Who do we still have on the Watch List?" Colefield asked Bart, looking down at the fuel gauge.

The Watch List was the missing persons still unaccounted for and posted on the wall of the office. The list had grown over the holidays. The list never went away.

"There's the thirty-eight year old Asian woman who jumped off the Hawthorne Bridge three weeks ago. And there's the meth-head dude that freaked out when the cops pinned him down on the Fremont. He jumped last Friday. Then there's the fisherman who fell out of his boat. But he was further north. Oh and there's the man from Camas who ran aground and thought he could push his twenty-footer off the sand bar. We also have that drunken idiot who fell overboard during the Christmas ships parade."

"That was near Scappoose. He's too far North to surface by Sauvie Island. He'd be pretty bloated by now. I suspect he's near Cathlamet."

"Yeah, you're probably right there. But the current has been shifty lately. You notice that?"

"I noticed."

Bart hit the throttle. "It could be the Scarbough kid," he said, waiting to see Colefield's reaction.

But Colefield didn't comment. He left the helm in Bart's control and moved out onto the deck as the boat splashed through the rough waters near the confluence of the Willamette and Columbia Rivers. The wind seemed to slice off the top crests of the waves.

Bart gripped the wheel, maintained a clean line through the headwaters and continued veering north after the bend, opting to favor the channel markers along the Washington side of the River.

A thousand images ran through Colefield's mind as he listened to the aluminum hull slap over the waves at better than 40 knots. The river mist spilling over the bow pelted his cold face. His hands grew colder by the minute as he held on to the railing to steady himself. Weaver stood on the opposite side of the wheelhouse just staring off toward land with a pair of loose binoculars slung around his neck, lost in thought.

About four or five miles downriver, Colefield spotted a Carver 28 that fit the description of the pleasure craft the caller on the radio had identified. He turned around and gave Bart a thumbs-up and pointed out the vessel ahead. Bart eased back on the throttle and altered course. He made contact with the operator on the marine radio.

As they drew near the Carver 28 the woman aboard popped out of the cabin and pointed frantically off their port bow. The white-haired man at the helm held the boat steady and awaited further instructions.

The river boat backed off its engines and glided slowly forward. Colefield kept his eye on the water. A bloated body bobbed up out of the gray river. At the same time, the woman aboard the pleasure cruiser let out a scream that echoed through the still air. And she hopped around the deck like she was going to wet herself.

Weaver moved to port and scanned the water with his binoculars. But it was Colefield who spotted the floater surface north of where they were looking.

"Let's circle around," Colefield ordered. "I'll toss in the hook!"

The current had picked up again. It was drawing the body downriver. They'd need to hurry if they were going to snag this one. He grabbed the rigging – a special stainless steel T-shaped hook attached to a long coil of heavy rope, carried it to the stern and lobbed it into the water, looping the end of the rope around a cleat.

Weaver lowered his binoculars, moved aft and released a line on the recovery stretcher attached to the transom, and waited, watching Colefield play out the rope.

It was on the River Patrol's third pass that they hooked the body. Colefield felt the familiar tug. The hook had been set. It wasn't unlike reeling in a large salmon except this one wasn't about to fight back. Hand over hand, he muscled the rope, drew the waterlogged body closer to the boat. When it was within view, Weaver lowered the metal litter down into the water and let it sink a few feet below the body, awaiting Colefield's signal.

Colefield gave one last pull and the body suddenly shot upwards, bobbed right out of the water. Colefield got a good look at it before it sank down again below the surface. Weaver had positioned the stretcher dead-on. The two of them slowly hauled in the body.

Once the corpse was out of the water, swaying from side to side with the rolling motion of the boat, Bart opened the wheelhouse door.

"It's the kid," Colefield said.

33

The large modern house sat on Lake Oswego with a view of Main Street. Colefield parked Montgomery's battered sedan in the circular drive, climbed out and walked toward the front door.

The house was in a pricey neighborhood, a community comprised of wealthy respected families. Old money. The area was perfect for Penny because it was all about new environments and change, Colefield thought.

When she opened the door, he barely recognized her. Her face was smooth and healed. Her hair was cut in a sophisticated Goth style popular with teens. She had on new jeans and a patterned top that went well with her clear dark eyes and rosy skin. The angry lost kid was gone, at least on the surface.

"Penny? Is that you?" Colefield laughed as she spun around.

"Deputy Colefield? You are about the last person I expected to see."

"I was in the neighborhood. Thought I'd see how you're doing."

A woman in her late thirties wearing chic yoga wear popped around the corner. "Penny? Who's at the door?"

"It's a friend of mine, Sharon."

The woman opened the door wider and greeted the deputy.

"We met at Penny's hearing."

The woman stood behind Penny and put her hand protectively on the girl's shoulder, keeping her attention clearly focused on the deputy.

Her face darkened. "Is anything wrong?"

"No, Ma'am. This is a social visit. I was in the area and thought I'd stop by and say hello."

229

"Then please come in. We were just setting the table for lunch. There's plenty extra if you're hungry."

Colefield glanced down at his watch. "Thank you, ma'am. But I'm afraid I don't have enough time for that. I've got someone flying in from Alaska and I'm picking him up in an hour."

"Well I'll leave you two alone to chat." She smiled at Colefield. "Come by any time. You're always welcome here."

"Thanks, ma'am."

Penny pushed a loose strand of hair from her face, stepped outside and closed the door behind her. It took her a few moments to organize her thoughts. She leaned back against the house, crossed her arms and dropped her façade. The smile she had been wearing before faded. Something about her attitude shifted back to the loser from Sauvie Island.

"Everything OK?" he asked.

"They're really sweet. They dote over me like a new puppy, and it kind of feels weird. But it's not their fault. I don't remember much about my real mom, and Anita never showed me any attention so I don't know how to respond."

"It'll take time…"

"You have a cigarette?"

"I don't smoke."

"I'm trying to quit. But at least I stopped smoking pot."

"School OK?"

"It's a little freaky hanging with rich kids. But guess what? Most are just as fucked up as me. I did meet a couple chicks that are into music and want me to play the drums in their band."

"You play the drums?" This kid was full of surprises.

"Only the 5-gallon bucket kind. But my foster parents said they'd pay for a real set if I can hold my grades above a C."

"Sounds decent of them." Colefield paused. "Did you want to know anything about Jeb? I'm the one who retrieved the body."

"Not really." She turned her eyes down. "It's kind of strange but I don't miss any of them. Maybe, Timmy. But the others, they're just ghosts to me. My foster folks say they are all in Heaven together now and getting along, but I don't believe that and really I just don't care. Is that weird?"

"It's too soon yet to digest it all. Give it some time."

"Anyway, I never got a chance to thank you. You saved my friggin' life. In more ways than you know. It may feel a little awkward now but this move helped. And thanks for putting in a good word for me with the judge. He's hooked me up with a great therapist you recommended. That was pretty awesome since we didn't really hit it off in the beginning."

"I've thought a lot about that lately. It was my karma to meet you and save you," Colefield said.

"Karma?"

"My destiny." Colefield thought about holding her soot covered face in his hands. "You taught me something. You were a friend and true sister to Timmy and tried to protect him from Jeb. Later you used your skill and courage to stay alive."

"I doesn't take skill to live in squalor with the Adams Family." The tough girl was back.

"I was referring to you chasing after life, and not running from it. It's something I've been trying to mimic."

"I've been trying to mimic something you do too."

"What's that?" Colefield flashed a pleased smile.

"Drive the rattiest truck in town." She peeked over his shoulder toward the drive. "Hey, where's your old ride?"

"It's getting some new upholstery."

"I'm glad you still have it. I liked that old piece of shit. I think of it as my rescue chariot."

"I'll give you a ride next time I'm in the area."

"I guess my grandfather left me some money. Some lawyer called me a few days ago and told me how he had a heart attack in jail. He said when I turn eighteen I'll inherit some money. It's sitting in some trust fund now. Maybe I'll actually go to college."

"You're thinking in the right direction."

"That's still a few years off."

"It'll pass by before you know it."

In a few years, she may still have issues to resolve, he thought. But the fact that she looked healthy, seemed off dope, and had put on a pound or two of muscle, reinforced the notion that she was making the necessary adjustments to her new surroundings. And this gave him hope. The band idea might work out or not. But at least she had the gumption to try.

"Hey!" she said. "Did you get back together with your Ex?"

Colefield looked off toward the lake. "That didn't work out, but I've been stalking a bartender that I think is starting to like the attention."

"Well, everything happens for a reason. Isn't that what you told me?"

"I did indeed."

"I'm counting on it." She smiled and gave him a big hug. "Thanks, Colefield. Really. You're a pretty cool dude for being a cop."

To his surprise he squeezed her tightly too. She released him first, waved goodbye and slipped back inside the house. He thought about how breakable she still was. Beneath her tough exterior, a fragile young spirit sought shelter. *The line that divides is often an invisible one...*

How tough it must be to have gone through so much at her age. And yet he could relate. In his heart of hearts, he believed she was going to make it. They both were.

Colefield stood there a moment taking in the clean scent of pine trees wafting through the air before he made his way back to Montgomery's belching beast.

He hoped he remembered to leave the window open on the tender just in case Jack came by for a treat. He thought he'd drive along the river to the airport to fetch home the old pirate.

– THE END –

NOTES AND ACKNOWLEDGMENTS

RIVER CITY sprang to life one foggy morning while I was gazing at the massive Columbia River from my boat, the *Enterprise*, a fishing trawler I call home. At the time, I was watching the television series, *The Killing*, a moody thriller set in Seattle. I was drawn to the troubled characters, the dark settings and the types of physical and emotional violence it portrayed. It had also triggered a muscle memory of my own from childhood, an event where I had stared into the heart of a monster. But young boys imagine all sorts of things....

That morning I hatched the idea to rewrite my own history by creating a narrative as sullen and haunting for Portland. I'll let the reader decide whether I succeeded.

Many of the locations in this story are real though I've taken some creative liberties when describing Sauvie Island. When first researching this novel, I would often ride my motorcycle around the island, placing key scenes in my mind. I passed by Collin's Beach, the nude beach I had last visited during my college years. The willows and reeds along the shore line provided me countless opportunities to surreptitiously photograph models. Later, when the rains arrived, I drove instead, scouting the island wildlife that make up a key part of this magical sanctuary.

The Portland Rowing Club exists and is as eclectic as I have described it. The old pirate, William B. Montgomery, is a friend and even more remarkable in person than on the page. I used Mr. Montgomery's houseboat and tender for scenes to give the book a nautical touch. And the dredging project really did occur

233

234 - DOC MACOMBER

both at my own marina on the Columbia and at the houseboat
community on the Willamette. But that's another story.

The loft in the Pearl District also exists. I'd like to thank
Mike and Jeanne Stringer for renting it to my girlfriend while
her own loft was being remodeled. She temporarily moved her
cat and a few suitcases upstairs and stepped into an elegant
new environment, much like the protagonist did. The view
is spectacular and the early traffic made for a sort of surreal
morning-after setting.

I'd also like to thank Sally Ashley for her brief cameo
appearance as my landlady. She added her own unique touch of
class.

Writing takes a team effort, and I have one of the very best
teams going. I owe many thanks to my devoted group of readers
who have over the years stuck with me to the very end, reading
and re-reading, commenting wherever necessary, pointing out
plot and character issues and offering their independent opinions.
Many of their views were taken to heart and implemented in
this book. I'd like to acknowledge each and every one: Bill
Ashworth; Lee Anna Bennett-Ashworth; Dr. Stephen J. Hanns;
Jim Hendrickson, Jr.; Kat Majors; Lenny Perrone; Harley L.
Sachs; Dane Stanich; Laury #1 Swan, and a very special thanks
to Bill Johnson. Mr. Johnson is the author of *A Story is a Promise*,
and is a devoted screenwriting teacher and creative consultant to
a number of talented Northwest writers. I was honored to have
his help.

I also owe a very special thanks to Deputy Jason Tyrus of the
Multnomah County River Patrol. His willingness to introduce
me to his co-workers and assist on a number of subjects, both
in person and by email, showed me the ropes of what life is like
on the River Patrol. He personally took me out on the water
for the real deal adventure as they policed Portland's "Liquid
Highways". Hopefully my broad descriptions of the River Patrol
Headquarters, its procedures, and of the team of dedicated
officers who keep the waterways a safer place will meet with

Deputy Tyrus's approval.

And last, but not least, I would like to thank Birdie, my fearless partner in crime. Her early editing and long re-writing sessions ignited my writing and shot this story to life. Without her, I would just be another lonely River Rat, a Whaler of Words. She's the best first mate a captain could ever ask for....

About The Author

Doc Macomber is a native Northwesterner. His previous books include: *The Killer Coin, Wolf's Remedy, Snip, and Riff Raff* – a finalist in the Killer Nashville Claymore Award. He is a contributor to various national and international publications. Doc formerly served in a Special Ops unit. He currently lives aboard a trawler in the Pacific Northwest.

(Author photograph by Ty Hitzemann)